My Mama's Drama

My Mama's Drama

La Jill Hunt

www.urbanbooks.net

Urban Books, LLC
300 Farmingdale Road, NY-Route 109
Farmingdale, NY 11735

ISBN 13: 978-1-60162-097-2
ISBN 10: 1-60162-097-7

First Mass Market Printing April 2019
First Trade Paperback Printing November 2018
Printed in the United States of America

10 9 8 7 6 5 4 3 2 1

Distributed by Kensington Publishing Corp.
Submit Orders to:
Customer Service
400 Hahn Road
Westminster, MD 21157-4627
Phone: 1-800-733-3000
Fax: 1-800-659-2436

My Mama's Drama

La Jill Hunt

Prologue

"So, do we need to stop anywhere else?"

"No, I think I'm good," I said as I put the bags in the trunk of the car.

"Are you sure? You know I don't come on this side of town that often, so you'd better take advantage while you can."

"I'm sure, and I know. Thank you so much."

"The only reason I come over here is because you're my favorite niece." My Aunt Celia playfully bumped me as she closed the trunk.

"And you are my favorite auntie." I laughed as we got into the car. We were joking, but I was not lying. She was my favorite aunt, and to me, everything about her was perfect. My goal in life was to be just like her. She had the best of everything, from the sleek black Volvo she drove to her job as an accountant for an engineering firm. She and her handsome husband, my uncle Darnell, lived in a huge brownstone and went on fabulous vacations every year. They didn't have any children of their own, which was probably why my aunt doted on me so much.

"I just want to make sure you have everything you need for school. How're classes going anyway?" she asked me as we pulled away from the mall parking lot.

She had called me early this morning, inviting me to breakfast and a little retail therapy. Luckily, I didn't have class and wasn't scheduled to be at work until later in the afternoon, so I gladly accepted her invitation. Shopping with Aunt Celia meant her buying me cute outfits that she wished she could wear if she were twenty years younger and fifty pounds lighter. It also meant a break away from my chaotic house, where I resided with my mother and fourteen-year-old twin sisters, Avery and Ashley.

"They're going good. I really enjoy my teachers," I told her.

"Have you picked a major yet? You got all your books?"

"No, not yet. I'm still trying to decide on a major, and I'm good with my books." Technically, that was a lie, but I had already come up with a plan to get my books. Aunt Celia had done so much for me already that I didn't want to ask for anything else.

"Well, you still have time. You've always been a smart girl and a good student, Kendra. You're going to go far in life. I've always told you that," Aunt Celia told me. "You have a bright future and your entire life ahead of you."

"I know, Aunt Celia." I sighed. I appreciated her encouragement, but the truth was I thought I would've been way further than I was right now, literally. I had busted my ass in high school, taking honors classes and making damn near straight As. I was accepted into both of my top college choices: Hampton University, where Aunt Celia had graduated, and Howard University. I had even gotten partial scholarship offers to both, but the funds weren't enough to cover tuition, room and board, and expenses. The only way I would be able to attend was to get grants and loans. That shouldn't have been a problem, because my mom was a single parent who struggled every month to pay the bills. Her job as a home health aide was barely enough to cover rent. But, my asshole of a father refused to release his tax information for me to apply for financial aid. Aunt Celia and Uncle Darnell made decent money, but they didn't make enough to cover a $60,000-per-year tuition bill. My only choice was to attend a local community college that they helped me pay for. It was for the best, though, because had I gone away to school, my teen sisters would have been home alone while my mother wasn't home, which was a lot. Her work schedule required her to work three days on and three days off. Those three days that she wasn't working, she was out partying and running the streets. She may have been the mother, but I was the parent. I was the one who cooked our meals, made sure the girls did their homework and went to bed on time.

"And what's going on with your boyfriend situation?" Aunt Celia asked.

I shook my head. "Now, you know I don't have a boyfriend, Aunt Celia."

"That's why I call it a situation, girl. Kendra, I don't understand you sometimes. You're smart, funny, and outgoing. You should have plenty of boys you're choosing to be friends with."

"I don't. They don't even give me a second glance," I told her. I was damn near twenty years old and still a virgin. Hell, I was nineteen and never been kissed, to be honest, and it looked like I was going to stay that way. It was not by choice, because I really wanted to meet a nice, intelligent guy who would challenge my mind and fulfill my blossoming sexual needs. It just seemed like guys never saw me. I'd never been asked out on a date; no one asked for my number. It's like I was invisible.

"Oh, trust me, baby, they're looking. You just don't realize that they are," she said.

I wish I believed her. I knew that I wasn't the baddest girl on the block, but I was far from ugly. I had inherited my mother's petite figure and my father's almond-toned skin and curly hair. The few friends that I had from high school often commented on how pretty I was. I just couldn't catch the eye of any guy that caught mine. It could've been because I wasn't the flashy type of girl that guys seemed to be into these days. I was a jeans and T-shirt kinda chick and never wore makeup. The only pictures I put on social media were ones that I took of the skyline, or sunsets, or anything else in nature that I happened to capture with my cell phone, which Aunt Celia paid for.

"I don't really have time to date anyway. I have school and work and the girls to worry about."

"Those are your sisters, Kendra, not your daughters. Please don't miss out on enjoying life because you're so busy taking care of problems that don't belong to you. I know that's your mother, and that's my sister, but you're gonna have to step back, so she gotta step up and be a mother to those girls. If you don't, you gonna look up one day and you're gonna be thirty years old, and the only memories you'll have of your twenties is working, cooking, and cleaning. That's not what I want for you, baby."

"Now, you know better than anybody that my mama ain't gonna step up, Aunt Celia. I love you and everything you do for me, but I'm all Avery and Ashley have. I'm not gonna do that to them," I told her. We pulled up to the small house that my mother and I lived in. Both of us were surprised to see my mother's beat-up Corolla parked in the driveway.

"Well, thanks for spending time with me, Kendra Boo. I had fun." Aunt Celia leaned over and gave me a hug.

"You're not coming in?" I asked.

She gave me a crazy look while pursing her lips. "Now, you know better than that. Thanks, but no thanks. Pass me my purse out that back seat."

I stretched into the back seat and handed her the large designer bag. She reached inside and took out the matching wallet, then handed me some folded bills.

"Aunt Celia, you've done enough today. I'm good," I told her.

"Take this money. Buy you and your children—I mean your sisters—some Chinese or pizza tonight. Don't forget to get all your bags out the trunk, because if you leave anything, I ain't coming way back over here to bring it."

I took the money and hugged her one more time before stepping out of the car. "Thanks, Aunt Celia. I'll text you later. I love you."

"I love you too, Kendra. Kiss your sisters for me."

I took my bags out of the trunk then went inside. As soon as I stepped into the house, the potent smell of weed hit me. How my mother passed random drug tests on her job was a mystery to me. The woman smoked more marijuana than a Jamaican. There was a trail of clothes leading down the hallway. It was obvious that she didn't even wait to get to her bedroom before she got undressed when she got home. I shook my head and kicked her scrub top and work sneakers out of the way as I went to put my bags into my room. The last thing I wanted her or my sisters to see was that Aunt Celia had taken me shopping again. Although they didn't speak on it, I knew they all felt some type of way about the relationship she and I had. I went to kick another piece of clothing in the middle of the hallway when I realized it was a man's shirt. I exhaled loudly. I should've known the reason she was here was because she brought some random-ass dude home. Whereas I wasn't having any sex, my mother had plenty. At least she was getting her groove on while my sisters were at school.

As I passed by her bedroom, I noticed the door was open. Some old school Jon B song was playing in the background. I quietly walked past and went into my room, putting my bags on my bed; then I went back into the hallway to close her door, which was wide open. It wasn't the first time I'd seen her having sex. There was only a sixteen-year difference between my mother, Diane, and me. I don't think she'd ever really considered me her daughter, but more like her younger sister.

"Yes, fuck me," she moaned. "Oh, shit. Yes, right there."

I reached for the door handle but paused for a second before closing it. My mother was naked, in the middle of her bed with her partner, on top of the rumpled sheets. Her legs straddled a man whose hands were gripping her ass. Something on his hand caught my eye. It was a ring. He was married. My mother was fucking a married man.

"Yes, daddy. Fuck me just like that!" She tossed her head back and screamed. Her body leaned forward slightly, and then I realized who the married man was that she was fucking. His eyes were closed, and there was a look of pure ecstasy on his face. My heart broke into a million pieces, and I couldn't move as I stared at Uncle Darnell, Aunt Celia's husband.

Diane

It had been a rough week, and some good dick was exactly what I needed. Darnell certainly didn't disappoint. I swear that man had a way of hitting my spot just right. He would have me shaking so bad that I was damn near convulsing like Mr. Crawford, one of my patients with ALS. The orgasms he gave me were almost enough to make me feel guilty about fucking him. Almost.

I hadn't planned on coming straight home when I got off from work this morning, but when he called and told me Celia was spending the morning with Kendra, I suggested he meet me at the house and enjoy a little "breakfast in bed." He obliged and did not disappoint.

Round one was over, and I decided to grab us something to drink before we commenced to start round two. I climbed off of Darnell's sweaty body, not even bothering to cover my naked ass because, like most men, he enjoyed looking at it so much.

"Damn, you got a fat ass, D," he said as I was walking out of my bedroom.

I turned and smiled at him. "Did you just call me fat? Clearly, you're getting your people mixed up."

"Trust me, ain't no way I could ever do that. That ass you got is one of a kind." He laughed.

"And don't you forget it." I winked then walked down the hallway and into the living room where I nearly jumped when the sound of Kendra's voice caught me off guard.

"Mama." Her face was full of hurt, anger, and disappointment.

"What the fuck are you doing home? Why the fuck aren't you at school?" I demanded, wondering how long she'd been home. I'd made sure to lock the front door, but I didn't remember if I'd closed my bedroom door before Darnell and I went in. It definitely wasn't closed when I walked out. Kendra wasn't a dummy, and she knew how I got down. There I was standing butt-ass naked in the living room, so it was clear. But, even still, I hoped that even if she knew what I had just finished doing, there was a chance she didn't know who I'd done it with.

"My teacher cancelled class today." She stared at me.

I folded my arms against my chest and asked, "Don't you still have work?"

"I don't go until later. Mama, what are you doing? Why would you do this?"

"Don't you question what the fuck I do, Kendra. I'm a grown-ass woman, and even though you act like you my mama, you ain't. I'm yours," I snapped at her. There were only fourteen years between us, and there were times I treated her like my sister instead of my daughter. I wasn't about to stand there and let her berate me like some teenager who just got caught. "I thought you were out with Celia anyway."

Kendra stood up. "How do you know I was out with her? I didn't tell you or anyone else I was going anywhere with her. Who told you?"

"Stay the fuck outta my business, Kendra," I warned.

"This ain't even about your business, Mama. This is about you sleeping with Uncle Darnell. You do some jacked-up stuff, and I try not to say nothing, but this is just wrong. I can't believe you. Why—"

"Kendra, shut the fuck up." I went to walk away, but she stepped in front of me.

"He's your sister's husband. Out of all the dudes in the world you can deal with? Really, you choose to fuck him, Mama? Him? Aunt

Celia's husband?" Kendra was breathing so hard that I could see her chest rising and falling as she yelled. She wasn't a crier, so I knew the tears forming in her eyes meant that her anger was on a whole other level.

"Girl, you better get the fuck outta my face. Who the fuck do you think you are? Who I choose to fuck ain't got nothing to do with you. I'm a grown-ass woman."

"I can't tell, because you damn sure don't act like one," she spat.

Before I could stop myself, I grabbed her by the collar. Her eyes widened in fear, and I loosened my grip a little. I hardly ever put my hands on her; she was such a good kid that I rarely had a reason. I could count on one hand the number of times I spanked her. And yeah, I knew how much she loved my sister, and I knew she was upset. But there was no way I was gonna let her, or any other bitch for that matter, talk to me any kind of way.

"Have you lost your damn mind? Who the fuck do you think you are?" I put my face close to hers. "Don't get yourself fucked up."

Kendra snatched away from me. "Get your hands off me."

"Little girl, you better calm the fuck down before I calm you down."

"I don't expect much from you, Mama, because when I do, you always disappoint. God knows you've done some messed up stuff, but I expected a little more than this. This is just evil."

"You don't know what you're talking about. You know what? I don't have to explain myself to you anyway."

"Hey, is everything okay out here?" Darnell walked into the living room and asked casually as if nothing was wrong. Fully clothed and showing no signs of having me riding his dick a few minutes earlier, he looked quite dapper in his gray slacks and a yellow button-down. Not only did his body look like it belonged on the cover of *Muscle and Fitness*, but his face was reminiscent of Blair Underwood back when he was on every black woman's wish list. His wavy salt-and-pepper hair and matching goatee gave him a distinguished look. I was slightly disappointed that our playtime for the day was over.

"Everything is fine, baby," I told him.

Kendra didn't say anything. She just stared at both of us in disgust.

"What's up, Kendra? You good?" he asked, walking toward her. She backed away, wiping the tears from her cheeks.

"She's fine. You know how emotional she can be." I shrugged and stepped closer to him. He raised an eyebrow, and until I saw him glancing at my perky breasts, I had forgotten that I was naked. For a second, the look of lust in his eye turned me on, and I arched my back a little more so my chest stood a little higher.

"Well, I'm gonna go ahead and get out of here," he said. "Are you sure everything is okay?"

"I'm positive." I looked over at Kendra, who was still pouting and said, "She ain't gonna say shit to nobody. She knows if she says one word, she's gonna find her ass homeless. And her sisters, too."

Kendra looked up at me. My threatening to kick her ass out didn't matter to her, but I knew she would go to hell and back for Avery and Ashley, so that was my ace in the hole.

"Good." Darnell reached into his pocket and took out a handful of folded bills and passed them to me.

"Thank you so much." I winked and took it from him.

Kendra stormed out of the room and down the hallway.

"You sure she's gonna keep quiet?" He gave me a concerned look.

"I'm sure," I said and wrapped my arms around his neck, kissing him full on the mouth before he walked out the door. When he was gone, I counted the money and smiled. Not bad. It was more than what I needed and way more than I expected. I wondered if he had given me the amount because of our being caught by Kendra. In that case, her coming home unexpectedly had actually been a good thing. But now that she knew what he and I were doing, I wondered if her knowing would cost me more than I imagined.

Celia

It took two trips for me to take all the shopping bags out of the trunk of my car. I locked the door of the car and then entered my house through the side door of the garage. I had just made it upstairs into my bedroom with the last of my newly purchased items when my cell phone rang. I reached inside my Michael Kors bag and pulled it out. When I saw it was a number from the office, I didn't answer. I had taken a much-needed day off, and the last thing I wanted to talk about was work. Whatever it was, it was gonna have to be handled without me. I was about to put it back in my purse when it rang again. This time, after seeing the caller's name, I answered.

"Where are you?" Nikki, my best friend, asked. "And don't lie. I came to surprise you and take you to lunch, and you're not even at work."

"Oh, that must be why the office was calling. I saw the number and didn't answer." I laughed. "I took a day off. Lord knows I needed one. You know that place has been stressing me out the past few weeks."

"I know, and I'm glad you took off. You should've called me, though, so we could hang today."

"I started to, but I decided to spend some time with Kendra this morning. We went to eat and then to the mall."

"How is she? She's still in school, I hope."

"Girl, yes, and she's doing good. You know I like to grab her when I can and make sure she's good. With her being in school, working, and taking care of the twins, it's been hard for me to catch up with her."

"She's still being the mama, huh? Where is Diane these days?"

"Kendra says she's a CNA and works for some home health company. I guess it's working out for her, though, because she ain't hit me up in a couple of months for no money. So, I guess that's a blessing."

Normally, my younger sister constantly had her hand out, asking for me to help her out with bills, food, etc., so I was surprised when I hadn't heard from her. That was another reason I invited my niece out. I wanted to talk to her face to face and make sure everything was okay. Kendra had a habit of telling me things over the phone that were fine when really, they weren't. One thing she would not do was lie to my face.

"Well, I'm glad she's finally getting herself together. It's about time." Nikki sighed.

"It is. So, why the hell were you taking me to lunch? What did Patrick do now?" I asked, sitting on the bed and preparing myself for the latest relationship fiasco involving Nikki's bum-ass boyfriend of two years. I had tried telling her time and time again that he was no good for her, but she seemed to think that somehow, he was miraculously going to stop lying, cheating, and spending all of her money. Her acceptance of him, despite the bullshit he brought with him, was due to the fact that he was a deacon at their church. That, to me, was an oxymoron. Deacon or not, he was trifling. Nikki swore he had potential, but I didn't see it. I definitely couldn't understand how someone who couldn't get their own lives in order could direct folks on how to live theirs. But Nikki adored him, and so did a bunch of others, not only in the church, but the community, too.

Patrick was as slick as a snake oil salesman. He was one of those guys that grew up in the streets but decided to turn his life around. He spent a lot of time still hanging out in his old stomping grounds, under the guise that he was encouraging young guys to turn away from crime and turn to God. Let Nikki tell it, he was the next Rev. Run. But even if he did suddenly see the light and become the decent man she thought he could be, nothing was gonna change the fact that he had a baby mama from hell.

"Why do you think what I gotta tell you has something to do with him?"

"Just tell me what he did." I sighed.

"Fine. Why did I get a call from some apartment complex looking for him because he's behind on his rent?"

"Wait. He moved out? When?"

"Hell no, he didn't move out. He's been living with me for the past year. How about he let his baby mama get a place in his name? Here I am trying to help him get his credit together so we can buy a bigger house, and he's over here creating more bills with Tiesha's ass," Nikki whined.

"Girl, listen, don't let this stress you out. As long as he ain't get it in your name, then don't even worry about it. How the hell did they get your number anyway?" Not only did I wonder if Patrick had been stupid enough to list Nikki as a reference or something, but I also was curious as to why Nikki felt the need to get a bigger house than the one she currently owned. Three bedrooms, three bathrooms, a den, and a family room were more than enough room for the two of them. Surely she wasn't thinking about having a baby with this fool.

"I don't even know. I swear, every time we get closer to our blessing, the devil gets busy and tries to tear me and him apart," Nikki responded.

I decided I wasn't even going to try to reason with her. It was pointless, because all the advice I'd attempted to give her in the past had fallen on deaf ears. She'd come to me with a complaint, and I'd encourage her to leave him alone and try to point out that she could do bad all by herself. Truthfully, she was the one in the relationship doing well, so in all actuality, she wouldn't be doing bad at all if she told him to leave her the hell alone. Nikki was the Director of Nursing at one of the most prestigious nursing care facilities in the city. She made an exceptional salary, which was good, because neither one of Patrick's current career choices, deacon or community activist, were paid positions. His only source of income was Nikki.

"Well, let me put all this stuff I bought away before Darnell gets home. I don't wanna take a chance of him seeing it and hearing his mouth." I hurried and made an excuse to get off the phone.

"You know Darnell doesn't care. He loves for you to have nice things. Heck, didn't he just buy you that MK purse and matching boots last month? You need to be thanking God every day for blessing you with such a good man. I told Patrick the other night he needs to hang out with Darnell. I'm hoping they can be a positive influence on one another."

"What? How?" I asked, wondering what kind of positive influence Patrick could have on my husband, who had been a postal employee for fifteen years, paid not only our mortgage but the majority of our household bills, and was attentive and faithful. Nikki was right about one thing: I had a good man.

"Patrick could motivate Darnell to come to church with you."

She had me there. One thing Darnell didn't do very often was attend church. He believed in God, but he wasn't very religious and would only go on Christmas or when I was doing something special on the program like the Women's Day celebration.

"Well, maybe. Listen, I'll call you later, and you may wanna pull your credit report and make sure Patrick hasn't jumped out there and gotten anything in your name behind your back," I suggested.

"You think he'd do that? Naw, he wouldn't." Nikki answered her own question.

We said goodbye, and I ended the call. I began unpacking my shopping bags and thought about how blessed I was. I couldn't imagine being single and having to deal with men like Patrick.

I knew when I met Darnell ten years ago that he was a good man, and when he saw I was a good woman, he made sure to make me his wife. We made a good team.

I picked up my phone and called him, but he didn't answer. He told me he had a doctor's appointment this morning, and I wanted to make sure everything went okay. I sent him a quick text, finished putting my things away, and decided to take a quick nap. I woke up an hour later, surprised by Darnell, who walked into our bedroom.

"Darnell?" I asked groggily as I sat up.

"Uh, yeah, baby. Who else would it be? You expecting someone else?" he teased.

"You're not funny. What are you doing home early? I called to see if you wanted to meet for dinner somewhere, but you didn't answer." I looked at him. "How was your appointment?"

"My what?" He seemed confused by my question.

"Your doctor's appointment?"

"Oh, yeah. It went fine. How was your, uh, outing with Kendra?" He reached for the TV remote and turned to ESPN before sitting at the foot of our California king-size bed.

"It was good. You know we had a good time as usual, but I do need to talk to you about something."

Darnell quickly turned around with a worried look on his face and muted the television. "What is it? What's wrong?"

"Well, you know how close Kendra and I are, Darnell."

"Yeah." He frowned.

"She's the closest thing I have to having my own child, and I love her and her sisters, and despite our differences, I love my sister too."

"Celia, where are you going with all of this? If you have something to say, just say it."

"Well, I want us to go on a family vacation. All of us: you, me, Kendra, the twins, and maybe Diane," I told him.

"What? A vacation?"

"A family vacation. A cruise, or maybe just rent a beach house for a week. We can all get away. Kendra truly deserves it, and I know she won't wanna go without her sisters." I waited for him to say okay. Darnell enjoyed traveling, and we had started tossing around ideas of where to go next. I figured now that my nieces were older, he wouldn't mind them tagging along.

"You want to bring a bunch of kids with us on vacation, Celia? I don't know about that." Darnell exhaled and rubbed his temples.

I was totally shocked by his response. *No* wasn't a word that I heard from Darnell very often. Not that I was spoiled, but because I never really asked for anything extreme. To me, inviting my family to join us on vacation shouldn't have been that big of a deal, so I was kind of put off when he resisted.

"They're not children, Darnell. They're teenagers," I told him.

"That makes it even worse. You know how teenagers are: they drink, smoke. . . ."

"You know my nieces aren't like that. Don't even try it. They're good girls."

"I'm not saying that they aren't. And Diane? Y'all can hardly be in the same room with each other, and now you're talking about going on a cruise with her? That's crazy." He shook his head. "I don't want to spend my vacation playing referee between you and your sister. You know how crazy you sound right now? Naw, Celia. That's a horrible idea. I can't believe you would even suggest that."

"It was just a thought, Darnell." I sighed, realizing that maybe he was right. My sister and I got along about as well as a KKK member at a Black Lives Matter rally. I allowed my desire to do something life changing for my nieces to overshadow the fact that Diane and I hated one another at times.

"I know, Celia," Darnell said, turning the TV back up.

I looked over at him, as handsome as ever, and crawled across the bed behind him. Putting my arms over his shoulders, I whispered in his ear, "I have another thought, Darnell."

"Really? What's that?" He smiled.

"Instead of arguing about a vacation, how about we do something else?"

"Like what?"

"Like this." I eased around and straddled his body, kissing his neck as I unbuttoned his shirt. A slight moan escaped him, and his hands cupped my ass, turning me on even more.

It had been weeks since we'd made love, and I was horny. Our mouths met with a passionate kiss, and I guided his hands into my loose-fitting jeans, then between my legs, so he could feel how much I wanted him.

"Damn, Cele, you're so fucking wet," he said, playing with my clit.

My hands left his and found their way inside the front of the sweatpants he was wearing. My fingers wrapped around his thick hardness, and it was my turn to smile. I eased off his lap and kneeled on the floor. I slipped my shirt over my head, and Darnell's eyes went to my full breasts.

"You like?" I asked, posing in the new bra I had recently purchased.

"Hell yeah!" He nodded.

"Good. I got something else I hope you'll like too," I said, again reaching for his manhood, this time taking it out of his pants. I eased in to kiss it, but Darnell's hand stopped me.

"Cele, stop," he said, nudging me away. "Come on."

"Nope," I said, once again attempting to take him into my mouth.

"I'm not playing, Cele. Don't."

"Darnell, just let me try," I said, my hands planted firmly on his thighs as I stared at him.

"No, I don't want you to try. I told you I don't want that," he said. "Now, you wanna have sex, I'm fine with that—"

"What I want to do is please my husband with my mouth." I sat back on my knees in frustration. "But he won't let me."

"Celia, why the fuck do we always go through this?" He adjusted himself and his penis, and I knew the moment was over before it even started. I had hoped that tonight would be different. Sex with Darnell was good, but I wanted something more—something he wasn't willing to do, or in this case, wasn't willing to allow me to do. Darnell refused to let me perform oral sex on him. He also didn't allow me to be on top when we were in bed. We basically had two positions: missionary and doggie when I could persuade him. There was the occasional morning wakeup "spoon" sex also, but that was it. At first, I thought it was because he suffered from some sort of childhood trauma, or maybe he'd been molested. I'd even suggested we go to a sex therapist. But he insisted it wasn't any of that, and that it was truly out of respect for me. He felt that there were certain things that wives shouldn't do in bed and only skeezers or whores, as he called them, did. As his wife, he said, I wasn't either one of them.

"Darnell, I swear, your sexual hang-ups are so damn frustrating." I stood up and headed toward our bathroom. "You don't want me to suck dick, you don't want me to get on top, and God forbid I want you to hit it from the back."

"What are you trying to say, Celia? I don't satisfy you?" He walked behind me and stood in the doorway.

"I'm saying I need to take a shower," I told him then closed the door in his face.

Kendra

After discovering my mother and my uncle in bed, then damn near coming to blows with her, the last place I wanted to be was in the house. Normally, I hated having to work on a Friday, but today, I was glad to have somewhere else to go. I had been working at Cell City for a year, and Fridays were our busiest days. We had a continual line of customers who either wanted to pay their prepaid bills or buy new phones. Despite having two other coworkers, it was my friend Sierra and I who would hold the place down and make sure the customers were handled. We stood behind the counter beside one another, taking payments and answering questions.

"It'll take about three or four days. Right, Kendra?" Sierra asked. When I didn't answer, she called my name again, this time a little louder. "Kendra?"

I glanced up from the computer screen that I had been staring at for the past two minutes and realized she was talking to me. "Huh?"

She gave me a strange look, then repeated, "Turnaround time on a Galaxy repair is three to four days?"

"Oh, yeah." I nodded. "That's right."

"What the hell is wrong with you today, girl?" she asked after the customer had left.

"Nothing, I'm fine," I lied. My mind was all over the place with thoughts about what had happened at my house and my mother's threats. All I wanted to do was call Aunt Celia and tell her everything, but I knew Mama wasn't playing when she said she would kick my sisters and me out. If that happened, we didn't have anywhere to go. As much as I knew Aunt Celia loved us, she always said she could only take Ashley and Avery in doses. There was no way we could go and live with her. My hands were tied.

"You've been spaced out ever since you got here. You sure you good?" Sierra asked again. I could see the concern in her face. Normally, I was bubbly and polite, but today, I knew she could tell I was distracted.

"Yeah, I just got into it with my mom, that's all." I sighed.

"Oh, I know how that bullshit is. You know my moms stay tripping. I can't wait to get my refund check so I can get an apartment. I've been saving all my coins, child, because I can't stay there much longer."

"Yeah, I can't leave, though. You know I have my little sisters to look after."

"I'm glad my brothers are older. They've been gone. As soon as they graduated, they were both out the damn door before they took their caps and gowns off." Sierra laughed, and so did I.

The door buzzed, indicating that a customer was entering. We both looked up and couldn't help but notice a tall guy with an athletic build walk in and start looking at the phones.

"Can I help you find something?" Dante, the store manager, came flying past us and strolled over to the guy. Sierra bumped my arm, and I shook my head. Dante was normally in the back of the store, where he was too busy doing inventory or some other imaginary task that prevented him from dealing with customers. However, whenever a handsome customer that he deemed approachable came in, he would mysteriously appear and offer assistance.

"Uh, I'm just looking right now. Thanks," the guy told him.

"Well, I'm Dante. If you need any help, just let me know."

"Thanks." The guy went back to looking at the phones.

Dante came and stood behind the counter and murmured, "Umph, umph, umph. I love a tall glass of water."

"Thirsty much?" Sierra teased. "And where the hell have you been? We were swamped out here ten minutes ago."

"I was in the back taking care of paperwork. You know it's almost the end of the month," he replied.

"Well, you can go right on back there and finish taking care of it. We got this out here." Sierra rolled her eyes at him.

A moment later, the guy walked up and stood right in front of me and held out a cracked iPhone. "Do you guys fix screens? My phone isn't insured, and my homeboy told me I could bring it here."

I looked at the severely cracked phone and said, "We do. Wow, what did you do? Throw this?"

He laughed, and I glanced up. Our eyes met, and I was caught off guard by how he was looking at me. He had the prettiest teeth and sexiest smile I had ever seen.

"Yeah, something like that. I was watching the game, and I guess I got carried away when my team won."

"Well, I would hate to see what would've happened if they lost," Sierra told him.

"Let's just say it's a good thing they didn't," the guy said then asked me, "So, can you fix it?"

"I can't fix it, but we have a technician who can. This phone is really damaged, though. How long have you had it?" I kept looking at the phone.

"About two years," he said. "I've been meaning to upgrade, but haven't had the time, I guess."

"Well, I can go ahead and help you with that," Dante offered.

"Nah, I think I'll just get it fixed for now, and then get the new Samsung when it comes out next month. Don't you think that's a better idea?" His eyes never left mine.

"Well, I'm an Apple girl myself, so I'm a little biased." I shrugged, trying not to seem intimidated by his stare, which I was. "You don't like your iPhone?"

"I do, but I was just considering trying something a little different, that's all. Sometimes you gotta change it up. Know what I mean?"

"I definitely know what you mean," Dante said as he reached for the phone that I was holding. "Change is always good. I have a Samsung myself, and I love it."

The guy looked over at him and said, "She has a point, Team Apple has been working fine for me."

"Good choice." Sierra laughed, and Dante rolled his eyes at her as he walked off.

"Our technician is booked for the day, so you'd have to leave it until tomorrow evening," I told him.

"Damn, I can't go that long without a phone." He exhaled. "You got a loaner phone I can use in the meantime?"

"I'm sorry, we don't. Do you have an old phone maybe you can use until we get this one fixed for you?" I suggested as I finally stopped looking at his sexy face to notice his fly outfit. There was no doubt about it; this dude had swag, from the red Polo sweater to the jeans he wore that fit him perfectly—not too tight, not too baggy, and damn sure not falling off his ass. His hair was thick, wavy, and cut into a nice fade, and his thick beard was well groomed.

"You know what? I do. I forgot all about that phone. Thanks."

"No problem. Let me go ahead and get some information from you, and we'll get you squared away," I said. I pulled up the customer information screen on my computer and asked him for his phone number. At first, he didn't answer. I looked up and saw that he was still staring at me. "Um, I need your phone number to pull you up in the system."

"My bad. I know I keep looking at you. Are your eyes green?"

It wasn't the first time someone had questioned, commented, or mentioned the color of my eyes. But there was something about the way he asked me that set off a spark inside of me.

"No, not green. They're hazel," I said.

"They're beautiful. Reminds me of this song 'Caramel' from back in the day: five-five, with light eyes, smile like the sunrise," he said, causing me to blush even harder than I already was.

"I think it's five-five with brown eyes," Sierra corrected him.

"Same thing." He laughed, then gave me his number.

I typed it in and pulled his account up in the system.

"Okay, Mr. Parker, is it?" I said, looking at the screen.

"Bilal," he said. "Bilal Parker, that's me."

Damn, even his name is sexy, I thought. "All right, Bilal Parker, the estimated cost of the repair is one fifty, unless we find something else wrong other than the screen."

He took out a wallet and opened it. I couldn't help noticing the amount of cash he had. It had to be at least a thousand dollars. He took out two hundred-dollar bills and passed them to me.

"Here you go."

"No, you don't pay until you pick it up," I told him.

"Oh, okay. So, you're gonna call me?" He raised an eyebrow at me as he put the cash back in the wallet.

"Huh?" I said.

"When it's ready tomorrow. Are you gonna call me?"

"Oh, yeah. The tech will give you a call once it's ready, or if they find something wrong that needs fixing," I said, embarrassed that I had misunderstood his question.

"Well, I appreciate your help—uh, I didn't get your name."

"Kendra," I said, handing him a receipt.

"Thank you, Kendra," he said, taking the slip of paper from me. "I'll see you when I come back."

"Thanks for choosing Cell City. Enjoy the rest of your day." I delivered the closing statement we were supposed to give all of our customers but usually didn't. I know it sounded corny as hell, but it was the only thing I could think to say to him.

"You enjoy yours too, Caramel—I mean, Kendra. Damn, you would make some pretty babies with those eyes of yours," he said just before turning to walk out the door.

As soon as he was gone, Sierra didn't waste any time stating, "That nigga was fine as hell! Oh my God. Why didn't you shoot your shot, girl? You shoulda got his number, Kendra."

"Well, I did, technically," I told her, holding up his phone and the order form for the repair.

"You know what I mean. Clearly, he was digging you. Quoting corny-ass song lyrics and shit," she teased.

"That was cute," I told her.

"And you're just as corny as his ass 'Thanks for choosing Cell City.' Your ass ain't said that to a customer since your first week of training."

We both laughed loudly, and Dante came from the back.

"Y'all need to calm down up here. This is a place of business, and we need to remain professional," he said.

"You're just salty because old boy was Team Apple and not interested in trading teams." Sierra giggled.

"Both of you can go to hell," he said.

"Now, Dante, that's not very professional of you to say," I told him.

In typical Dante fashion, he smacked his lips, rolled his eyes, and returned to do whatever it was he was pretending to do in the back of the store.

"One thing for sure: ol' boy can definitely get it," Sierra said.

"You're right," I agreed.

"What? I know you didn't just say that, Miss Purity, with your virgin ass." She looked just as shocked by my statement as I had been when I made it. "I thought you were saving yourself for someone special."

"I am." I looked down at the computer screen and said, "Bilal Parker."

"Even his name is sexy," Sierra said.

"True, but sexy or not, I've seen dudes like him all my life, and I can definitely spot a dope boy when I see him. And you know I don't do dope boys. Bilal Parker is the last dude I'll be giving anything to."

Bilal

"Damn, B. Where the hell you been? I been calling you all damn day!" Dell yelled as soon as he opened the front door.

"Man, my phone is all fucked up. I had to take it to get fixed. It should be ready tomorrow," I told him.

"Why you ain't just fix it yourself?"

I followed Dell into the living room, where he was in the middle of playing Madden and eating pizza.

"It wasn't something I could fix." I sat in one of the oversized chairs in the living room and peeked into the open cardboard box on the table with one remaining slice.

"Don't even think about it," Dell warned me, picking up the piece of pizza and biting it. Once he had chewed it to the point to where he could talk, he said, "You can break Firesticks, damn near hack databases, and install all types of fucking software, but you can't fix a cell phone?"

"The screen was cracked." I shrugged. Had I really wanted to, I probably could have just ordered the parts and fixed the phone myself, but I really didn't feel like going through the hassle, so I just took it into the store.

"Nigga, why didn't you just buy a new one? Them shits only like five, six stacks."

"And it only cost one fifty for me to get it fixed. Man, what's the big deal?" I laughed. five or six stacks was no money to Dell, who made ten times that in a month, but in my mind, five or six stacks meant half of my rent or two months of car payments. A new phone wouldn't set me back, but I just wasn't trying to spend it if I didn't have to.

"The big deal is that I couldn't reach you, cheap motherfucker. That's what."

"Man, the only reason you was calling was to talk shit about the damn game, which, by the way, we won," I told him. "Pay me my money."

"Shit." Dell reached into his pocket and took out two crisp fifty-dollar bills and threw them at me. "Take your change, chump. Maybe you can put it toward buying a new phone."

I picked up the money, which had landed on the floor in front of me, and put it in my pocket. Dell had always been a sore loser, even as a kid. When we'd be playing ball in the park, he was the one who would get mad and take his ball so that no one else could play if he lost. His poor sportsmanship didn't just end there. Dell and Marlena, his girlfriend of the past five years, had been engaged five times, because whenever he got mad, he would demand that she give him the ring back. I guess she had gotten used to it, because the last time he got down on one knee, she accepted the proposal, but not the ring.

"Where is everybody?" I asked. It was Friday evening, and usually, Dell's crib was the hangout spot for his brothers and cousins when they got off from work.

"I don't know. But I need you to take a ride with me right quick," he told me.

"Ride where?"

"I gotta pick up a package from D-Lo, and he needs to holla at you."

"Man, please. You know D-Lo ain't tryna holla me. That dude don't even like me ever since that shit between me and his cousin Fee went down," I told him.

"Ain't nobody thinking about that shit. This is business." Dell laughed. "D-Lo know his cousin is a ho. He ain't tripping about that. This is business."

"I hope it's business for real, because I ain't got time for bullshit, D, and you know I don't fuck with everybody for real."

"And I do? Come on. You know me better than that, and if I'm sending business your way, you know it's gotta be some decent money I'm putting in your pocket. Especially since your ass need a new phone."

I smiled at Dell. He'd been my best friend since we were in third grade. He was smart as hell, and we both graduated from high school with honors, but Dell had always been drawn to the drug game and all that came with it. I went to community college and studied computer science; he studied street narcotics. After I completed school, I worked tech support for a software company for a while but quickly realized that sitting behind a desk eight to ten hours a day wasn't something I enjoyed at all, so I found something that suited me a little better and paid a lot more. With Dell's help, I started my own legitimate, legal business and had been successful ever since.

"You know D-Lo ain't got no real money, though."

"I wouldn't say that. He ain't pushing as much weight as I am, but he got some cash flow."

"I can't tell," I said. D-Lo was only known to sell dime bags to high school kids. Based on where he lived and the car he drove, he wasn't making no real money as far as I could see. But I trusted Dell, and if he said D-Lo was legit, then I had to go with it.

"Just talk to the man, that's all." Dell shook his head at me.

"Fine, and for the record, I appreciate all the business you send me, even D-Lo's broke ass." I laughed.

"A'ight, let's roll."

Dell and I got into his Escalade to head over to D-Lo's raggedy-ass house across town.

"Where's Marlena?" I asked, noticing her Audi sitting in the driveway.

"Ain't nobody thinking about that girl," Dell said. "She got mad and went to stay at her sister's house, so I went and got my car."

"That's her car," I reminded him. "You gave it to her for her birthday, remember?"

"That was before she started acting stupid."

"Aw, hell. Trouble in paradise again? What did she do now, buy skim milk instead of two percent?" I teased. "No, wait. She probably folded the towels the long way instead of in half."

"Fuck you. She had the nerve to snap on me because some chick said long time no see to me in Walmart the other day," Dell said.

"What chick?"

"Don't matter." The way he said it let me know that Marlena had a good reason to snap. Dell loved her, but he also had a weakness for other women.

"Damn, Dell." I laughed.

"Whatever, and when is the last time you even had a girl? I damn sure can't remember."

"I get women all the time, and you know it," I told him, somewhat offended by his comment. It had been a minute since I had been in a relationship, but I got ass when I needed to. I had been so focused on starting my business and my busy schedule that a girlfriend was the last thing on my mind. There was also the fact that I hadn't really met anyone that caught my attention—until today. I thought about Kendra, the pretty girl from the cell store.

"I ain't talking about pussy from randoms, either," Dell said knowingly.

"Why are we even having this discussion?" I asked. "We're talking about how you're gonna get your woman back."

"What makes you think I want her back?"

"Because I know you better than anybody on this planet, and you love her."

Dell shrugged and said, "I do love her."

He was about to go into details about who the girl was when we turned into D-Lo's neighborhood and pulled into the dirt driveway in front of his house. His raggedy Impala was sitting out front, along with an old Chevy Blazer riddled with bullet holes. A couple of guys were sitting on the porch, playing dominoes and drinking.

"Man, make this quick," I told Dell when we got out of the truck.

"I will. This ain't gonna take long at all," he told me, reaching under the seat and taking out his 9 mm. I touched the waistband of my pants, making sure my own pistol was intact, and we both headed inside. I may not have engaged in the same line of work as my best friend, but I knew better than to roll out and not be strapped up in case something popped off.

"What's up?" Dell spoke as we got to the front door.

"'Sup," one of the dudes said without looking up.

"What's good?" The other one nodded.

Dell tapped on the door and opened it at the same time. I followed, and we entered the smoke-filled living room. I damn near caught a contact high before I even made it completely inside. I scanned the room but didn't see D-Lo anywhere.

"Where this nigga at?" Dell asked.

"I know you ain't asking me," I told him.

"What the fuck are you doing here?" a female voice asked.

Dell and I both turned to see Fee, D-Lo's cousin and one of my former randoms, standing in the doorway. My first thought was that this was some kind of setup, especially when I noticed Junie, her baby daddy, standing behind her.

"What's up, Fee? We here to meet D-Lo," Dell told her.

"D!" Fee called out. "D-Lo!"

D-Lo came walking down the hallway. He was a short, stocky guy who always wore sunglasses whether it was night or day and whether he was inside or out. "What the fuck are you calling my name like that for?"

"These clowns are here to see you." She rolled her eyes at me.

"Clowns? What the fuck?" I snapped. She wasn't calling me a clown when I was fucking her a couple of months ago while her baby daddy was locked up.

"Chill, Fee. They here to talk business," D-Lo told her.

"Business? Not with him, I hope." She pointed at me. I knew she was still salty because, for some reason, she really had it in her head that we were going together, although I told her time and time again I was only interested in the ass she was offering and nothing more. There was no way in hell that was going to happen. Even if I was interested in having a girl at the time, it wasn't going to be her hood ass.

"You need to listen to your cousin and chill out." I laughed.

"And you need to shut the fuck up," Fee snapped.

"Yo, D-Lo, you need to handle that shit," Dell warned.

"Fee, chill out, for real," D-Lo told her.

"Whatever, D-Lo. Don't act like you wasn't just in here talking shit about Dell the other night. And you swore you wouldn't ever fuck with this nigga because he—" She stopped when she realized Junie was listening.

"I think we need to go ahead and leave," I told Dell.

"Naw, it's all good," D-Lo said. "She's gonna shut the fuck up."

"I doubt that," I mumbled.

"Yo, who the fuck is this nigga?" Junie stepped to me.

"You definitely don't wanna do that," Dell told him.

"Junie, man, chill," D-Lo said again.

"They're right, man. You don't wanna do this." I shook my head.

"Fuck you." Junie took a step closer.

"Son, I'm telling you this ain't the dude you wanna try," Dell told him.

"Man, ain't nobody thinking about this dude. You warning me about him when you should be warning him about me," Junie said. "Ask about where I'm from."

"Well, considering you ain't listening to them, it seems that they're a whole lot smarter than where you're from," I said.

"What did you say?" Junie came and stood in front of me. We were about the same height and size, but my shoulders were slightly broader than his.

"Junie, man, you need to calm down. You don't understand—" D-Lo reached for him, but he snatched away.

"Understand what? That I'm 'bout to knock this—"

Before he could finish, I had balled up my fist and punched him in the face with so much force that he crumpled to the floor. He covered his eye where the punch had landed. The two guys that had been on the porch ran in. Seeing Junie on the floor, they started laughing.

"Damn it, Junie. I told you." Dell sighed.

"Bitch ass mother—" Junie hopped to his feet and was about to charge at me, but two guys grabbed him.

"Take him outside and let him walk it off," Dell told them.

Junie was still struggling to get at me when they escorted him out the door.

"You good?" Dell asked me.

"Yeah, I'm cool," I said, checking my knuckles to make sure they were still intact. It had been a minute since I'd gotten into a fight, but it was good to know that my punch still carried some power behind it.

"I tried to warn him. You heard me, right?" D-Lo shrugged.

"Me too. People don't realize. Bilal ain't no killer, but don't push him." Dell laughed. "That nigga called you soft, and you knocked his ass to the ground."

I turned and looked at Fee, who stood staring and too stunned to move. Before I could say anything to her, D-Lo snatched her ass.

"Next time you talk shit in front of your boyfriend, you're gonna get fucked up right along with him," he said.

Diane

The last place I planned on spending my day off was at Celia's house, but when I finally woke up Sunday afternoon, the entire house was empty. No one mentioned anything about going anywhere, so I sent a text to Avery, asking where the hell they were. I knew she was the best one to ask, because Ashley's attitude toward me was just as bad as Kendra's, who still wasn't talking to me. Out of all my daughters, Avery was the one who remained loyal no matter what. She was the one who always checked on me to make sure I made it to work safely, let me know that she made me a plate and put it in the microwave, and kept me abreast about what was going on in the house. I knew Kendra and Ashley weren't too pleased with how she looked out for me. I had overheard them criticize her for her concern on more than one occasion. I appreciated her sticking up and defending me, and I was grateful that I shared a bond with at least one of my daughters. The other two could go to hell as far as I was concerned.

Sure enough, Avery texted me back, telling me that Celia had picked them up and they were at her house and about to have dinner. I told her to bring me a plate. A few minutes later, my phone rang.

"Aunt Celia said if you want a plate, you gotta come and get it yourself." Avery sighed.

"What?" I snapped.

"This ain't no takeout restaurant. If she wants to eat, she can come and sit down at the table with the rest of us. Tell her the food will be ready in forty-five minutes," Celia yelled in the background. "Ashley, baby, hand me that pan for this macaroni and cheese."

"Yes, ma'am," Ashley said cheerfully. I could just see her fawning over everything in Celia's kitchen and making her feel like the queen she already thought she was. "Can I stir it?"

"You sure can," Celia told her.

"I told her you were resting today, Mama. You been working all week," Avery whispered.

"Don't worry about it. Screw her and her fucking dinner. She just wants me to drive all the way the hell over there to brag about some new shit she bought and don't need. Ain't nobody—"

"Gimme that damn phone. Diane, shut up and put some clothes on and come on over here. Now, ain't nobody gonna beg you to come and eat," Celia stated.

"I ain't say nobody had to beg me, Celia. You know today's my only day to rest. I been working for the past three days straight. I'm tired and don't feel like coming all the way over there," I told her. "I don't know why that's so hard for you to understand. You can't just send me a plate?"

"Di, when is the last time you've sat down and had dinner with your family, specifically your girls? Like, at a table, and had a real conversation with them over a meal?"

I thought about her question. I couldn't remember the last time we sat down and had dinner. Shit, I couldn't remember the last time I had cooked a meal. Most of the cooking in my house was done by Kendra, along with the cleaning, laundry, and other household chores, many of which she delegated to her younger sisters. It wasn't that I wasn't capable of being more maternal, but my oldest daughter never gave me the chance to be the mother in the house. Not that I was eager to do so anyway.

"You don't know what you're talking about, Celia. You act like—"

"Darnell has some steaks on the grill. I made crab cakes and fish. I'll give you forty dollars to put in your gas tank when you get here. Now, bring your ass," Celia said then hung up.

Hell, after speaking with her, of course I was gonna go to her house. I would get a free meal consisting of my favorite foods, enough money to fill my gas tank twice, and I would see Darnell's fine ass. I would be crazy not to go. I figured now was as good a time as any to introduce Terry, the guy I'd been dating for the past two and a half months when I wasn't fucking Darnell, to the family. I called him and told him I would pick him up in twenty minutes. After a quick shower, I put on my tightest jeans, a button-down shirt, and a pair of peep-toe booties. I piled my braids on top of my head, then dabbed on some lip gloss and some of the Marc Jacobs Daisy perfume that Celia had given me for Christmas.

Terry was eagerly waiting when I arrived to pick him up. He wasn't the brightest guy I'd been with, but he was tall, sexy, and worked at the Target warehouse, so he was always hooking me up with what I needed.

Celia's oversized five-bedroom, three-bathroom brick home sat in the center of a cul de sac. I never understood why she and Darnell needed that big-ass house, especially since it was just the two of them. Everything about my sister just seemed so damn excessive to me. She was extra when it came to everything—her job, her clothes, her house. Seemed funny to me that the only thing she wasn't excessive in was pleasing her man. Darnell said he never got head, and they mainly only had sex in the missionary position; hence, why he came to me. I may not have had a well-paying career or an overflowing bank account like she did, but my bedroom skills and talents were top notch, and I made sure to be quite impressive each and every time I was with him.

"Damn, this place is nice as hell," Terry said when we arrived. Celia's car was in the driveway parked beside Darnell's Audi and a huge Dodge Ram truck. "Your sister and her husband must be paid."

"They do all right. Please don't go up in here commenting about their shit. Act like you been somewhere. She already thinks that she's better than we are," I warned him.

"I feel you. My brother acts like that too, like because he got that good job being the manager at Jiffy Lube, he's the man," Terry said as we walked to the front of the house.

I rang the doorbell and glanced at Terry's outfit, which consisted of baggy jeans, an oversized white T-shirt, and some Timberland boots. Celia probably wouldn't be pleased with his attire, but I didn't care. It wasn't her reaction that I was concerned about anyway.

The door opened, and Darnell stood smiling. Like Terry, he was also dressed in jeans and a white T-shirt, but his were well-fitting designer jeans, and he wore an apron on top. He went to greet me with a hug, until he saw Terry standing beside me. His face went blank for a second. I hadn't seen him since our midday rendezvous had been interrupted by Kendra. That was almost a month ago. Now, here I was, standing on his doorstep, wearing braids that he'd paid for, with another guy by my side. He was not pleased, and I was glad that he wasn't.

"Hey, Darnell." I grinned, then said, "This is my friend, Terry."

"What's up, man?" Terry gave Darnell a pound with his fist. "This a nice crib y'all got."

I cut my eyes at him, but he was so busy looking past Darnell that he didn't see me.

"What's up? Y'all come on in." Darnell moved so we could come inside.

I gave him a seductive wink as I walked by. I led Terry down the hallway and into the den area.

"Hey, good. You're here," Celia said when she came into the room; then added, "Oh, you brought a guest."

"Yes, this is my friend, Terry," I said.

"Uh, nice to meet you, Terry." Celia's voice was an octave higher than normal, and her smile was fake. She hated unexpected guests in her home.

"Same here. Wow, that TV is huge. Is that a 4K?" Terry asked, pointing at the plasma television hanging on the wall.

"Yeah, it is," Darnell said. "You want a beer?"

"You know I do," I said.

"Yeah, I'll take one," Terry added.

"Where are the girls?" I asked Celia.

"They're in the sunroom, setting the table. The food is almost ready, and we're gonna eat in there. I guess I need to tell them to set another place," Celia said. "I'll be right—"

"No, I'll tell them. Come on, Terry, so you can meet the girls," I told him.

The irritated look on Celia's face now matched the one on Darnell's. The day was getting better and better.

"Mama!" Avery ran over and hugged me when I walked into the sunroom. Kendra and Ashley barely looked in my direction.

"Hey, Avery," I told her. I looked at her sisters and said, "Hello, Ashley, Kendra. Girls, this is Terry."

My three daughters were polite but nonchalant as they spoke. Darnell walked into the sunroom carrying two beers, handing one to Terry, then the other to me. I took a long sip.

"I'm going to help Aunt Celia," Kendra said, rolling her eyes at both Darnell and me.

"Me too." Ashley followed Kendra out the door.

"I guess I should go help too." Avery shrugged.

Darnell made small talk with Terry and me while we waited for Celia and the girls to bring the food out, and then we all sat down for dinner. Darnell and Celia each sat at the heads of the table. The twins and Kendra, who avoided looking in my direction, sat across the table from Terry and me. The conversation during the meal was mainly Terry and I talking to one another. Darnell contributed a comment every now and then about a sports team, and everyone else just sat and listened. Once we were done eating, Celia finally spoke.

"So, y'all know my birthday is coming up. I've decided to treat myself this year," she announced.

"What are you gonna get, Auntie?" Ashley asked excitedly.

"Something I've always wanted," Celia said.

"A puppy?" Avery said.

"Hell no, not up in here," Darnell spoke up. We knew he didn't like dogs, which was ironic to me.

"No, not a dog." Celia laughed. "Although I have always wanted one. Uncle Darnell is scared of dogs."

"You scared of dogs for real, man?" Terry laughed.

"No, I ain't scared of no damn dog. I just don't like them." Darnell shook his head. "I had a bad experience when I was a kid, that's all."

"A trip to Italy." Kendra's voice was so low that I almost didn't hear her.

"Ohhhhh, yeah." Ashley clapped.

"No, not yet. I'm saving that for when you graduate," Celia told her. "We're gonna go together to celebrate. Now, hurry up and finish."

Kendra smiled at my sister, and for a second, I felt a twinge of jealousy.

"I am, Aunt Celia, with honors. I promise."

"Well, what the hell is it?" I asked.

"A BMW." Celia grinned.

"Oh, yes! Aunt Celia, a BMW is perfect for you," Ashley told her.

"That's so cool," Avery commented.

"Great gift, and you deserve it." Kendra smiled.

"Which one are you getting? You'd look good in an X5." Terry nodded. "It's classy."

"It's funny you say that, because that's exactly what I'm getting," Celia told him.

"I knew it," he said. Again, I rolled my eyes at him.

"And I've decided to give you the Volvo," Celia said to Kendra.

My mouth fell open, and so did everyone else's at the table. I couldn't believe she was giving Kendra a car that was only three years old.

"Are you serious?" Kendra asked.

"Yeah, once I get my new car at the end of next month, it's yours. And you'd better take care of my baby," Celia told her.

"Kendra, you're gonna have your own car. Oh, snap!" Avery nudged Kendra, who had tears in her eyes.

"It's about to be on." Ashley gave Avery a high five.

"No, she ain't," I said. "You are not about to give her that damn car. That makes no sense."

Celia looked at me like I was crazy. "What are you talking about? She needs a car to get to school and to work."

"And to take us places," Ashley whined.

"Why would you give your car to her and not me? I'm the one who drives all over the fucking city going to clients' houses. You know how old and run-down my car is. Hell, you've had to help me pay to get it fixed."

"I'm not giving you my car," Celia stated matter-of-factly.

"Why not? That would make more sense than giving it to Kendra. Shit, she hardly drives," I snapped.

"Because I don't have a car!" Kendra spoke up.

"You can have my car if she gives me hers." I pointed to Celia.

"You're not getting my car," Celia repeated as she shook her head.

I decided I needed some reinforcements. "Darnell, can you please tell her that giving Kendra that car instead of me makes no sense? My car is in horrible condition."

"It is in pretty bad shape." Darnell shrugged.

"Well, you know my brother is the manager at Jiffy Lube. I can get him to look at it," Terry offered.

"Shut up, Terry." I finally said what I'd been wanting to say all evening.

"Why would you want Kendra to drive an unsafe car? That's why it makes more sense for her to have the Volvo. It's a safer car for her to drive," Celia said.

"She's not getting that damn car. If I can't have it, then she can't either," I told her.

"You sound so damn childish, Diane. Don't be like that." Celia sighed.

"Childish? Did you just call me childish?" I stood up.

"Yes, I did. You're pretty much throwing a temper tantrum at the table because I won't give you *my* car. I'm doing something nice for your daughter. I would think you'd be a little more appreciative."

"Appreciative of what? It ain't like you did shit for *me*, Celia. You never do. Hell, you wouldn't even let Ashley bring me a plate home. And I know why you did this shit. You ain't slick. You wanted me to come all the way the fuck over here so, once again, you could floss and shine and force me to sit here while you brag about taking Kendra on exotic trips and then giving her your car. Fuck you, Celia. Let's go, Terry," I yelled.

"Diane, calm down. That's not what she was doing," Darnell told me, and I gave him a threatening look.

"Mama, please," Ashley pleaded.

I looked over at Kendra, who stared at me in disgust. I was pissed and ready to go. I stormed out the front door. Terry was on my heels.

"Diane, baby, wait. I don't think you should leave like this," he suggested.

"Get in the fucking car!" I screamed, and he jumped in the car.

"Mama, come back!" Ashley came running out the front door. "Are you just gonna leave us?"

"Get Kendra to bring you home in her new fucking car!" I yelled before spinning out of the driveway and speeding off down the street.

Celia

I didn't know what the hell was going on, but it seemed as if my entire family had lost their damn minds. First, I had to damn near force Kendra to come to the house. After leaving early morning church service, I called and said I was on my way to pick her and her sisters up, and she said she couldn't come. Normally, when I called to say I was cooking Sunday dinner, she and her sisters would be ecstatic, so I immediately became concerned. When I asked why, she began stuttering and giving bullshit excuses that I wouldn't accept, until finally, she said okay. When I pulled up to the house and saw Diane's car parked in front, I knew my sister probably had something to do with her initial hesitation. Then, when we got to the house, she hardly spoke to Darnell and spent most of the time alone upstairs in the bedroom that we kept reserved for her. Then, Diane finally showed up, but she had some random man with her. She flipped out when I told Kendra that she could have my car; then she stormed off, leaving all three of her daughters in tears.

"You guys okay?" I asked as I drove them home. I had tried to salvage the remainder of the evening with ice cream sundaes and a trip to the nail salon, but the girls still seemed melancholy.

"We're fine," Kendra answered, taking a glimpse at her sisters in the back seat.

"Yes, ma'am." Ashley and Avery both nodded.

"Well, I had fun with y'all," I told them. "Despite what happened. And I meant what I said. I'm giving you my car, Kendra. Your mama may not like it or agree with it, but it's my car, and I can give it to whoever I want to give it to. You need a car, and you deserve it."

Kendra looked over at me and said, "You don't have to give it to me, Aunt Celia. She can have it. I'll be fine."

"Ain't no way in hell I'm giving her my car. It's yours, end of story," I told her.

"Aunt Celia?" Ashley called my name.

"Yes?" I looked at her in the rearview mirror.

"Can we stop at the store?"

"No, Ashley. It's getting late. We gotta get home. Besides, Aunt Celia has to drive all the way back after she takes us." Kendra frowned.

"But we don't have anything to drink at home," Avery said.

"Stop begging. We have plenty of water," Kendra told her.

"And Avery and I need some soap," Ashley said.

"It's fine. We can stop, but I'm not getting out. Target is the devil, and he won't win all of my money today." I laughed and pulled into the front of the store. I reached into my purse and handed both of them a twenty-dollar bill—the same twenties that I had been planning to give their mother. They hopped out of the back seat and ran inside the store.

I looked at Kendra and asked, "Do you need anything?"

"No, I'm fine," she told me before getting out of the car. "But I better go in and make sure they hurry."

I was waiting for them to come out when I looked over and saw a guy waving at me as he walked out of the store. I waved back, and he walked over to my car.

"I thought that was you. How are you doing?" he asked after I rolled my window down.

"I'm good. How about you?" I smiled.

"I'm great. Busy as ever. Still waiting on that call from you."

"I know, I know. You'll hear from me soon."

"Okay, I'll be waiting. You still got my number?"

"I do." I nodded.

He reached into his pocket and handed me a business card. "Just in case you don't."

I took it and said, "Thank you."

"All right, well, you enjoy the rest of your Sunday."

"You too. And I'm going to call."

He grinned and walked away. I couldn't help but watch him as he went to his car. Lord knows he was fine as hell. If I wasn't married and was a few years younger, there was no telling what would happen. I glanced back over to the front of the store and saw Kendra standing and staring for a few seconds before coming to get back in the car.

"Is everything okay?" I asked when she got in. "Where are the twins?"

"They're paying for their stuff. You know that guy?" she asked with a strange look on her face. "The one you were just talking to."

"Yeah, Bilal. You know Ms. Nikki's boyfriend, Patrick?"

"Yeah."

"That's his nephew. Why? Do you know him?" I asked her.

"No. Well, yeah. Well, no," she stammered.

"What in the world? Either you know him, or you don't."

"Well, he was a customer in the store last month. He came in to get his phone fixed. So, I don't *know him* know him." She shrugged.

"Well, damn. Do you wanna know him?" I teased.

Kendra immediately blushed and shook her head "Oh my God, no, Aunt Celia. I was just wondering how you knew him, that's all."

"It's nothing to be embarrassed about. That's one fine man, and he's smart. Hell, I was just thinking if I wasn't married to your uncle, I would holler at the brother."

"Aunt Celia!" Kendra gasped.

"What? You know he's fine. That's why you asked about him yourself. He can get it, huh?"

"Oh my God, Aunt Celia. Please don't talk like that. I'm begging you." Her face reddened even more.

The back doors opened, and Ashley and Avery got into the car, chatting about what they had bought. Kendra looked relieved as she conveniently joined their conversation.

I drove them home. They all seemed disappointed when they arrived and saw that Diane's car wasn't in the driveway.

"Don't forget to get those plates out of the trunk," I told them as they were getting out of the car.

"Thanks, Aunt Celia," Ashley told me.

"Love you, Aunt Celia," Avery said. They both gave me a kiss through the driver-side window before getting the leftover food that I had packed up to for them to take home.

"Love you too, sweeties. Have a good week at school. And text me," I told them.

Kendra remained seated in the front seat. "Sorry again about my mom, Aunt Celia."

"Stop apologizing for her ignorance. It ain't your fault," I told her. "Y'all gonna be all right?"

"Yeah, we'll be fine," Kendra said softly as she looked out the window. "Aunt Celia?"

"Yeah?"

"You and Uncle Darnell . . . you . . . he . . . Mom—" She stopped.

"Kendra, your Uncle Darnell and I know how your mother is. She's family, and there's nothing we can do about her or her bad behavior. But we love you and your sisters, and we're gonna do everything we can to help you girls," I assured her.

"Thanks for coming to get us today."

"Anytime, darling." I leaned over and kissed her forehead.

She got out and went inside the house, waving to let me know she was safe inside.

Later that night, I was getting ready for bed when Darnell came into the bedroom. "Can you believe Diane acted like that?" I asked him.

"I can't believe a lot of shit you and your sister do," he replied with such an attitude that it caught me off guard.

"What is that supposed to mean?"

"I'm just saying that sometimes you antagonize her, and you know it."

"How did I antagonize her? Giving Kendra my car is antagonizing? Really? Bullshit," I said as I brushed my hair.

"You have a tendency to cross a line when it comes to her children, that's all."

"Again, that's bullshit. I love my nieces, and I make sure they are taken care of."

"That's my point. You make sure everyone knows that you take care of them, especially Diane. You ain't have to make a whole fucking announcement at dinner and shit, Celia. You made her look bad."

"She made herself look bad. And since when did you start taking up for her?" I demanded.

"I ain't taking up for her. I'm stating facts. And when did we decide that you were even getting a new car?" he asked.

"I didn't know I needed to discuss it with you."

"I'm your husband. Of course you needed to discuss it with me. You were quick to discuss the fucking money we took out for all them damn IVF treatments that ain't work."

Darnell's words stung, and I felt like I'd been slapped without him even touching me. The last thing I needed to be reminded of was my inability to have children. It was a fact that I dealt with every single day.

"You were the one who wanted to try in vitro, Darnell," I said, fighting to hold back the tears.

"Because both of us wanted to have a baby, Celia. The in vitro was for us, not you."

"Well, I was the one who had to go through it—the injections, the stress, and the miscarriages—so I know they didn't work. You don't have to remind me. And for the record, I just got a promotion and a raise. I can afford to buy a car if I want to. It won't affect our household account one bit," I said matter-of-factly. "I work hard, and I deserve it—unlike my sister, who you're so quick to defend."

"Listen, you're the one who started this conversation by asking me a fucking question, and now, because I won't side with you, you got an attitude." He snatched a pillow off the bed and headed out the bedroom door.

"Darnell, what the hell? What are you doing?"

"I'm not gonna stay in here tonight with you acting like this. I'm going to sleep in the guest bedroom. Wait, no, that's Kendra's bedroom. I'm going to sleep downstairs," he said.

I couldn't believe my husband was acting like this. I didn't know what the fuck was going on with him lately, but he needed to get it together and get it together quick, because one thing I wasn't about to do was deal with him and his tempter tantrums much longer.

Kendra

I walked into the house still in a state of disbelief. When I had walked out of Target and saw Bilal standing by the car and talking to Aunt Celia, I thought I was seeing things. I had been thinking about him ever since the day he came into the store. When I found out he had come back to pick up his phone when I wasn't at work, I was disappointed. It didn't help that Dante bragged about how he'd been the one who was there when Bilal came in "looking like a whole snack." Dante even helped Bilal pick out a new protective phone case. Sierra suggested that I give Bilal a "courtesy call" to make sure his phone was working properly, but I was too afraid. I accepted the fact that I would probably never see him again, until tonight. I had to call Sierra.

"Kendra, are you still gonna twist my hair?" Ashley asked as soon as I walked in the door. "You promised."

"Uh, yeah, in a little while. Go take your shower first," I told her, heading into my bedroom.

"Mine too?" Avery asked.

"No, don't even try it. You are *not* getting your hair like mine. I asked her to do this last week. You wasn't even thinking about getting your hair twisted. You told Mom you wanted braids like hers," Ashley snapped.

"But she said she ain't got the money to get them done yet," Avery told her then turned to me and said, "Please, Kendra."

I looked at her, then back to Ashley, who was waiting for my response with her arms folded and an attitude on her face. I shrugged and said, "We'll see. Go take a shower, both of you."

"Okay." Avery smiled. Satisfied with my response, she hopped up and ran down the hallway.

"Don't worry about it. You can just do hers. I'll do my own hair." Ashley gave me a disappointed look.

"Ash, don't be like that. I told you I would do it. Just go take a shower and make sure you wash your hair good." I winked. "I'm not twisting any hair that ain't washed."

Ashley grinned, realizing that there was no way Avery was going to wash her hair without being told, minimizing her chances of my twisting it. She gave me a hug, then just like Avery had done moments before, took off down the hallway.

I smiled and headed toward my bedroom. As I passed my mother's door, I could hear the sound of nineties R&B playing. The aroma of marijuana hit my nostrils, alerting me to what was going on inside. I figured she had to be in there with that Terry dude she had brought with her to Aunt Celia's house. He seemed innocent enough. Although I was disgusted by the fact that, once again, she had brought another random man into our home for sex, I was glad that it wasn't my uncle this time.

As soon as I got into my room, I dialed Sierra's number. She had barely said the word "hello" before I started talking.

"Guess who I saw at Target today?"

"Was it somebody famous?" she asked.

"No, nobody famous," I told her.

"Was it a regular?"

"No, not a regular, but it was a customer," I hinted.

"From your excitement, I'm thinking it's a guy. Oh my God, Kendra, did you see him?" she gushed, and her excitement now matched mine.

"Yes, it was him." I laughed.

"Did he see you? Did you look cute? I hope you looked cute, Kendra. Please tell me you looked cute. What did you say to him?"

"I didn't say anything, and it doesn't matter if I was cute or not. He didn't see me."

"What? Why not? You didn't speak to him? Was he with a girl?"

"No, he was alone, I think. And the only girl I saw him with was my Aunt Celia." I laughed.

"Wait. What? I'm confused. He was in Target with your aunt?"

"No, when I walked out of the store, he was talking to her while she was sitting in her car. But she does know him. It's her friend's nephew."

"Oh, shit! So this whole time we've been tryna find out how you can see this dude—"

"I haven't been tryna figure out anything. That's all you."

"Come on, Kendra. Don't act like you wasn't feeling that dude. Y'all had all types of sparks and fireworks and shit going off while he was in the store. And you said yourself that he could get it. Now you wanna act like this?"

"I ain't say he wasn't fine. But right now, I'm tryna focus on school and taking care of my sisters. The last thing I'm gonna be doing is getting involved with a dope boy. That ain't me," I told her.

"I'm ready." Ashley stepped into my room with her hair dripping and a towel around her neck. She had a plastic bag full of hair products in her hand.

"Listen, I gotta go twist my sister's hair. We'll talk more when I get to work tomorrow."

"Definitely, because this ain't the end of this conversation, heffa," Sierra said before hanging up the phone.

"Come on in here, silly rabbit." I beckoned for Ashley to come in. I grabbed a throw pillow off my bed for her to sit on and put it on the floor in front of me. She plopped down and shook her head, spraying water everywhere "What the hell?"

"Oh, sorry," Ashley said innocently "Who was that?"

"None of your business, nosy," I said and began towel-drying her wet tresses.

My mother may not have given us a lot physically or emotionally, but two things my sisters and I had been blessed with that definitely came from her were our thick, wavy hair and our cute figures. I looked at her hair hanging past her shoulders and knew it was going to take at least an hour and a half to complete.

As soon as she sat down, Avery walked into the room.

Ashley wasted no time telling her, "Your hair ain't washed, so it ain't getting twisted."

Avery rolled her eyes at both of us. Just before walking out, she said, "Fine. Mama said I could get braids next week anyway."

When she was gone, Ashley asked, "Do you have a new boyfriend?"

"What?"

"I heard you talking about being with a dope boy."

"See, this is what I tell you about ear hustling. You always get stuff wrong. What I said was that I'm *not* going to be with a dope boy. I have more important stuff to do with my life, and I have too much to risk, so being with a dope boy ain't happening."

"Don't you want a boyfriend with money? Dope boys always got money," Ashley said.

"I have a job. I make my own money. When I graduate from college, I'll get a better job and make more money. And I plan to date a guy who has a job and makes his own money, too—legally. Anything worth having is worth working for. Guys that sell dope may make a lot of money, but it's easy money and easy to lose their life or their freedom over. Remember that," I told her.

I constantly tried to teach my sisters to make the right choices, especially since my mother constantly made the wrong ones.

"Remember when Mama was dating Doobie?" she asked. "He used to give her money all the time. And us. And he had that nice car. He was real nice. I liked him, and he was a dope boy."

"And where is Doobie now?"

"Mama broke up with him," she said mat-ter-of-factly. "That's why he stopped coming around."

"He's in jail, Ash. He got pulled over, had a gun under the seat. They ended up raiding his house and finding a shitload of powder. And now he's behind bars. All that money he had ain't doing him a bit of good," I told her.

"For real?"

"For real. Now, turn your head around so we can get these twists done."

I spent the next hour twisting her hair and watching *Power*, making sure to remind her that there was a difference between what happens on TV and what happens in real life. I was nearly finished when Avery came back in.

"Kendra! Come here!"

"She's not doing your hair!" Ashley told her.

"You're mean," I said to Ashley, laughing with her.

"Kendra!" Avery called my name again. This time I could tell it was serious, so I got up and went to see what she wanted. She beckoned for me to come farther down the hallway

"What?" I asked, confused until I heard yelling coming from the other side of the door.

"Listen," she whispered.

"What have I told you and Ashley about ear hustling?" I hissed, not even wanting to know what kinds of sexual sounds she was hearing. "Get away from that door."

"Something is wrong. I think they're fighting." She had a panicked look on her face.

I listened closer, and sure enough, I heard my mother cursing.

"I don't know what the fuck you're talking about. You're crazy. Get the fuck out of my house!"

"I ain't going no fucking where until you give me my fucking money. Now, where is it?" Terry's voice was loud, but I could tell he was trying not to yell.

"I don't have your fucking money."

"You're lying. I know how much money I had in my fucking pants pocket. I had two hundred and thirty-seven fucking dollars, and now it's only thirty-seven. You stole two hundred dollars from me, and I want it back now."

"Get your fucking hands off me, bitch. I don't have your fucking money! Let me go!"

There was a loud crash, and before I could stop her, Avery grabbed the door and ran in.

"Avery!" I took off behind her. Inside the room, Terry, wearing only his sweatpants, had my mother pressed up against the dresser. The loud crash was the sound of the mirror crashing to the floor.

"Get the fuck off my mama!" Avery screamed.

"Move back, little girl." Terry tried to hold my little sister back with his one free hand as Avery charged at him.

"Avery, get back here." I grabbed at her, but she was too quick.

"You'd better not touch my fucking daughter!" my mother screamed at him.

"You'd better give me my fucking money!" Terry yelled, squeezing her arm tighter.

"Let her go!" I yelled, as I still tried to grab Avery, who was now clawing at Terry.

Suddenly, Ashley came running in and joined in the chaos. The three of us were too much for Terry to handle. We proceeded to pounce on him until he released my mother from his grasp. Once she was free, she lurched at him again, but I restrained her. Ashley stood behind me, crying and sweating. Her hair that moments ago was neatly twisted was now unraveled and wild. Avery stood against the wall near my mother's nightstand, barely moving.

"Get dressed and get out!" I yelled at him.

"I will as soon as she gives me my fucking money!" he yelled back.

"I don't have it. I keep telling you," Mama panted. She was completely naked, so I had to wonder if she was telling the truth.

"She doesn't have it," I told him.

"She's a fucking lie, and I ain't leaving here without it!" He went to grab her again.

Ashley screamed, "Averyyyyyyyy, noooooo!"

I turned and saw Avery with a gun pointed directly at Terry. Everyone stood and stared at her.

"Avery, it's okay," I said, my voice trembling as much as her hand that was holding the pistol was.

"Get your shit and get out of our house," Avery told him.

"You heard her, Terry. Get the fuck out before she shoots your stupid ass," Mama warned him.

I pleaded with him, "Terry, just leave, please. Before anyone gets hurt."

Terry's eyes stayed on Avery for a second before he said, "I'm leaving. I need the rest of my clothes and shoes."

"See, Avery, he's leaving. Put the gun down," I told her.

"Not 'til he gets the fuck out," Avery said, tears mixed with sweat on her face. I could see that she was just as scared as Terry was.

I reached down and grabbed Terry's shirt that was near my foot and tossed it to him. Ashley snatched his Timberland boots and pushed them into his hand.

"You got your shit. Now leave, motherfucker," Mama said.

"Mama, please." I sighed.

Terry turned and ran out of the room and down the hallway. We all followed behind him, making sure that he continued out of the house.

"Go back in the house," I told them as I stood on our small porch and watched Terry running down the street, still holding onto his shirt and boots. I walked back inside, making sure to lock the door behind me and praying that he wouldn't come back with a gun of his own in search of his money.

I went back down the hallway. Ashley and Avery were huddled together in the doorway of my mother's room. She was inside, sitting on the side of her bed, smoking a cigarette.

"Is he gone?" Ashley asked me.

"Yeah." I nodded "He's gone."

"Mama, are you okay?" Avery asked.

"I'm fine," Mama told her, then said, "I'm glad y'all had my back. Avery, where's that damn gun?"

"I put it back in your drawer, Mama," Avery said.

Mama walked over to the dresser and took out the gun, looking at it. "It's a damn shame that motherfucker spazzed out like that. His ass ain't have no damn two hundred and thirty-seven dollars. Lying ass. It was only a hundred and eighty-seven."

"What?" My eyes widened in surprise, and I gulped loudly as I realized what her statement meant.

"See for yourself." She reached under the mattress, took out some folded bills, and spread them on the bed. Sure enough, it was a hundred and fifty dollars.

"Mama!" Ashley gasped.

"Mama, do you realize what just happened? What could've happened?" I snapped.

"Kendra, don't start with me. I ain't in the mood. Avery, go get the broom and help me clean this shit up. After all, you're the one who needed this damn money to get your hair braided."

Diane

I spent the remainder of my days off hanging with my girl Ronda at her apartment. I tried to stay away from the house during the day in case Terry decided to pop up. I knew that as long as the girls were at the house, I was pretty safe, but while I was there alone, I wasn't so sure. I also wasn't sleeping all that great. It wasn't the first time I had taken money from a guy, but this was the first time things had gotten crazy and involved my girls.

I couldn't believe Avery had pulled the gun out of my nightstand and aimed it at Terry. She was truly my ride or die, and I had no problem handing over the two fifty-dollar bills and hugging her tightly after she swept the mess from my floor. As usual, Kendra and Ashley were treating me like a heathenous slut. I stayed out of their way, and they stayed out of mine.

And now, to top everything off, I was running late for work. Most of my clients didn't mind me

being tardy, but the latest one I was assigned to
was a real bitch. She called the agency for the
slightest infractions. The last time I was late, not
only did I get a call from HR, but I was given a
written warning. I was treading on thin ice, and
I knew this might lead to me getting fired, if not
suspended, and I couldn't afford to have either
one of those happen. I put my foot on the gas to
speed up so I could make it to my client's house
faster.

"What the fuck?" I said out loud as my car
began to jerk. I looked at the gas needle, making
sure it wasn't all the way on E. It was at almost
a quarter of a tank, which normally would make
me feel happy, but now caused me to become
worried. The driver behind me began blowing the horn, and I pulled over to the side of the
road. I turned off the engine and let it sit for a
few minutes, then turned the key. It started right
up with no problem, and I relaxed a little bit. I
pushed the gas, and it took off, but as soon as
I got in the middle of the street, it began putter-
ing again, and I pulled back over.

"Shit!" I tried to think of what to do. I grabbed
my cell phone and dialed Ronda, the first person
that came to mind who would possibly come to
my rescue. She didn't answer, probably because
she was just as hung over as I was from all the

drinks we'd had at her house the night before. I
decided to take my chances and dialed another
number.

"What do you want?"

"Darnell, my car is tripping," I told him, trying
to sound as pitiful as possible.

"Yeah, right. I'm at work, Diane. I don't have
time for this," he said.

"Darnell, listen to me. My car—"

Darnell interrupted me. "This isn't gonna
work. Celia said she ain't giving you her car, and
I can't make her."

"Fuck Celia and her car. I'm about to be late
for work, and I need you to come and help me.
I'm sitting on the side of the road," I whined.

"Call Terry. Isn't that your corny-ass boyfriend's name?"

I knew Darnell was still a little salty about me
bringing Terry to their house, but this was an
emergency, and there was no way he was going
to leave me in a bind.

"Darnell, please. I can't be late for work again.
I'm gonna get suspended," I told him.

"Sorry. I'm not even nearby. I had a meeting two hours away with district management.
They're waiting for me now, and I gotta go."

The call ended, and I screamed again and
hit the steering wheel. I was fucked. I inhaled

deeply and told myself to calm down and think. I closed my eyes and asked the universe to send help quick. For some reason, Terry kept popping into my head, which made no sense. He was the absolute last person in the world that would help me. Then, it hit me. Terry mentioned that his brother was a mechanic and the manager of the Jiffy Lube on Denmark Street, which was right around the corner. I restarted the engine and sputtered down the street, praying the entire way.

"Can I help you?" a guy in his early sixties asked when I walked into the tiny building. He looked old enough to be Terry's father instead of his brother. The name on his uniform shirt said *Hugo,* and his hands were covered in grease, even though he constantly wiped them with a rag he was holding.

"Um, yeah. Are you the manager?" I asked, wanting to make sure he was the right person.

"Naw, that ain't me. I just work here. Is something wrong with your car?" he asked. "I can probably help. I know more than him anyway."

"No, I need to speak with the manager. Terry told me to come and see him." I smiled.

"Oh, I shoulda known. Gimme a sec. I'll go get him." Hugo shuffled out a side door that led to a side garage that was attached. A few seconds later, a guy looking very much like Terry came walking in. They were the same height and had the same build, but this guy was a few years younger and more serious than Terry, who was laid back.

"Hi, I'm having a little trouble with my car, and I was wondering if you could check it out for me. . . ." I spotted his name and added, "Ricky. My cousin works with Terry. He said to come through and you'd take care of me."

"Oh, okay. What's wrong with it? What's it doing?" he asked.

"Well, it'll start, but when I drive, it starts sputtering and jerking," I answered, then pointed. "It's the green Honda."

"Okay, well, I can take a look at it this afternoon, but I have a couple of customers in front of you."

"I have to go to work." I smoothed out my scrub top as if to make a statement to let him know I had a job. "I don't get off until seven."

"We close at seven thirty, so you should be good." He nodded.

"Cool. I appreciate it. I gotta catch an Uber, but I'll be back." I winked at him.

His eyebrow raised, and he softened a little bit and smiled back. That was all the reassurance I needed that I would be able to "persuade" him to fix whatever was wrong.

"A'ight, I'll see you when you come back."

I pulled out my phone and logged onto the Uber app, but for some reason, it wouldn't let me request a ride. I began to panic even more when I checked my bank account and realized the reason the app wasn't working was that my card was being declined. I had the cash I had taken from Terry, but I didn't have enough money in my bank account. I hurried back inside.

"Listen, do you guys have some kind of shuttle or something that can take me to work right quick?" I asked the old guy behind the counter.

"Nah, we ain't that fancy around here." He shook his head at me.

"I'm gonna be fired if I don't get there soon. Isn't there somebody that can take me?" I pleaded.

"Well, I can't leave, and neither can anyone else. But Josh over there is about to leave to go pick up a car. He might be able to give you a lift." He pointed to a pickup truck that was parked outside. "Go ask him."

I rushed into the parking lot and over to the truck, where a middle-aged guy was typing on his cell phone. "Excuse me, Josh."

He looked over at me. "Yeah?"

"I was wondering if you could possibly give me a lift to work. Hugo said you would help me out. It's not that far. I have to leave my car here, and I'm not trying to get fired," I explained.

"Um, I don't know. . . ." He rubbed the side of his head. "I'm supposed to go and meet another customer for a tow."

I tugged down on my scrub top and leaned over a little, giving him my most pitiful look. "Can you please help me out? Hugo said you wouldn't mind because you're a really nice guy."

"Hugo said that about me? That old fart normally talks shit about me." Josh glanced over at the garage.

"Do you think I would've asked if he hadn't sent me?"

"Well, I guess not. You sure it's not far?"

"It's only like ten minutes away," I said, rushing over to the passenger side and climbing in.

Luckily, it didn't take long for Josh to get me to my patient's house, and I arrived to work only thirty minutes late. I apologized to the family, and after pointing to Josh's truck that I had just hopped out of and showing them his card, I convinced them not to call the agency and report my tardiness. I made sure to remain extremely pleasant the entire day, just to make sure. I even promised to arrive early the next morning to make up the time.

Ronda picked me up when I got off. When we arrived back at the Jiffy Lube, it was seven forty.

The lights were off, and my car was nowhere to be found.

"Are you kidding me?" I said, opening the door of the Ronda's Ford Fusion. "Hold tight. I'll be right back."

I walked over and pulled the door, but it was locked. I was walking back to the car when I heard someone yelling, "Hey, hey! Over here."

I turned around and saw Ricky coming from the side of the building.

"Oh my God, I thought you were gone," I told him.

"Naw, I told you I would hang around until you got here," he said. "Your car's right over here."

We walked around to the side of the building where my car was sitting. "What's wrong with it?"

"A lot." He rubbed his head and looked at the car "For starters, your fuel pump is shot, your carburetor needs work, and you need a tune-up and oil change."

"Shit." I was hoping it would be something simple, but the way he said it, I knew it would be more than the hundred and twelve dollars I had in my purse, fifty of which I had stolen from his brother days earlier. "Okay, I know about the oil change and the tune-up. That can probably wait. But the fuel pump and the carburetor, how much is that?"

"Parts and labor? About five hundred."

"Five hundred dollars? Man, come on."

"Yeah, and most of that's for parts. I gave you a deal on the labor since your cousin works with Terry and sent you."

I said, "I don't have five hundred dollars."

"I don't know what to tell ya." He shrugged. He got into my car and turned the ignition. The engine started up, but when he pushed the gas, it began sputtering as it had before. "See, there's no fuel getting to the engine. That's the main problem."

"I believe you, but I still ain't got five hundred dollars. I barely have fifty." I reached into my purse and took out my wallet. I opened it up, and a picture fell out. He reached down and picked it up, taking a moment to look at it before passing it to me.

"Here you go. She's pretty. Is that your daughter?" he asked.

I looked at Kendra's graduation picture and nodded. "Yeah, that's my daughter. And yes, she is pretty."

"She get it from her mama, huh?" He laughed, turning the car off and stepping out.

I decided to try my luck and see if he was as gullible as his brother. "You think so, huh?"

"Mm-hmmmm," he said, his eyes looking me up and down.

"Well, look, Ricky. Being that I don't have five hundred dollars up front, is there any way we can work out some kind of payment plan?" I took a step closer to him and laid my hand on his chest.

"What kind of payment plan?" he asked.

"Well, what I got is worth way more than five hundred dollars, that's for sure," I said, taking his hand and slipping it under my shirt so he could feel my hardened nipples. Sure enough, I felt his thumb rubbing back and forth. I looked down and saw the bulge in his pants.

"So, we can do this one of two ways: I can fuck the shit out of you right here, right now, and then fuck you again when my car is ready." I reached down and stroked the growing bulge.

"Or?" He moaned.

"Or I can give you five blow jobs. The choice is yours." I smiled. "The choice is yours."

We were standing there, rubbing on one another, when a pair of headlights came around the corner. He quickly snatched his hand from under my top, and I laughed as I recognized the car.

"Calm down. It's just my girlfriend, Ronda. She probably drove around to check on me," I told him.

The window of Ronda's car rolled down, and she yelled, "What's going on? You good?"

I looked over at her and said, "Yeah, my car's not ready, but give me one second. I'm trying to make some payment arrangements."

"Ohhhhhh, okay." Ronda gave me a nod, then rolled the window back up.

"Well?" I said, turning back to Ricky.

He looked at me, licking his lips, and said, "Tell your friend you're good. I'll take you home."

An hour later, we pulled up to the front of my house. I was sore and satisfied. I had bragged about fucking the shit out of Ricky, when in reality, he had fucked the shit out of me. He may have been younger than his brother, but he was definitely better in bed. Hell, I shoulda been the one paying him five hundred dollars.

"There's your pretty daughter." He pointed to Kendra, who was checking the mail.

"Yeah, that's her," I mumbled, not wanting his attention on her, but on me. I turned his face to mine and kissed him fully on the mouth. "So, when will my car be ready?"

"Uh, three or four days. I'll call you and let you know. Then you can make your final payment," he said, running his finger along my neckline.

"I can't wait," I told him.

"I bet," he said.

I got out of the car and waved as he pulled off.

"Mama, who was that?" Kendra, who was standing on the porch, asked me as I passed.

"None of your damn business," I told her and continued inside.

"Mama, you've gotta stop this. You can't keep bringing these dudes to our house like this. It ain't right. Look at what happened the other night."

"First of all, this is my house, and I can bring whoever I want up in here. Second, that was the mechanic who's fixing my car that broke down this morning when I was on my way to work," I told her.

"The mechanic, huh? Then why were you kissing him like that? And why are your braids all messed up? And why are there bruises on your neck?" Kendra asked.

My fingers touched the area where Ricky's mouth had been a little while ago. I was too busy enjoying the way he bit my neck to think about whether he was gonna leave any marks. It was his hands that had grabbed my braids and pulled them down from the bun they were in as he was fucking me from behind at one point.

"Look, I have to get my car fixed, and I don't have the money right now, so I gotta do what I gotta do, understand? Now leave me the fuck alone," I grumbled.

"Mama, you don't have to do this. You can have Aunt Celia's car. I don't need it, I swear," Kendra cried out.

I looked at her and saw that she was being sincere. For a second, I felt guilty for what I had done. Then I thought about how she and Celia had laughed and talked with one another in the kitchen while they were preparing dinner. I couldn't remember the last time my daughter and I had laughed together. She barely even talked to me because she was so busy being up Celia's ass.

"Fuck Celia and her car. I don't want that shit. She can keep it. I got my own car. And another thing: if you wanna keep living here, then you better not take that car either," I said, leaving her standing in the middle of the living room.

Kendra

"Daddy?" I answered my phone, which rang just as I was walking to work. Although we talked on the regular, he rarely called me. We mainly communicated via text a couple of times a week.

"Hey, sweetie. How are you?" he asked.

"I'm fine. What's wrong? Is everything okay? Is Grandma Ruby all right?" My father's mother, Ruby, had been sick for the past few months. My mind began filling with all kinds of reasons he could be calling, all of them negative.

"Everything's everything, and she's fine."

"Oh, okay." I exhaled slightly and realized I had been holding my breath without even knowing it.

"The school called me and left a voicemail. It seems that your sister Avery hasn't been dressing out for her PE class, and if she don't start, she's gonna fail for the year," he said.

All of the anxiety that had left my body moments before returned. "Oh, I'm sorry, Daddy. I guess they still have your number on file. I'll take care of it."

Although my parents hadn't been together for ten years, for some reason his number still wound up as a point of contact for the school, and every now and then, he would get a call. He acted like it was no big deal, but I knew better. Ashley and Avery were a sore subject for him, and ultimately the reason for the demise of my parents' marriage. Not that it was even peaches and cream before, because most of my childhood memories included the two of them constantly arguing, fussing, and fighting. My mother was volatile in nature, and my father's drinking and smoking didn't help. How they even lasted as long as they had was beyond me.

It was days before Ashley and Avery's fourth birthday when the shit hit the fan. My mama had planned this huge party for them and was asking my daddy for more money to pay for it. He refused, saying that he wasn't footing the bill for her and her friends, and they weren't getting drunk on his dime. Mama's friend Ronda came over to the house, and they were in the kitchen talking when the words that changed my entire family dynamics came out her mouth.

"Shit, Di, he need to stop tripping before you go see them girls' real daddy for the money." She laughed, not realizing Daddy was right outside the door and could hear every word they were saying.

"You ain't neva lied. That might not be a bad idea. Maybe I should pay Abraham a visit and see if he can help out." Mama giggled.

Before they knew it, my daddy rushed in, demanding to know what they were talking about. Mama tried to say that she was joking, but the seed of doubt had already been planted. Daddy had always accused Mama of being unfaithful. Now his suspicions were confirmed, and his heart was broken when the results of a paternity test that he paid for and had done on me and my sisters came back. He didn't waste any time packing up and moving out, despite my begging him to stay. He promised that he would always be there for me despite my mother's attempts to force him out of our lives.

"You either take care of all of my girls or none of them. You don't get to pick and choose," She would scream at him when he would come to pick me up or bring me things that he had bought.

"What the fuck is wrong with you, Diane? I ain't taking care of no kids that ain't mine. You go get their daddy to take care of them, not me," he told her, which was easier said than done. The results of the second DNA tests for the twins, this time ordered by Child Support, revealed that Abraham wasn't their father either. It was then that Mama decided they didn't need a father, and neither did I. For years, she forbid Daddy from having any contact with me, until I finally became old enough to reach out to him myself, without her knowing. He would sneak to see me, secretly give me money, and check on me. Now that I was grown, it shouldn't have been Mama's business that I had a relationship with my father, but after all these years, if anyone even mentioned his name, she would lose her mind. Needless to say, I had a fake name for him in my phone, and whenever we met up, it was nowhere near the house.

"You sure everything is a'ight, Kendra? The teacher mentioned that she'd tried calling your mama several times before calling my number," he said with a concerned voice.

"Yes, Daddy," I assured him.

"Well, I know you mentioned needing some money for books the other week. I ain't forgot, and I'm working on shifting some stuff around to get it to you. Grandma Ruby's medicine cost a little bit more than expected this month," he explained.

"I know you're working on it. It's okay. But I gotta go to work." I sighed.

"Okay, well, talk to your sister about that gym class. She don't need to fail."

"I will." I laughed.

"Love you, baby girl."

"Love you too, Daddy."

I ended the call and headed toward the store. In a way, I was glad that he had gotten the call from the school instead of Mama. Lord knows if she had, she probably would've killed Ashley on sight. I was going to have some choice words for my little sister myself when I got home. I sent her a text, instructing her not to go outside at all when she got home from school. Then, noticing the time, I hurried.

Sierra greeted me. "I already clocked you in."

"You did? Thanks," I told her.

"Yeah, I saw you boo-loving on the phone outside and didn't want you to be late. See how I look out?"

"Whatever, Sierra." I laughed. "You know I wasn't boo-loving. I was talking to my damn daddy."

"Mm-hmmm. Well, heads up, because your *daddy* is walking through the door."

I looked up, and sure enough, the door was buzzing as Bilal walked inside. I tried my best to seem unbothered, but when he reached the counter and smiled at me, I couldn't help but acknowledge the slight excitement I felt.

"Hi, welcome to Cell City. How can I help you?" I said in my best customer service voice.

"Why, thank you. I'm glad to see you here today. Last time I came in to pick up my phone, you weren't here." He grinned.

The fact that he had missed me when he came in made me even more giddy than I was already feeling. Sierra nudged me behind the counter, and I tried to kick her but missed.

"Don't tell me your team won again," I said.

"Naw, the screen is still good." He held the phone up. "But I think I wanna go ahead and take your advice and get a new phone."

"Oh, okay," I said. "I can definitely help you with that. Let me get your phone number again so I can see what kind of upgrade you're eligible for."

He gave me his number, and as I was pulling his information up, he said, "I think I wanna get the iPhone 8, and I don't wanna do an upgrade."

I looked up at him. "I don't think you're gonna get much for your trade-in."

"I don't wanna trade it in. I'm gonna keep it," he said matter-of-factly.

"So, you wanna—"

"I'm gonna pay cash for it." He shrugged, reaching into the pocket of his jeans and taking out the biggest wad of bills that I had ever seen. "I don't want to pay a monthly bill for two years for something I can just buy outright. That's crazy."

Again, Sierra nudged me. This time I aimed my foot at her leg and connected, causing her to flinch and move away.

"Uh, well, alrighty then," I told him.

"You do have one in stock, right?" he asked.

"Yeah, we do. How many gigs of storage do you need? You know the higher the gig, the higher the price," I warned.

"I use my phone a lot for my business, so cost ain't really a concern," he said.

"And what color did you want?"

He stared into my eyes and said, "How about you choose for me? I'm sure you'll make the perfect choice for me."

Something about the way he said it made me pause, and for a second, I forgot what I was supposed to be doing. "I, uh, I'll be right back."

I went into the locked room where the phones were located and tried to get myself together. *Kendra, calm the fuck down. You're acting nervous as shit, like you've never helped a customer before. He's just a dude buying a phone*

*the same way all your other customers come in
and buy every day.* But I knew that this wasn't
a regular dude. Everything about him seemed
to draw me in: his voice, his smile, his eyes, his
swag. I also knew that he was exactly the type of
dude I needed to stay the hell away from. I had
seen my mother deal with those types of dudes
time and time again—the flashy guys who stayed
fly, had plenty of money, drove the hot cars, and
talked a good game. They were the so-called
"business" men who ran the streets and ran
women. I knew better, and I wasn't falling for
him or his games. I had future plans, and they
definitely didn't include dating a thug. I didn't
care how sexy he was.

I found a phone, took a deep breath, and went
back out to finish his transaction, reminding
myself to keep it professional. When I got back
to the register, he was on the phone talking to
someone. I tried my best not to listen as I opened
the box and activated the phone, but it was hard.

"Yeah, I'm almost done, and I'll be out in a
minute. Chill, girl. I told you I was giving you my
old phone, but I gotta get it switched over. And
don't touch my radio," he mumbled.

I glanced up and saw Sierra easing over to the
window. She looked back at me, and I gave her a
look that said, *I told you so.*

"Okay, your total is $808.26," I told him.

"Cool. Let me ask you something. You work on commission?"

"Yep," I said coolly.

"On accessories too?"

"Uh-huh." I nodded.

"Great. Let me get an Otter box, screen protector, and a car charger."

"No problem." I grabbed the items he'd asked for, and after ringing them up, I placed them into a bag and told him the new price. It was more than nine hundred dollars.

He handed me ten hundred-dollar bills and said, "Keep the change."

"Sorry, we can't accept tips. Company policy. But here's your phone and your accessories. I've already transferred your number over." I counted out his change and gave it to him, along with the phone and the bag.

"Thank you. Let me make sure it works. What's your number?" He smiled at me.

I gave him a phone number, and he dialed it. The phone at the register began ringing, and I picked it up. "Thanks for calling Cell City. This is Kendra speaking. How can I help you?"

"Wow, it's like that?" Bilal gave me a disappointed look. "I asked for your number, not the store's number."

"I can't do that." I shook my head at him.

"Company policy, or yours?"

"Mine."

"I guess your man wouldn't appreciate me calling you anyway. I understand. Well, thanks again for all of your help. And since I can't have your number, feel free to use mine." His fingers brushed along mine as he took the bag from my hand.

"Thank you for choosing Cell City. Enjoy the rest of your day," I said.

"Nice seeing you again, Caramel Kendra." He winked and headed out the door, making sure to say goodbye to Sierra as he passed by.

"What the hell is wrong with you?" Sierra wasted no time asking as soon as he was gone.

"What are you talking about?" I shrugged as I casually walked over to the window and stood beside her. We both stared into the parking lot and watched as Bilal got into a black Yukon Denali with rims. Although the windows were tinted, I could clearly see the silhouette of a female passenger. "I know you heard him on the phone, and you can clearly see who he was talking to."

"A'ight, I get that, and he is hella disrespectful tryna holla at you with his bitch right outside. She's a good one, because ain't no way I'm gonna sit outside in the car like I'm some kind of pet while my man goes into a store. But real talk, Kendra, I damn sure woulda took that tip." Sierra looked at me out of the corner of her eye.

I thought about the three-hundred-dollar textbook I needed for my statistics class and the two other textbooks that I hadn't even priced. Then I thought about Bilal having a girl in the car and felt a twinge of jealousy. "Nah, you can't always take what people try and give you. Especially when you don't know what they want in return."

Later that evening, after the store had closed, I was waiting at the bus stop on the corner when the familiar black Denali pulled over in front of me. The window rolled down, and Bilal began speaking to me.

"Hey, pretty lady, you need a ride?" he asked.

"Nah, I'm good," I said.

"Come on. It's no problem, and you don't need to be out here by yourself at night. It's not safe. Where are you headed?"

"I catch this bus every day. I won't be out here alone that long. Thanks for the offer, but I'm good," I said, this time with more attitude, recalling the chick that was sitting in the passenger side just a little while ago. He had some nerve trying to pick me up.

"A'ight, well, I can sit here and wait and make sure you're good," he told me. "If you'd like, I can pull into the lot, and you can wait in the truck. We can talk."

Again, I shook my head. "Nah, I'm good."

"You are one stubborn woman." He laughed. Then, to my surprise, he turned into the parking lot and parked his truck. He got out and walked over to me.

"What are you doing?" I asked.

"Waiting to make sure you're safe."

"You don't have to do that."

"I know I don't have to." He took a step closer to me, and I got a whiff of his cologne. I was almost tempted to take him up on his offer when I saw the headlights of the bus approaching.

"See, the bus is right there. So, thanks, but like I said, I'm good," I said, taking a step back.

"Well, I'll just make sure you get on. But maybe you'll reconsider and give me your number now since you're not on the clock."

"I don't think your girlfriend would appreciate this at all." I shook my head at him just as the bus pulled up.

"Huh? What?" He gave me a strange look.

"Your girlfriend? The one who was waiting in the car while you were inside. The one who you're giving your old phone to." I laughed, thinking about how he tried to play me. I stepped on the bus and showed my student ID and paid the discounted fair.

"Hey, Kendra," Bilal called out, and I turned around.

"What?"

"Just so you know, that was my sister. I don't have a girlfriend," he answered just as the doors to the bus closed and we pulled off.

I walked to the back and took a seat, wondering if I was the one who had played myself.

Bilal

I couldn't get that chick Kendra off my mind. She was cute as hell, and even though she was kinda young, the way she carried herself let me know she was about her business and not about the bullshit. Truth be told, she was one of the few chicks in life who had ever declined to give me her number when asked. As if that weren't surprising enough, she then turned down the offer for a ride. Rejection wasn't something I was used to, and it was kind of refreshing. Normally, I wouldn't have even cared, but it was something about her. The only reason I didn't pop back up at her job was because one, I didn't want to look super thirsty and seem like a stalker, and two, I had no free time. As much as I hated that the neighborhood crime rate was up, it meant that so was my business. I was glad that I had broken down and gotten a new phone, because it was ringing nonstop.

I had just finished up with a client when Dell called. He had sent me a text earlier that I hadn't had a chance to respond to, so I knew his calling meant that whatever it was, it must've been important.

"What's up, D?" I answered as I walked to my truck. "I got your text, but I just got out of my meeting."

"It's cool, bruh. Look, I been trying to catch up with Unc the past couple of days, but he kinda been ducking me. He was supposed to see me last week and didn't. You know I hate to even bring it to you, but that's family, and before it's handled on another level, I just wanted to come to you first."

"Man, I told you to leave that alone when he came to you."

"I know, but he was in a bad spot, so I helped him out. It was Uncle P. What was I supposed to do?" Dell asked.

"Tell his ass no the same way I do every time he comes to me when he's in a bad spot," I told him. "That's my uncle, D, but you know how he is."

"Man, I get it."

"How much he owe you?"

"Don't matter. If you happen to talk to him, just tell him to hit me up."

"Man, just tell me." I knew it had to be a fairly large amount if Dell was talking to me about it.

"B, it's cool."

"Dell, how much?"

"A'ight. Three stacks."

"Three stacks! What the fuck? Why the fuck did you give him three fucking thousand dollars? Dell, have you lost your mind? You knew his ass wasn't gonna be able to pay back that much fucking money."

"I ain't give it to him all at one, Bilal. Calm the fuck down," Dell groaned.

"Man, ain't no calming down. You gave my clown-ass uncle three thousand dollars, and now his ass is ghost. You been knowing his ass as long as me, D. You know this dude don't even try and keep no damn job."

"I ain't give it to him all at once. And not all of it was in cash. Some of it was product."

"You know what? Don't tell me any more." I was furious at this point. "I'll holla at him and make sure you get your money."

"Bilal, I'm telling you right now, this ain't on you, it's on him. I ain't taking no money from you. You know how we do. This is Unc's debt, not yours," Dell said.

"It's all good. I'll holla at you later."

I don't know who I was more pissed at: Dell, or trifling-ass Uncle Patrick. I dialed his number, but he didn't answer. I was in the middle of sending him a text when my phone rang. Seeing my mother's picture flashing on the screen, I immediately answered.

"Hey, Ma."

"Bilal, when are you gonna bring me the phone?" my sister whined in my ear.

"Fatima, not now. Leave me alone about that damn phone."

"Well, you were the one who said you were gonna give it to me. That was the reason you even went and got a new phone, remember? I haven't had a phone in two weeks, and I really need it."

"That ain't my problem, Fatima. You were the one who lost your phone, not me," I reminded her.

"Uuugghhh! I don't know why you just won't buy me a new one anyway, Bilal."

"Hell no! I already bought you two phones over the past two years. You want a new phone, you buy it yourself."

"Fatima, bring me my damn phone!" my mother yelled in the background. "And you need to stop telling your li'l friends to call you back on my number. This ain't your phone."

"I'm talking to Bilal, Ma," Fatima told her.

"Oh, well, tell him I'm cooking the oxtails that he asked me for, and he can come and pick them up tomorrow."

"She's lying, Bilal. She ain't even been to the store to get no oxtails. You can bust her if you come over right now and bring the phone."

"Bye, Fatima. Tell Ma I'll call her later." I ended the call and drove over to my uncle's crib, thinking he would be home since he didn't have a steady job. I didn't see his car in the driveway, but the garage door was up, and his girlfriend was backing out. I beeped my horn as I pulled beside her in the driveway. I put my truck in park, got out, and walked over to her.

"What's up, Nikki? Your hubby home?"

"Now, you know that ain't my husband, Bilal. Don't even." She smiled at me as she stepped out and gave me a hug.

"Well, he calls you his wifey. That much I do know," I told her.

"Whatever, but to answer your question, no, he ain't home."

"Would you happen to know where he might be?"

"Not really, but he's probably over at the church. They have men's Bible study tonight that he's teaching, so he's probably setting up for that."

I thanked her and tried not to laugh. The thought of my uncle teaching Bible study was the funniest thing I'd heard since learning that he was actually a deacon at the church. How he'd managed to land that title was beyond me. He had always been a smooth talker and had fooled a lot of folks, including Nikki, who was not only pretty but warm, welcoming, and well liked. As smart as she was, she was as gullible as they came, and I felt sorry for her. My uncle's good looks and fraudulent charm had seduced this poor woman and snatched her into his sticky web of lies. I just prayed that she escaped before he sucked the life out of her like he did the other unsuspecting victims he bled financially, mentally, and emotionally.

After saying goodbye to Nikki, I drove over to Mount Hebron, the church that she and my uncle attended. The parking lot was empty, but I spotted a man coming out of one of the side doors.

"Excuse me," I said. "I'm looking for Patrick Parker."

"Deacon Pat? Oh, he's not here. He'll be back, though, later tonight, because we're having men's Bible study. You should come back and join us. That man has a way with God's word, and I'm sure you'll enjoy."

"Thanks, but I'm good," I said and drove out of the parking lot. It was almost five o'clock, and I still had to meet with my supplier across town. I became pissed all over again, because I was about to be sitting in traffic due to my being out chasing a grown-ass man over something that ain't have anything to do with me. I had to handle this and handle it quick. I wasn't about to let my dumb-ass uncle disrespect my best friend.

I dialed my mother's number and prayed that she would answer the phone and not my sister.

"Hey, Bilal, I was just about to start cooking. What time you coming by?"

"I don't know, Ma. I got some running around to do. Have you talked to your brother?" I asked her.

"What?"

"Uncle Patrick. Have you talked to him recently?"

"I talked to him earlier today."

"A'ight, if you talk to him again, tell him I went by his crib to holla at him, but he wasn't home."

"You went by there today?" she asked.

"Yeah, a few minutes ago."

"Now, Bilal, you know your uncle wasn't gonna be at home this time of day. His ass is probably over at Chubby's doing something he ain't got no business doing," she told me.

"Thanks, Ma. I'll talk to you later," I said, turning around in the middle of the street and heading off to find my uncle.

Celia

I ran my hands along the smooth leather seats. Sitting behind the wheel of the brand-new BMW X5 that I'd been eying for the past month felt like heaven. I originally planned to wait until my birthday, but the salesman that I'd been talking to at the dealership called and told me that his manager had given him the okay to give me a hell of a deal. A customer had ordered one but changed his mind once he saw the color. It was too good to pass up, and I was ecstatic, even though I had a feeling Darnell wouldn't be so pleased that I bought the car without even calling and telling him. I told myself that his attitude had been so horrible the past few days, it was easier for me to ask forgiveness rather than permission. I would face the consequences of my decision later. Either way, it was gonna be an argument.

"One thing about it, you make this car look good," the salesman said.

"Nah, I think it's the other way around," I told him.

"You sure you don't wanna trade your other beauty in? It's in excellent condition, and I know we'll give you a trade-in amount that would be more than decent."

"I'm sure. That beauty is going to stay in the family. As a matter of fact, I'm going to pick up her new owner right now, and then I'll be back later," I told him and stepped out of my gorgeous new car.

"Sounds like a plan. We'll be ready when you get back."

I drove over to Kendra's job, hoping to catch her before she caught the bus. It was Thursday, and she got off at four o'clock. I pulled into the parking lot just as she was walking out of the door.

"Aunt Celia, what are you doing here?" she asked with a worried look on her face.

"Everything's fine. I came to pick you up so you could ride with me." I smiled.

She got into the car and asked, "Go with you where?"

"I need someone to take me to pick up my new car, and I figured you could give me a ride in your new whip."

"What? Aunt Celia, are you serious? Don't play," she shrieked.

"I'm not playing," I told her.

"So, this . . . you're really . . . you mean?" She couldn't seem to get her words together.

"This is now yours, baby girl."

She reached over and threw her arms around my neck, squeezing me so tight that I almost couldn't breathe.

"Aunt Celia, thank you so much. I can't believe this." I could see the tears forming in her eyes, and I almost started crying myself.

"A promise is a promise, Kendra. Oh, and I'm supposed to give you this." I pulled the visor down and handed her the crumpled bills. "Your daddy sent this to you."

"He did?" Kendra asked.

I nodded. The truth was that Champ had called and told me about Kendra needing book money. He didn't have the total amount, but he did have most of it. I assured him that I would make up the difference. Despite Diane's horrible treatment of him while they were together—and even worse after their breakup—Champ and I remained friends. I knew that he wasn't blameless in the demise of their relationship, but he was still a good father to Kendra.

"So, let's go get this ride of yours all cleaned up, so we can go and pick up mine," I told her. "As a matter of fact, get over in this driver's seat."

Kendra and I swapped places. I sat back and enjoyed being chauffeured as she drove down the street. We continued until she pulled into a strip mall not far from her job, where cars were lined up, waiting their turn to be detailed by the small group of men on the side of the building.

"Um, this is where you want to get it washed?" I asked, looking at the line.

"Yes, Aunt Celia. This is Shine Boss. This is the spot. Can't you tell?" She pointed at the flashy cars waiting in line. Although a hood car wash wouldn't have been my ultimate choice, I knew Kendra was loving this moment, so I didn't protest.

"Well, it's your car." I shrugged, hoping nothing would happen while they were detailing, because I doubted if Shine Boss had any type of liability insurance.

We chatted while we waited our turn. A few moments later, a skinny guy walked over and handed us a red ticket with a number on it, then directed us inside another establishment called Zippy's to wait and pay.

"So, we go in there to pay?" I asked Kendra as we walked toward the strip mall.

"Yeah, the same guy who owns the chicken spot owns Shine Boss," she explained.

We were about to walk in when I spotted Patrick at the other end of the shopping center, laughing and talking to another group of guys. I thought about Nikki, who had just told me this morning that he had gone over to the church.

"Hey, Patrick!" I yelled over at him, making sure that he knew I saw him. He looked over and saw that it was me. He gave me a weak smile and waved at me.

I followed Kendra inside and paid for our ticket. When we came out, he was still there, and standing there with him was Bilal. I nudged Kendra's arm.

"Huh?" She looked at me, and I nodded toward the group of men so she could see what I was talking about.

"Look who's over there." I smiled.

She looked past me and then quickly looked away. "Oh." She glanced up at me.

I spoke loudly again so they would look over at us. "Bye, Patrick."

"Aunt Celia." Kendra gasped.

"What? I was just telling him goodbye." I laughed.

"Kendra?" Bilal asked as he walked toward us.

"Oh, hey, Bilal," Kendra said.

"Is that the only person you see?" I teased, surprised that he seemed just as excited to see her as she was to see him.

"Oh, my bad. Hey, Ms. Celia. How are you doing?" He grinned, his eyes still on my niece.

"I'm fine," I answered. "I didn't know you knew my beautiful niece."

"Yeah, she gives me great service at Cell City. Well, when I'm lucky enough to catch her at work. What's up, Kendra?" He smiled at her.

"Nothing much," she said.

"What are y'all doing on this side of town?" he asked.

"Kendra brought her car over here to be detailed," I told him.

"Car? Last time I saw you was at the bus stop—when you ain't want me to wait with you to make sure you were safe," he said. "I didn't want you out there all alone."

"Yeah, well, I have a car now. I'm really safe," Kendra told him.

"That's what's up," he said.

"Well, that was nice of you, Bilal," I told him.

"That's what real men do." He raised an eyebrow at me. "Which car is yours?"

"The white Volvo," Kendra said shyly.

"Wow, that's a nice ride." Bilal's eyes stayed on Kendra. "Hold tight. I'll be right back."

We waited and watched him walk over and talk to one of the guys detailing cars. He pointed to the car, then back at us. The guy nodded, and Bilal came back.

"What was that all about?" Kendra asked him.

"Just making sure my man takes excellent care of you, that's all," he explained.

"Wow, you are just a gentleman all the way around, huh?" I nudged Kendra again.

"I try," Bilal said. "So, I guess I'll see you whenever I need my phone serviced again, huh? Unless you wanna see me sooner and finally give me your number."

"Nah, I'm sure I'll see you when you come back to the store," Kendra told him.

I couldn't help but frown, wondering why she was acting nonchalant. It was obvious that he liked her, and I knew that she was attracted to him.

"Cool." Bilal shrugged, then added, "Well, it was nice seeing you two beautiful ladies again. I got some business I gotta go handle over here with my uncle."

"Take care, Bilal," I told him. When he was gone, I looked over at her and said, "What's wrong with you? Why won't you give him your number?"

"Aunt Celia, I am not trying to get involved with someone like *that*. You know better. You taught me better," she said.

"What do you mean?" I asked her, concerned about what she was referring to.

"Don't act like you don't know what I'm talking about. Look at Bilal." She nodded toward where he was standing with Patrick and the other guys.

"Okay, what am I looking at?" I asked, staring at the well-dressed, articulate young man who had just tried to impress her.

"You know just as well as I do what he's about. His swag, his demeanor, his talk, it's all game. His money. Have you seen his truck?"

"Yeah, I've seen it. Kendra, what are you getting at?" I was still confused.

"I've seen guys like him my entire life. I know what he does and how he gets all that."

"He's a business owner." I shrugged.

"Okay, business owner. You see that store they're in front of, Chubby's? You do know that's a dope spot, right? That's what those guys over there are doing. Most of them are corner boys. My mama's had more than her fair share of street dudes, and I don't have time for that. Besides, I definitely ain't about that life." Kendra shook her head. "I'm trying to get away from the hood, not stuck here with some dude. You even showed me that. That's all we've ever talked about."

"Kendra, have you asked Bilal what he does? Have you had a conversation with him?" I asked her.

"No," Kendra said matter-of-factly.

I shook my head and inhaled. "I swear, y'all young girls these days are so damn smart that you're dumb sometimes and don't know a real man when you see one."

"What does that mean, Aunt Celia?"

"That means I think you may wanna get to know someone before you judge them. You might miss out on a good thing. I would definitely give him my number if I were in your shoes," I told her.

She looked at me and hesitated before turning around and saying, "Bilal, can I speak to you for a moment?"

As she walked over to meet him halfway, my eyes went to Patrick and what she had said about Chubby's. I thought about calling Nikki and telling her where her man was. I even thought about taking a picture and sending it to her, but my best friend was in love, and I knew that even with evidence in hand, she was still going to stay with that loser. It was going to take something way more damaging to get her to see him for what he truly was.

Bilal

I hadn't been this excited over a woman since, well, I really couldn't remember ever being excited about one. I had dated chicks and smashed more than my fair share, but none of them had ever really intrigued me the way Kendra did. The first time we talked on the phone, she was a little apprehensive and shy. For a second, I thought I had misread the attraction I had for her when we first met. There were brief moments of silence in the conversation that made it kind of awkward.

"If now isn't a good time to talk, you can call me back," I offered after one of the fifteen-second pauses.

"No, I mean . . . I'm good. I'm sorry. It's just that one of my younger sisters is working on a science project that I'm helping her with, and the other one is trying to finish her math homework. But they're all finished and gone off to bed, so I should be undisturbed. But I can't make any promises." She laughed.

"Oh, I thought I was boring you," I told her.

"No, not at all. I kept muting the phone so that it wouldn't be disruptive, but I guess it didn't work."

"It's all good." I realized that it wasn't her being quiet; it was the phone being muted. "How old are your sisters?"

"They're fourteen. Ashley and Avery. They're twins," she said. As she continued to brag about her sisters, who were both on the honor roll, and how one was a cheerleader and the other on the dance team, I instantly knew how important they were to her. I also learned that in addition to working at the cell phone store, she was a full-time student and on the dean's list. She was smart and about her business.

"You have a lot going for yourself. I respect that," I told her.

"So, can you tell me exactly what it is that you do?" she asked me. "My aunt told me you owned your own business."

"Yeah, I have my own security installation company," I said proudly.

"Oh, okay." She sounded like a cross between surprised and relieved.

"What did you think I did?" I responded.

"Um, I wasn't really sure," she answered.

"Naw, come on and tell me."

"There's nothing to tell." She giggled, then quickly said, "Security installation. Like burglar alarms?"

"Burglar alarms, that's funny. But yeah, along with video surveillance cameras, motion detectors, all of that," I explained.

"That sounds kind of cool. How did you get into that? Did you go to college?"

"I did. Graduated with an associate's degree in IT and was bored sitting behind a desk. One day a customer called in, and I was the only one he talked to that helped him solve a problem he'd called in about four times before. He was really appreciative and impressed. We got to talking, and I found out he worked for a home security company doing installations, and they needed part-time workers. He hooked me up with a job and taught me everything he knew, and I took it and ran with it. A year and a half later, I ventured out on my own, with his blessing, and I've been rocking it out on my own ever since," I explained.

"Oh, so you're super-duper smart, huh?" she said. "I'm impressed. Helped him solve his issue, flipped it into a gig, then took it to a whole other level."

"I'd never thought about it like that before," I said, surprised that she had pointed that out.

I had been called smart by teachers before, but never by a woman I was interested in dating. Most women just talked about how they liked my body, not about my mind.

"I think that's dope, though. Most people would've just been satisfied having a good job, but you took a risk and went for what you wanted, and it paid off," Kendra said.

"Nah, sitting behind that desk for eight to ten hours a day was driving me nuts." I thought about how miserable I was at my old job as a technical phone rep. "People told me I was crazy when I told them I was quitting to start my own company. They tried to fill my head with all types of doubt. If I'd listened to them, I'd still be there. But my boy Dell and my moms had my back, and they supported my decision."

"Well, I'm glad you ignored the naysayers and had your best friend and . . ." Kendra's voice drifted, and I wondered if she'd hit the mute button again.

"Kendra, you still here?" I asked into the phone.

"Oh, yeah, I'm here. I was just saying it's cool that your mom supported your decision too."

"Yeah, she did." I sighed. There was beeping in my ear, and I looked at my phone, seeing my mother's number on the screen. "Speak of the devil. Hold on for a sec."

"Okay."

I clicked over and said, "Hey."

"Bilal, can I get a ride Friday night to the basketball game?" Fatima asked.

"Tima, why do you keep calling me from Ma's phone?" I asked, instantly irritated.

"Because I don't have my own phone, that's why. And before you even ask me, I'm asking you for a ride because I don't have my own car either," she said.

"Bye, Fatima," I told her.

"Bilal, wait!" Fatima yelled right before I was about to push the button.

"What?"

"Can I get a ride?"

"I can't. I got a date. I'll call you tomorrow. I gotta go," I told her, hoping that putting it in the atmosphere would guarantee Kendra would agree to go out with me when I asked. I returned to the other line and said, "Hey, I'm back."

"Everything okay with your mom?" she asked, sounding even sexier than before I put her on hold.

"Yeah, it wasn't even her. It was my sister being worrisome." I laughed.

"I know how that is," Kendra said. "How old is she?"

"She's seventeen and a pain in my ass."

"Stop it. You're mean." Kendra giggled.

"Nah, I'm serious. Bugging me about taking her to a basketball game Friday night." I sighed.

"You'd better take her."

"I can't. I'm busy and got something else to do."

"Oh."

"Yeah, I'm taking you to dinner."

"Huh?" I could hear the confusion in Kendra's voice.

"Well, I'm hoping I'll be taking you to dinner. If you'll let me," I clarified.

She was quiet, and I was thinking I might be taking Fatima to the basketball game after all. Then she said, "I'd love to go to dinner with you."

Kendra

"So, pretty much I have your aunt to thank for this, huh?" Bilal asked, using his skewer to pick up a piece of steak and dipping it into the pot of melted cheese that sat in front of us. The steak was a part of a variety of choices we had to dip, which also included chicken breast, shrimp, cubes of bread, and one of the biggest lobster tails I'd ever seen. This wasn't just a typical dinner date; it was an experience. I'd expected him to take me to a typical Applebees or Red Lobster. When when we arrived at a fondue restaurant called The Melting Pot, where he had made reservations, I soon realized that there was nothing typical about Bilal Parker.

"Well, ultimately it was my decision," I told him. "But she did put in a good word or two about you."

Once I relented and told him he could call me, Bilal hadn't wasted any time asking me out. I was just as hesitant about going on a date with him as I had been about giving him my phone number. After talking and texting for a few days, I felt comfortable enough to accept his invitation and go out. Sierra and the twins were more excited than I was, and they helped me pick the perfect outfit, hairstyle, and apply my makeup. It was my first real date. I just knew that I was going to be a bundle of nerves the entire night when Bilal arrived to pick me up. But as he walked me to his truck and opened the door, teasing me about making sure I felt safe getting in with him, I laughed and began to relax.

"I'm glad she gave me the okay. I knew I liked her for some reason." He winked. "But, seriously, she is really cool peoples."

"I can't believe you know one another. It really is a small world."

"So, are you going to tell me what kind of job you thought I had?" Bilal asked.

I looked down at the pot of melted cheese sitting in front of us and tried to think of a good response. When I learned what Bilal really did, I felt bad. I couldn't believe that I had been so judgmental.

"Don't get shy on me now."

I dipped my skewer into the cheese and twirled it. "I'm not acting shy." I glanced up and looked into his handsome face.

"I can't believe you thought I was a drug dealer."

Clearly, I was busted, but he didn't seem too bothered by it. "I'm sorry about that, I really am."

"It's cool. I'm fairly used to it. A lot of people aren't used to someone like me being a legit entrepreneur, especially since I'm so young." He shrugged and seemed amused, which made me feel less guilty about my assumption.

"Exactly how old are you?" It was one of the questions I had meant to ask but never got around to.

"I'm twenty-two."

"Twenty-two?" I gasped. I knew he was older, but I hadn't expected him to be that old.

"What's wrong? How old are you?" he asked with a concerned look.

"I'm nineteen," I told him.

"Oh." He smiled, and I could see he was relieved. "For a second I was afraid you were gonna say seventeen. You look mad young, but I figured you were legal. I guess that explains why you said you didn't want anything from the bar."

"Yeah, I'm old enough to vote, but not old enough to drink," I said.

"Do you drink?"

"Nope."

"Smoke?"

"Nah, I don't," I said, suddenly feeling like a prude. "My life is kind of boring. I pretty much work and go to school."

"I guess we're gonna have to change that," he said.

"And how do you suggest that we do that?" I asked.

"We're gonna have to put a little excitement in your life. As a matter of fact, there's a concert at the end of the month I was gonna check out, and I would love for you to join me."

"What concert?"

"Hip-Hop Allstars Tour."

I couldn't believe he was sitting there inviting me to go with him to one of the biggest rap concerts in America. This wasn't just a concert; it was a two-day event. The average ticket cost was around four hundred dollars and had been sold out for months. He was acting like it was no big deal, like he had just asked me to go shoot basketball at the neighborhood park.

My eyes widened, and I said, "You're kidding, right?"

"No, I'm dead-ass serious. My boy Dell and I bought tickets months ago."

"That concert is like four hours away and two days long," I said, still waiting for him to reveal that this was some kind of joke. Going to the concert meant an overnight stay, like, in a hotel. I'd barely been on a date with a guy, and here he was inviting me to spend the night with him in a whole other city. Not to mention the fact that it was happening months in the future. Did that mean he anticipated us to still be dating? It was a little overwhelming for me.

"Yeah, we're driving up there and already have our Airbnb booked. But his girl is going too, and there is plenty of rooms in the spot we got, so don't worry. It'll be a fun little getaway."

There was no way I was going on a four-day road trip with a guy I just met. I ain't care how fine as hell he was, or funny, or smart, or how much I enjoyed talking to him. That would be crazy. I went to tell him thanks but no thanks, but when I looked up and saw Bilal staring and smiling, I couldn't. There was something in his eyes that drew me in—a soft and inviting look that let me know that he was happy, and that happiness was because of me. He reached across the table and grabbed my hand, and I felt a surge of energy go through my body that I had never felt before.

"I don't know. I'll have to think about that one," I said.

"Well, you have time, and I can understand you saying that. After all, we did just meet and are still getting to know one another. Besides, I plan on taking you on plenty of exciting outings before you make a final decision. We can ease into the whole exciting life thing. Is that cool?"

"I think I can handle that." I laughed.

"Great, because after dinner, I figured we'd go go-karting, and I can beat you right quick."

"What makes you think you'd beat me at go-karting?"

"Uh, because I've been driving way longer than you have. Trust me. You're getting your tail kicked."

"Well, for your information, I'm an excellent driver. Don't sleep on my skills."

"You're gonna have to prove to me you have some skills. We can wager, and loser pays for dessert afterwards?"

"Bet." I nodded, and we shook hands, once again causing the surge of energy to go through me.

We laughed and joked as we enjoyed the remainder of our dinner. He told me about growing up without his father, who had been killed by a drunk driver when he was nine. His uncle, Patrick, moved in with them, supposedly to be a role model, but he definitely wasn't anyone Bilal looked up to. Based on some of the stories I'd overheard Nikki tell Aunt Celia, I understood why.

After leaving the restaurant, we went to the indoor go-kart track. There was a slight crowd, and we had to wait, so I decided to call home and make sure everything was okay.

"Hey, Kendra. Are you having fun?" Avery asked when she answered the phone.

"Yeah, is everything cool there?"

"Yep, she's not here, and she hasn't called. We're fine."

I was glad Avery knew exactly what I was asking without my having to explain. Although I figured my mom hadn't called or come home early from work, I wanted to make sure. I checked the time and saw that I still had a couple more hours to enjoy my date with Bilal before I had to head back.

"Okay, lock that door, and don't answer it for anyone," I reminded her.

"I know. Have fun," she said.

"Everything okay?" Bilal asked, handing me one of the helmets we were required to wear.

"Everything's fine. I just wanted to check in on them."

"Your sisters are adorable, like you," he said.

"Thanks," I said, blushing. "They're a handful, though."

"Yeah, I know the feeling. My younger sister is hella nervewracking."

"Well, well, well. What's up, Bilal?" A female voice came from behind me.

I turned around to see a group of women staring at us, and I tensed up.

"What's up, Fee?" Bilal's voice was calm, and his face was stoic.

"This must be the spot you bring all your women to, huh?" She looked me up and down then turned to her posse and said, "Y'all remember when I told y'all he brought me here and we made that little side bet?"

"Yeah, didn't you beat him and win?" one of the girls asked. "So, he had to pay up?"

"He damn sure did." Fee nodded. "And boy, did he."

I looked over at Bilal, who seemed amused by this entire conversation, unlike me. I was growing more pissed by the second.

"Parker, Fuller, and Courtland, report to the starting line, please." The announcer's voice came over the loudspeaker.

Bilal eased his arm around me and said, "You ready, Caramel?"

"Caramel? What the fuck kinda name is that?" Fee turned her nose up.

"The kind that will get you knocked the fuck out the same way your punk-ass boyfriend did," Bilal snapped at her. I didn't know what that meant, but she quickly backed off and walked away with her friends.

When they were gone, I eased from under his arm. "Can we please go now?" I asked him.

"What? We're up next. Come on, Kendra. I'm sorry that shit happened, but she was wildin'," he tried to explain.

I wasn't in the mood to hear anything he had to say. I was embarrassed and ready to go. "It's fine. I just want to leave." I took a deep breath and fought the urge to cry.

He reached for the helmet I was still holding and said, "Yeah, we can go. Let me go turn these in."

"I'll wait for you at the door," I told him. I walked to the front door, ignoring the stares and comments of Fee and the other chicks.

"Guess Caramel ain't that sweet," one of them commented.

"Fuck that light-bright-ass girl. She don't even look like she can handle him the way that I did. I fucked the shit outta him, and he knows it," Fee said loud enough for damn near everyone in the crowded arena to hear, causing me to be even more humiliated than I already was.

I picked up the pace of my steps and hurried out the door. By the time Bilal made it outside, I was already leaning against his truck.

"Why did you walk out here by yourself? I thought you were gonna wait at the front door."

"Your li'l girlfriend and her cronies were harassing me, so I left," I told him.

"That ain't my girlfriend," he said, reaching to open the door for me.

I grabbed the handle before he could and opened it myself, closing the door before he could say anything else.

When he finally got in, he looked over at me and said, "Kendra, I'm sorry."

I continued staring out the window into the dimly lit parking lot. I was angry at myself for even giving him my number. I had let my guard down and allowed myself to like him, and now I felt like a fool.

"Kendra, can you please say something?"

I remained silent.

"Can you at least look at me?"

I turned and gave him the most evil look I could.

"Damn," he said. "Even when you're mad you're beautiful. Those eyes are everything."

"That's not gonna work," I told him.

"What's not gonna work?"

"Your tired attempts at flirting."

"I'm not flirtin. I'm stating facts."

I rolled my eyes before looking away again, deciding that our first date would definitely be our last.

"So, where do you wanna go now?" he asked as we drove from the parking lot.

"Home."

"Come on. It's still early."

"I have class in the morning, and I need to get back to check on my sisters," I told him.

"I can't believe this. We were having a great time, and you're gonna let those ignorant chicks interrupt a perfectly good night?"

"You're the one who interrupted it."

"How?"

"You didn't even say anything. You just stood there smiling." I shook my head at him.

"Because they looked stupid as hell. Didn't you think so?" He had the nerve to smile at me.

"Yeah, but—"

"But what? You wanted me to get loud and cuss her out while she was standing there? That's not how I roll. I let her talk and look dumb. I wasn't bothered by nothing she was saying."

"But I was," I told him.

"And that's why I put my arm around you and told you to come on. That right there was enough of a response. I wasn't thinking about them, and they knew it," he said.

"You brought her and me to the same place and made the same wager," I snapped at him.

"I go to that place all the time, and not just on dates. I go with friends, my sister—hell, I've been there a couple of times with my mother. Real talk, the owner is one of my best clients, and I like supporting him the same way he supports me. That's how I treat all of my clients," he said, then pulled over into a nearby parking lot.

When we were parked, he looked over at me and said, "Listen, Kendra, I like you. I enjoy talking with you. I've enjoyed taking you out tonight, and I'd like to do it again. Maybe I could've handled Fee's ignorant ass a little different, and for that, I'm sorry. I truly am."

I turned and faced him once again. I could hear the sincerity in his voice and see it in his eyes. I tried to hold onto my anger, but after hearing his explanation, the tension began to ease away from my body.

"I just don't like being put in a position where I feel like I'm being confronted, especially by someone I don't know," I told him. I dealt with enough confrontation at my own house from my mother. I had learned early on to avoid it in public, even when it meant being teased because of my skin tone, my good grades, or anything else people chose to tease me about. I realized

Bilal had nothing to do with how Fee had treated me, nor how people had treated me in the past.

"I understand, and I promise I'll never put you in that type of situation again. You have my word." He leaned toward me and touched my face.

"I appreciate that." I nodded and gave him a slight smile.

Then, he pulled my head closer to his. I instinctively closed my eyes and felt his lips press against mine softly. His mouth opened slightly, and I gasped and kissed him back, enjoying the taste of his tongue for what seemed like an endless minute. It was my first kiss; it was perfect, and I didn't want it to end. When he finally pulled away from me, I was breathless and smiling.

"Does this mean I don't have to take you home?" he asked.

"Well, you do owe me dessert." I shrugged.

"Uh, I think you're the one who owes me dessert," he said, kissing me again.

"How?"

"You forfeited the race," he replied.

"You better hope the ice cream machine is working at McDonald's." I laughed.

After finally finding a McDonald's with a working ice cream machine and indulging in hot fudge sundaes, Bilal took me home. I was glad that we had gotten past Fee and the incident and continued to enjoy our evening. The more I got to know him, the more I liked him.

"I had a nice time—well, except for meeting your little friend Fee," I said when he walked me to the door.

"Uggghhh, we're not gonna bring that up again," he groaned, then said, "I had a nice time too."

"Thank you for dinner."

"Thank you for dessert." He put his arms around my waist and kissed me again.

My second kiss was even better than the first. This time when he pulled away, I put my arms around his neck and pulled his mouth back to mine.

When the kiss ended, he sighed. "Damn, Caramel, you're dangerous."

I was about to respond when the flicker of headlights coming down the street caught my attention. I would notice the uneven lights anywhere.

"Well, I gotta get inside," I quickly said.

"Okay, I'll give you a call later." He leaned in to kiss me again, but I turned around and fumbled with the doorknob.

"Sounds great," I told him. "Good night."

"Good night," he said.

I rushed in and prayed he had made it back to his truck before the car made it down the street. I peeked out the window and saw him opening his door just as my mother pulled up. My heart began racing, and I silently prayed that he would quickly drive off before she got out of the car. God must've been listening, because he did.

I went straight into my bedroom, and as soon as I sat on the side of my bed, Avery and Ashley were tapping on my door, which was open.

"Why aren't y'all in the bed?" I asked them.

"Did you have fun? Was he nice? Where did y'all go?" They fired off the questions so fast that I couldn't tell who asked what.

"Go to bed. I'll tell you about it tomorrow," I told them.

"Celia! Come move your damn car out of my driveway!" my mother yelled.

I looked up at my sisters, who looked just as worried as I felt. Since she had been working all weekend, she didn't know about the car. I had hoped that Aunt Celia would call and tell her, but clearly, she hadn't.

"Go to bed, now!" I whispered to the twins, and they didn't waste any time following my instructions.

"Celia!" my mom yelled again.

I hurried into the living room where she was standing, and said, "Hey, Mama."

"Hey, who the hell was that leaving my damn house? And where the hell is Celia? Tell her to come move out of my fucking driveway. She don't live here, so I don't know why she even parked there."

"That was my friend, and Aunt Celia ain't here. How was work?" I asked innocently.

"What friend? And what the fuck you mean she ain't here? Her car is here." She glared at me.

"My friend Bilal, and she, uh, well, that's—"

"Why the fuck is her car here and she ain't, Kendra?"

"Mama, she gave me the car. She got her new car the other day."

"Didn't I tell you you couldn't have that fucking car? What the fuck do you mean?" She took a step toward me, and I took a step back.

"It's just for me to drive to school and work, that's all, Mama," I said.

"I don't believe this shit. My car is falling a-fucking-part while I go back and forth to work to keep a roof over your head and food on the table, and you think you're getting ready to live here rent free and drive a fucking new Volvo?" she shrieked.

"Mama, it's not new." I tried to calm her down. I didn't dare remind her that she got food stamps monthly that we bought food with—when she wasn't selling them to her clients.

"Bitch, that car is only four years old. Don't get smart with me. I will whoop your ass."

"I'm not trying to get smart, Mama. I'm just saying, the car is for our family. Avery can stay back for cheerleading now because I can pick her up. You know she's been wanting to cheer forever." I thought that throwing my sister's wishes in would help my attempt to reason with her.

"Fine, since it's for our family, give me the keys." She held her hand out.

I froze. The one condition that Aunt Celia set when she turned the keys over to me was that I was not to allow my mother to drive the car. I couldn't give her the keys.

"I can take you to work in the morning, Mama."

"I don't need you to take me no-damn-where. Give me the keys." She was within striking range now, and I braced myself.

"No, Mama. I'm not giving you the keys," I told her.

Sure enough, she grabbed me by the collar, and I pushed her away with so much force that she stumbled. Surprised by my actions, she became even more angry and went to hit me again, but I grabbed her arm and pushed her again. This time, she didn't fall. She charged at me, knocking me backward, and I pulled her down with me. In a flash, we were in a full-out tussle and rolling on the floor.

"Mama!" Avery yelled and ran to separate us.

"Kendra!" Ashley was right behind her.

I maneuvered away from my mother and jumped up, panting. My face was wet with both sweat and tears. It was the first time I had ever gotten into a physical altercation with her, and my emotions were all over the place. Avery helped my mother get to her feet, while Ashley held onto my arms.

"You either give me that key or you get the fuck out of my house," she demanded.

"I'm not giving you the key," I told her, shaking my head.

"Fine. I hope you like living in your new car. Get out."

"You can't kick me out. If I leave, who's gonna raise your kids? Not you, because the first call I'm making is to social services, and not only will you lose them, but you'll also lose that check and that EBT you get and don't spend on them," I said.

She stared at me, until finally, she said, "I don't want that fucking car anyway. And I don't know who you think you are, but just because you got a so-called friend and a new ride, your ass ain't grown, and I will still fuck you up."

I looked over at my sisters and said, "Come on. Let's go to bed."

Diane

At one point in time, my sister Celia was my best friend. We were only two years apart, and I could and would tell her everything. I trusted her more than anyone in the world. So, during my junior year of high school, when I fell in love with Randall Carter, the captain of the basketball team, she was the first person I told. I told her about him kissing me behind the gym after practice one day. I told her how he held my hand and sucked on my neck when we went to the movies for our first date. I told her about how he put his hand under my shirt and got mad when I stopped him from going any further. She was my shoulder to cry on when Randall broke up with me for a girl who was known to put out. Then, Celia tried to warn me when I started dating Champ to make Randall jealous and decided to lose my virginity to him and made sure Randall found out.

"You what?" Celia screamed when I told her what I'd done.

"I gave it up to Champ, and you know he got a big mouth, so he's gonna tell someone. When Randall finds out, he's gonna be begging for me to take him back." I laughed.

"Diane, that's the dumbest thing I have ever heard. What is wrong with you? Why would you do that?" She stared at me like I was crazy.

"Calm down, Celia. It was just sex. It wasn't even that good. Hell, Champ was a virgin too, and I think that's why he ain't know what he was doing. I know it's gonna be even better with Randall, though, because I love him, and he loves me," I explained.

In my sixteen-year-old mind, I had everything figured out. Sure enough, after dating Champ for a couple of months, Randall asked me out again. Everything was going exactly as planned, until I ended up ironically at Planned Parenthood, where they confirmed that I was pregnant.

"Di, what are you gonna do?" Celia asked when I came to her with my latest announcement.

"I'm gonna get rid of it. What do you think I'm gonna do?" I said as if nothing else was an option.

"You're gonna have an abortion?" she said, her face full of shock. "How?"

"You know, Cele, sometimes I feel like I'm the older sister and you're the baby. What do you mean, how?"

"Where are you gonna get the money? Isn't it like three hundred dollars?"

"It's two fifty," I said.

"What did Champ say?"

"About what?"

"About your English project, Di," she said sarcastically. "About your being pregnant, fool! What do you think?" Celia snapped.

"He didn't say anything because he doesn't know. I'm not gonna tell him. The only person who I'm telling is you, and Cele, you'd better not tell anyone," I warned her. I wasn't worried about my sister telling anyone at school, but whereas I had been a Daddy's girl, Celia clung to my mother like she was a saint. They had a tight bond.

"Diane, this is crazy. First of all, you don't have the money, and you don't have a job, so there's no way for you to get it. Second, I just think this is an overall bad idea."

"You have money, Cele," I said.

"What?" Celia frowned.

"You have money. You can give it to me."

Celia had been working and saving money for college for the past two years. I knew she had a nice sum that she could tap into and help me.

"That's money for school, Di. You know how hard I've been working, and I don't have nearly enough for my tuition," she said.

"Celia, you know you're gonna get a scholarship anyway. I don't know why you're stressing. This is way more important, and I promise I'm gonna pay you back," I said, grabbing her arm.

"Pay me back how? You don't have a job." Celia shook her head.

"Celia, please. You're the only person that can help me," I pleaded.

"Diane, this is crazy, and this is something I don't think I can help you with. You really need to talk to—"

"Dammitt, Cele, will you please listen? I don't need to talk to anyone else. I'm talking to *you*. Now, all I need is for you to loan me the money, so I can go and get this taken care of. Shit, it's not that big of a deal." I stood up and began pacing the floor of the bedroom that we shared. I was starting to think going to her might not have been the best idea, but I really didn't have anyone else.

Celia took a deep breath and paused for a moment, just looking at me. Finally, she said, "When are you supposed to go get it done?"

"Thursday at three fifteen," I said.

"Are you sure you even want to, you know, do this?" Her voice was shaking, and you would've thought she was the one needing the abortion, not me.

I walked back and sat next to her on the bed. "Hell yeah, I'm sure, Cele. Why would I not want to do this? I'm seventeen, for Christ's sake. What do you want, for me to end up like Mama?" I frowned. My mother was seventeen and my father eighteen when she got pregnant with Celia, which was why they got married. Daddy worked wherever he could, until he died from Leukemia when I was thirteen.

"Mama is a good woman. What's that supposed to mean?" Celia asked defensively.

"It means I don't want to be forced to spend the rest of my life paying bills, which is all a baby is. Once she got knocked up, their lives stopped. That ain't gonna be me. I want to be free to live my life, and I can't do that with no baby. So, I'm getting rid of it. Well, if you give me the money," I said.

"But what about Champ? It's his baby too," Celia said. "He should have some say-so."

"It's not even a baby yet. It's more like a lima bean. I get it; you don't believe in abortion. But, trust me, Cele, this is for the best. Please just give me the money."

"Di, you know Mama puts my savings into her account so I can't touch it." She shook her head at me. "I don't have two hundred and fifty dollars to give you, really."

"How much do you have?" I asked her, desperate to take whatever I could get. "I know you have money in your sock drawer."

"How do you—"

"How much, Cele?" I sighed.

"About eighty dollars. And that's not enough to—"

"I'll take it," I told her.

She stood up and walked over to her dresser, taking out a small, beaded coin purse and handing it to me. "Here. I hope you know what you're doing. I don't agree with this at all."

"I know you don't, Cele, but thank you. I appreciate it. I really do," I told her as I jumped up and gave her a hug. "Thank you, Celia. You're the best sister ever. I promise I'm never gonna get knocked up again. I'm gonna make sure when Randall and I get busy, not only am I gonna be on the pill, but he's gonna wrap it up."

"What about the rest of the money?" she asked.

"I'll figure it out. But believe me, I'm gonna get it," I assured her.

Two days later, I was sitting in the waiting room of Planned Parenthood when the glass door opened and I heard my mother screaming my name.

"Diane Celeste Hughes, have you lost your damn mind?"

"Mama, I—"

"Get your ass up right now and let's go," she demanded.

"But, Mama, I—they're about to . . . I have an appointment," I told her. My heart was beating so hard and fast that I could feel it in my neck. She was the last person I had expected to see.

"You don't have to do nothing but what I tell you to do," Mama said, grabbing me by the arm and pulling me up.

"You're hurting me, Mama," I said. Other people in the waiting room were staring at us.

The receptionist stood up from the desk. "Ma'am, you're going to have to—"

"Lady, this ain't got nothing to do with you. This is my daughter, and she's leaving!" she yelled so loud at the poor woman that she instantly sat back down.

"There are no refunds," the lady said to me.

I closed my eyes and told myself that I was in the middle of having a bad dream and when I opened them, it would all be over. There was no way in hell that this was real life. It couldn't be. I shook my head in an effort to wake myself from the nightmare. Sadly, I was still standing in the middle of the waiting area, being yanked out of the front door by my mother, who was cursing in between quoting Scripture.

I reluctantly got into the car, and she screamed at me all the way home. When we arrived, I walked in the front door, and there was Celia, sitting on the sofa, her eyes red and swollen from crying. Her eyes met mine, and instantly I knew how my mother had found out where I was and what I was doing.

"Diane." She hopped up and went to hug me, but I pushed her away.

"Leave me alone," I growled. "You promised you wouldn't say anything."

"You took the money from the can, Di," Celia said, referring to the coffee can my mother kept on the top shelf over the stove. I had taken the rest of the money I needed that morning. "She went crazy."

"And you had to tell her why, huh? Don't ever speak to me again. I mean it. I hate you," I told her.

Celia had betrayed me in the worst possible way, and from that moment on, the relationship I had with my sister was never the same. Throughout my dreaded pregnancy, I barely said two words to her. After Kendra was born, I allowed her to care for her, but I still hated her for what she had done. Celia eventually accepted the fact that our relationship was forever broken, and the love she once had for me, she now poured into my daughter, and the two of them shared a close bond. Celia doted on Kendra, and at times, it felt like a slap in my face.

"I don't know why you're so mad. You should be happy that she has a damn car," Ronda said, passing me the joint we were smoking. "That's gonna make shit easier for you."

"I'm mad because she acts like she calls all the damn shots. I'm Kendra's mother, not her. She ain't better than me, that's for sure," I told her, taking a drag. "I wish she would quit acting like it."

"Calm down. Hell, you need to be keeping a low profile, considering the fact that you're screwing her husband." Ronda laughed.

"Shit, I ain't even been doing that lately. He won't even take my damn calls. Lord knows I miss that dick, too." I took another drag and blew the smoke out of my mouth and into my nostrils before passing it back to her.

"You losing your touch?" Ronda laughed.

"Never that. I just had to put up with that nigga Ricky while he fixed my car, but now that it's done, I'm 'bout to be back on my game. You know how I do."

"You live a dangerous life, that's for sure."

"Nah, I just live life."

It was my day off, and as usual, I was spending it at Ronda's house, where there was plenty of weed and liquor and I could relax. Tension at my own house was thick, and Kendra and I still weren't speaking. She would go her way, and I would go mine.

My cell rang, and I looked at it. It was my job. I immediately sent it to voicemail. I knew they were calling for me to work overtime, and as much as I could use the extra cash, I wasn't about to work for it. My phone rang again. This time it was Ricky, and I sent him to voicemail as well. I tried calling Darnell again, but he didn't answer. It was around the time he normally went to lunch, so I decided to pay him a little visit.

Sure enough, by the time I parked my car in the parking lot at his job, he came walking out of the building. I beeped my horn, and when he looked up, I got out of the car and waved. He stared and kept walking until I yelled his name, not caring about the other folks walking nearby who were now staring at me. He didn't waste any time coming over to where I was.

"What the hell are you doing here?" Darnell said when he got to my car.

"Is that how you're gonna greet me, Darnell? I thought you'd be a little happier to see me." I faked a pout. "I'm here because you keep ignoring my calls."

"Why the hell do you keep calling?" He glared.

"Because I miss you. Both of you," I said, reaching down and fondling his crotch. I smiled when I felt a familiar bulge. "Oh, and I see you miss me too."

He took a step back. "Nah, I don't."

"Liar." I smiled. "Where are you about to go?"

"None of your business. What do you want, Diane?"

"It's my day off, Darnell. I want to spend some time with you, so I came to see if you wanted to go somewhere for lunch."

"Somewhere like where?" he asked. "I damn sure ain't going to your crib."

"We don't have to go to my crib, Darnell. We can go somewhere and talk like we used to." I shrugged.

"Shouldn't you be taking your man to lunch and talking to him?" Darnell was trying to be hardcore, but I could see him loosening up. The anger in his face when he first saw me wasn't as strong, now replaced by mild irritation.

"I keep telling you he ain't my man. I don't even deal with him anymore. I promise."

"Whatever."

"We can go to Applebee's over by the mall," I suggested, making sure whatever location I picked would be optimal for everything I planned on doing. I had to get back into his good graces, and today was going to be the start. My raggedy-ass car wasn't going to last much longer, and I would need his help to either get Celia to take the car from Kendra and give it to me or get me another ride. Either way, Darnell was my best option, so I had to work my magic.

He stared at me for a moment before saying, "Fine, let's go."

Not only did I convince Darnell to take me to lunch, but also to take the rest of the day off to take me shopping. It didn't take much effort to get him to check into a nearby hotel so I could thank him properly—although he was the one who did all the work. I was spent after two rounds in bed, and so was he.

"I knew you missed my ass." I laughed, playfully running my hand along his naked chest.

"Yeah, whatever. I'm still pissed that you brought that clown-ass dude to my crib."

"Why are you jealous? You said yourself he's a clown." I laughed.

"That was disrespectful as fuck, Di, and you know it."

"It was no more disrespectful than Celia giving Kendra that fucking car. It's like my word doesn't mean shit to anybody these days. And then, you ain't even have my back."

"Man, fuck Celia and that car."

I was about to ask him why when my phone vibrated for what seemed like the hundredth time since we'd gotten to the room.

"Damn, your man checking for you like that? He been blowing you up all damn day." Darnell sighed.

"Shut the hell up. I told you I ain't got no man. Well, except for you." I winked as I climbed out of bed and walked over to the dresser. I picked up my phone and saw that it was Kendra.

"What the fuck do you want?"

"Mama, have you talked to Avery?" she asked.

"No, and I'm busy right now," I said, hitting the END button before she could say anything else. I was about to put the phone back down when she called back.

"Avery didn't come home from school," she said. "And she's not answering her phone."

"Where the fuck is she?" I asked.

"I don't know. Ashley says she thought she was gonna ride the late bus, but she isn't home yet. I called her phone, and she ain't answer. I know you're off today, so I thought she might be with you, or you might've talked to her."

"Well, she ain't called me, and I don't know. But I tell you what: you better fucking find her by the time I get home later, or I'm gonna fuck all of y'all up," I said. This time when I ended the call, I turned my phone off then climbed back into bed with Darnell. I still had to discuss the car situation with him, and I didn't have time to deal with this dumb shit. Knowing Avery, she was somewhere with her dumb-ass friends, and Kendra was panicking for no reason. Then again, I wondered if I should try to reach her. If she answered the phone for anyone, it would be me.

"Everything a'ight?" Darnell reached over and caressed my thigh.

"Yeah. Avery ain't catch the bus home."

"Oh," he said. "We need to leave?"

I looked at my phone across the room, then over at Darnell lying beside me. My eyes drifted from his handsome face to his lower abdomen, and then rested on his manhood, which was semi-hard. I decided to let Kendra deal with finding her sister since she thought she was the woman of the damn house anyway.

"Nah, we got some unfinished business to take care of first," I said, taking him into my mouth and enjoying the sound of him moaning my name.

Celia

Where the fuck are you? I typed then hit send.

I had been trying to reach Darnell for almost four hours when I got the call from Kendra saying Avery was missing. He hadn't answered his desk phone, his cell phone kept going to voicemail, and he hadn't responded to any of my texts. I didn't know where the hell he was, and I was pissed. Here we were at the hospital, in the middle of a family crisis, and he was nowhere to be found, and neither was my sister.

"Your mama still not picking up?" I asked Kendra.

"No, I guess her phone is dead," she said, pacing back and forth.

"I'm sorry, Kendra," Ashley said, hugging her sister. "I should've went and found her when she wasn't on the bus."

"It's okay, Ash. You did the right thing by calling me when you did." Kendra comforted her.

I got up and put my arms around both of my crying nieces, and I became angry all over again. My sister should have been there with us, and instead, she was in the wind, no doubt doing something that she had no business doing.

"Hey, did you try calling Ronda?" I asked.

"No, I didn't call her. I didn't even think about that," Kendra said, taking her phone from her pocket.

"How is she?" We all turned to see Nikki coming into the waiting room.

"They haven't said anything yet," I told her as she gave me a big hug. "Thanks for coming, girl."

"I can't believe this," Nikki said; then, looking around the room, she asked, "Where is Di?"

I gave her a knowing look and shook my head, then motioned for her to step out into the hallway so we could talk in private.

"We can't find her ass. Kendra called her when Avery first went missing, and she told her to find her, and that was it. Hell, she doesn't even realize that the girl is here in the hospital," I told her.

"You really need to get custody of those kids." Nikki shook her head at me. "Diane ain't no kind of mama for them. She never has been."

Nikki was right in a way. Diane wasn't the best mother in the world. Still, a part of me wanted to believe that she loved those girls in her own way. Having my nieces come and live with me had crossed my mind time and time again. It was Darnell who pointed out that if I took those kids away from her, not only would Diane lose her mind, but it would probably split our family apart. With my parents being dead, Diane was the only sense of family that I had, and as much as we didn't get along, I didn't want to lose her. So, I resorted to helping out as much as I could. It wasn't easy, especially when Diane felt like my help should've been more toward her than her children. But she was a grown-ass woman who could take care of herself, and if she made better choices, she would've had a better life.

"I ain't thinking about that right now."

"So, what exactly happened?" Nikki asked.

"Well, it looks like she missed the bus. She decided to walk home the back way, and somebody found her laying in the ditch on Burnside Road. They don't know if she was hit by a car or what. Like I said, we're still waiting." I gave Nikki all the information we had gotten so far.

"Poor baby."

"Yeah, it's a mess, girl," I told her.

We were about to walk back into the waiting room with Kendra and Ashley when my phone buzzed.

"Where the hell are you?" I snapped when I answered.

"I had a meeting out of district. I'm headed back in now. What's wrong?" Darnell asked.

"I'm over at the hospital."

"Hospital? What hospital? For what?"

"Granby West. Avery's been admitted."

"Oh, shit. Is she okay?"

"We don't know yet. They haven't said."

"Mrs. Fuller?" A police officer approached me in the hallway.

"Darnell, I have to go talk to the police. We're in the fourth floor waiting room. Hurry up," I told him then hung up.

"Yes?" I said to the officer, who I couldn't help but notice was tall and attractive.

"I'm Detective Donaldson, and this is Detective Shaw. We have a couple of questions we need to ask you about your niece."

"Okay." I nodded. We went into the waiting room, and I sat on the couch beside Kendra, who was still holding Ashley. "These officers have some questions," I told her.

We were in the process of answering their questions when Diane finally called.

"What the hell happened to Avery?" she demanded.

"Calm down, Diane. We're still waiting to find out. We're talking with the police now," I explained.

"Police? Why the fuck are the police there?"

Everyone was staring at me, so I said in a calm voice, "This is my sister, Avery's mom. I need to update her. Excuse me for a sec."

I stepped back into the hallway and said, "First of all, you need to calm down and act like you got some damn sense. Second, you need to bring your ass to Granby West."

"I'm on my fucking way now. And don't tell me to calm down when my child is laying in a hospital and you're talking to the police," Diane told me.

I wanted to ask her why she was a concerned parent all of a sudden, but instead, I told her, "I'll see you when you get here."

The two officers walked out, and Detective Donaldson handed me a business card. "Here's my card. We have some officers still out at the scene gathering information, and we'll keep you updated."

"Thank you so much," I told him, taking the card from him.

"We'll stay nearby until the doctors give an update," he said before they walked off.

Twenty minutes later, the doctor walked into the room. Kendra immediately jumped up and asked, "How is Avery? Is she awake?"

"She's still unconscious right now, but she's stable. She has a broken leg and a few cracked ribs, some cuts and bruises," the doctor told us. "She's a tough young lady."

"Can we see her?" Ashley asked.

"In about an hour. We're still monitoring her closely right now, and we want to keep her in ICU for now as a precaution. But I'm pretty sure she's going to make a full recovery."

"Pretty sure? What the hell does that mean? Is she gonna be fine or no?" We all looked past the doctor at Diane, who was standing in the doorway.

"I'm sorry, you are?" the doctor asked.

"I'm her fucking mother. That's who I am. Now, where is my daughter? I want to see her," Diane told him.

"As I just stated before you arrived, she can't have visitors now. But in an hour or—"

"No, fuck that! I want to see her *now*!" Diane yelled.

"Mama, please don't do this," Kendra pleaded.

"You shut the hell up. This is your fault," she growled at her.

"What? How? Mama, I was at work when all of this happened," Kendra tried to explain through her tears.

"It's not her fault, Mama." Ashley defended her sister.

"And you? Where were you when she went missing? Why weren't you with her?" Diane grabbed Ashley's shoulder, causing her to cry out in pain. Before I could move, Nikki jumped between her and the girls.

"Ma'am, I'm gonna have to ask you to calm down," the doctor told her.

"Diane, you're being ridiculous," I said, embarrassed by my sister's behavior.

"I'll let you know when you can see her. You may continue to wait here, and I'll send a nurse to bring you back," he said then quickly walked out.

"Hell no, I want to see my daughter now! He can't keep me from seeing my daughter!" Diane began yelling again. She went to take off after the doctor at the exact same time Detective Donaldson and his partner walked in. Behind them, I was surprised to see my husband.

"What's going on?" Darnell directed at no one in particular.

"Is there a problem?" Detective Donaldson asked.

"Hell yeah, there's a problem. That cracker doctor won't let me see my kid. That's the problem," Diane told him.

"Detective Donaldson, this is Avery's mother. She's just upset by this whole ordeal. We apologize," I said.

"I don't need you apologizing for me. I wanna see my daughter. And what do the police have to do with this anyway? Somebody better tell me what the hell is going on before I set it off up in here!" Diane snapped.

"Ma'am, you're gonna have to lower your voice. We can't talk to you while you're acting like this," Detective Shaw warned.

"Maybe we should talk somewhere else," I said, reaching for Diane and hoping she would calm down. "There are other patients on this floor."

"I don't give a damn about them. I wanna know what's going on with Avery."

"As best as we can tell so far, she was struck by a hit-and-run driver," Detective Donaldson answered.

"As best as you can tell? What the hell is wrong with everyone around here? The doctor is pretty sure. . . . I betcha if Avery was some little white girl, she woulda been found and y'all would have some damn answers." Diane folded her arms and began pacing back and forth.

"I'm sorry you feel that way, Ms. Nixon," Detective Donaldson started.

"That ain't my damn name. My last name is Hughes," she told him.

"I'm sorry. Your daughter's last name—"

"I can't deal with this," Diane said, brushing past them as she rushed out.

"I'm sorry," I said.

"It's okay. We understand how emotional these situations can be." Detective Donaldson gave me a sympathetic look.

"Detective, you guys have confirmed that it was a hit and run? That means that nothing else happened to her?" I asked him.

"Not that we know of. A witness said that it looks like a vehicle veered onto the side of the road where she was walking, hit her, and kept going. But we'll keep you updated," he said and left.

I was slightly relieved once he confirmed that there wasn't any sign of rape or assault. My eyes went past him, and I realized that my sister wasn't the only one missing. My husband was too. Come to think of it, they had both just happened to show up at the same time.

A strange feeling came over me, and I turned and asked Kendra, "Did you tell your mom where we were?"

"No." Kendra shrugged. "Her phone kept going to voicemail, and I didn't bother leaving a message because you know she never checks them."

I took out my phone and dialed Diane's number. Sure enough, her voicemail picked up after the first ring. Thinking maybe she had me blocked, I turned to Nikki and said, "Let me see your phone."

When she gave it to me, I dialed the number again and got the voicemail.

"Did you tell Ronda where we were when you talked to her?" I asked Kendra.

"No, I just asked if she had talked to my mom, and she said she hadn't," Kendra answered. "As a matter of fact, let me go find her. Come on, Ashley."

I felt my legs weaken, and I sat down trying to get my thoughts together. I passed Nikki her phone.

"What's wrong?" Nikki asked, looking at me strangely.

I made sure we were alone before I spoke. I stared at her and said, "If no one got a hold of Diane, how the hell did she know where we were? How did she know we were here at the hospital?"

"What are you saying, Celia?" Nikki's eyes widened.

"I'm saying wherever the hell Diane was, Darnell was there with her."

Kendra

To hear that my sister was alive was a relief. It had been the longest, scariest eight hours of my life. I had been at work when Ashley called in a frenzy, saying that Avery hadn't made it home. I immediately left work and went home, where we began searching for her. When we hadn't found her an hour later, I called Aunt Celia, and she made it to the house in record time. We called the police, but they said my sister had to be missing at least twenty-four hours before we could file a report. We searched everywhere: the school the park, and friends' houses that she would visit. She was nowhere to be found.

I knew my mother would be no help at all, but I called her anyway. In my desperation, I even called my father, and at least he was more empathetic than she was. He was on the phone when two police officers arrived at the house and informed us that Ashley had been found and was being taken to the hospital. Hearing this, my aunt, sister, and I rushed to the hospital, where we waited until they updated us. My mother finally arrived and threw her tantrum.

In the middle of the chaos, I had forgotten about my date with Bilal until he called while I was searching for her.

"Hey, I'm on my way," he had said when I answered.

"I'm sorry, Bilal. I can't make it tonight. I have a family emergency," I told him.

"What's wrong? Are you okay?" he asked.

"Yeah, I'm fine. I'll tell you what happened later. Okay? I have to—"

"Yeah, yeah, go ahead. Just give me a call when you can."

"I'm so sorry," I told him.

"Kendra, I get it. It's cool. Go handle your business and let me know if you need anything."

Had I not been so distracted by everything that was going on with my sister, I would've been impressed by his understanding and his offer to help. I promised to call him as soon as I was able and continued to search for my missing mother, praying that I wouldn't find her huddled up with Darnell, who also seemed to have disappeared.

God must've heard my prayer, because when Ashley and I walked to the front entrance of the hospital, my mother was standing near the visitor's desk, and Uncle Darnell was nowhere in sight. She wasn't alone, though. Standing beside her was Nikki's boyfriend, Patrick. They looked like they were having a serious conversation.

"Mama?" I said, walking over to where she was standing.

"Hey, Kendra. How you doing, beautiful?" Patrick gave me a brief hug then did the same to Ashley. "Hey, cutie pie. You holding up okay?"

"Hello," I said politely.

"What the hell are you doing down here? Why aren't you upstairs making sure Avery is okay?" She glared at me. I almost asked her the same question.

"We came to check on you, Mama," Ashley told her.

"I don't need nobody checking on me. Get back upstairs with your sister," she snapped at us.

We went to follow instructions when I heard Patrick say, "We might need the little one down here when the cameras get here."

"You think so?" Mama asked, rubbing her chin and looking at Ashley.

"Yeah, that's her twin sister, right? She ain't gotta say nothing, just stand there next to you."

Ashley frowned at me, and I motioned for her to hurry inside, but it was too late.

"Ashley, you stay here. Kendra, get back up there," Mama said.

Ashley grabbed my hand and stepped closer to me. "I wanna go wait with Kendra."

"I don't give a shit what you wanna do. You gonna stay down here and do what I tell you." Mama pulled her away from me.

"Mama, why can't she go back with me?" I asked. "You know she's gonna be the first person Avery will be looking for when she wakes up."

"She'll be up in a minute," Patrick told me. "And can you let Nikki know I'm down here helping your mama handle some business?"

"What kind of business?" I frowned.

"Grown folks' business. Now get back up there," Mama said, her voice so loud that the old ladies sitting at the visitors' desk put their fingers over their lips to quiet her down. They didn't know that doing so would only make her talk louder.

"Don't shush me! My daughter is up there dying because someone decided to mow her over with a car and left her on the side of the street like roadkill, and you wanna shush me? Fuck you, lady. You get to sit here behind this desk, talking and judging each person that walks in here like your opinion matters, and you want me to shush so your little sidekick can hear you.

I don't think so!" Mama yelled at the top of her lungs.

"Diane, come on." Patrick pulled at her arm.

A pretty black woman walked up and asked, "Um, excuse me. Are you Diane Hughes?"

"Why?" Mama barked, startling the lady.

"I'm Shanna West with WJLS TV-10. I was wondering if we could talk to you for a moment about what happened to your daughter." The woman put her hand out.

"Nice to meet you, Miss West. I'm Patrick Cunningham, a friend of the family and a deacon at Mount Hebron Baptist Church. We can speak with you over here." Patrick shook the lady's hand and smiled.

The lady motioned to a guy carrying a TV camera who was walking through the door. Avery and I stood there, confused by everything that was going on.

"Mama?" I said.

"Are these your children also?" Shanna West asked, taking out a pad and pen.

Mama walked over and put her hand on my shoulder and said, "Get your ass upstairs now like I told you." She then looked at Ashley and said, "You stay next to me and don't say nothing unless I tell you. Do you both understand?"

I looked at my mother and nodded, then gave Ashley a reassuring look. I didn't know what my mother was up to, and I was going to get to the bottom of it, but now was not the time or place.

"Yes, ma'am," I told her and rushed back upstairs.

When I got to the waiting room, Nikki was the only one sitting there. My heart began pounding. "Where's Aunt Celia? Did the doctors come and get her? Is Avery awake?"

"No, they haven't come back yet. She and your uncle went to get something to drink from the vending machine."

"Oh," I said.

"Is that your mother?" Nikki said, pointing to the television. "And is that Patrick?"

"Yeah, he's here."

We both stood up and stared at the television screen. My mother, Ashley, and Patrick were standing at the front of the hospital, being interviewed by Shanna West, live on the news.

"This is Shanna West, and I'm here with the mother and sister of the hit-and-run victim we reported about earlier, along with Deacon Patrick Cunningham, spokesperson for the family. Deacon Cunningham, can you update us on how the young lady is doing?"

"The young lady is currently in a coma. She sustained horrible injuries and is in ICU," Patrick said into the camera. Beside him, my mother sobbed as she held onto Ashley, who looked confused by everything.

"That's sad to hear. And she was found on the side of the road near the school?"

"Yes, in the ditch," Patrick said. "Our children aren't safe, not even walking home from school."

"And what are the police saying?" Shanna asked.

My mother sobbed. "They said that they're gonna see what they can find out. They don't care. My daughter had been missing for hours before they even decided to look for her. That's how much they care. Had she been some little white girl that had been missing, they would've had her picture all over the news and issued out all kinds of alerts!"

"Oh my God." I gasped, not wanting to believe what I was seeing.

"What the hell?" Nikki said at the same time, sounding as shocked as I was.

"We at Mount Hebron are going to support this young mother and her family, because they are a part of our community. We will be accepting donations over at the church, and a GoFundMe page will be available for those not in the area."

It suddenly dawned on me why my mother was doing this. It was all for attention and money, the two things in life that she loved more than anything. I had to go find Aunt Celia so she could put a stop to it.

"I'll be right back," I said, leaving Nikki standing with her mouth open.

I followed the signs to the vending area and turned the corner when I heard her voice.

"Don't stand there and lie to me."

"I'm not lying, Celia. I was at a district meeting. You know I don't have my phone on when I meet with corporate. Then, I guess I ain't have a signal while I was on the road driving back. You're acting crazy," Darnell told her.

I froze, not wanting to interrupt the intense conversation.

"Naw, you're crazy, Darnell, if you think I believe anything that's coming out of your mouth right now."

"Celia, we don't even need to be having this conversation right now. You're upset about Avery and—"

"No, I'm upset because you're standing there lying to me. Now, tell me—how long have you been fucking my sister?"

I felt the air leave my body and felt myself become faint. I had walked up on a conversation that I hadn't wanted to hear. My heart broke for my aunt, and although my first instinct was to go in and have her back, I decided the best thing to do was leave—and leave fast.

Bilal

Since my date with Kendra was cancelled, I decided to follow up on another problem I had been dealing with. Uncle Patrick was supposed to have paid me at least half of the money he owed Dell that I paid, but I hadn't heard from him. I drove over to his crib, hoping to catch him, but no one was home. The church parking lot was empty, and Chubby's was closed. I decided to take a chance and call him, even though he'd been ignoring my calls and texts for the past two days. I was shocked when he answered.

"What's up, nephew? Did you see me on TV? I looked good, huh?"

"What? TV? What are you talking about?" I asked.

"I was just on the news. I gave a live interview," Patrick answered.

"On the news for what? Where are you?"

"I'm over at the hospital. One of Nikki's friends had an emergency, and I'm the family spokesperson."

Whoever it was must've been desperate if they had my uncle speaking on their behalf.

"Well, naw, I ain't see it. I was calling about my money you were supposed to have two days ago."

"I know, I know, but I promise you I'll have it in a couple of days."

"A couple of days?"

"As a matter of fact, I'll have all of it. I just need you to give me seventy-two hours."

"If you don't have half of what you owe me now, how the hell do you expect me to believe you'll have all of it in two days?"

"Three days."

"You said a couple."

"A couple meaning three. I meant to say a few days. Besides, I said seventy-two hours, and I'm gonna have it. Nephew, you gotta believe me. In three days, I'm gonna have your money."

I didn't trust my uncle as far as I could throw him, and I damn sure didn't believe him, but there was nothing I could do. This was all Dell's fault. He shouldn't have even done business with Uncle Patrick in the first place.

"Three days," I told him.

"Three days," Uncle Patrick said. "I gotta go. Some more reporters just got here, and I gotta go talk to them."

At that point, I didn't even wanna know what my uncle was up to. The only thing that mattered was him having my money in three days. Not that I was hurting for funds. Business had increased tremendously for me over the past few months. We were in the middle of a recession, and crime was on the rise. As bad as that sounded for everyone else, that was good for me, especially in my line of work. People were afraid and wanted to feel safe, and I was the man to call.

I decided to stop by Dell's house before going home.

"What the hell are you doing here? I thought your ass had a date," he said when he answered the door.

"She bucked on me. Had some kinda family emergency." I walked inside.

"Hey, Bilal!" Marlena called out from the kitchen.

"Hey, Lena!" I looked over at Dell and said, "I thought you said you were done with her."

"She got herself together and started acting like she had some sense, so I'm giving her one last chance." His voice was barely above a whisper, and I tried not to laugh.

"Does she know that?" I said, loud enough for her to hear.

"Do I know what?" Marlena asked as we passed the doorway of the kitchen.

"Know that he's met some new chick," Dell said quickly.

"Oh, yeah. Dell told me you feeling some youngin'," Marlena teased.

"She ain't that young," I said. "She's only three years younger than I am."

"Dawg, she still a teenager, and you're damn near thirty."

"Shut the hell up. You know that ain't the case." I was tempted to give examples of young chicks he had dealt with over the years, but I knew better than to go there, especially with Marlena in earshot.

"How old is she?" Marlena walked over and gave me a hug. Every time I saw her, she put me in the mind of a high school cheerleader. She was short, cute, bubbly, and instantly liked by everyone she met.

"She's nineteen, almost twenty," I told her.

"So, she's legal. That's all that matters." Marlena rolled her eyes at Dell, then asked, "Do you like her?"

"He just met her. How the hell is he supposed to know that?"

"Oh, he knows. Now, answer the question."
Marlena waited for my response.

I thought about the conversations I'd had with
Kendra, and how I felt whenever I saw her, and I
smiled. "Yeah, I think so. I do."

"I'm glad to hear that. Now, you can stop
going around here dealing with these skanks
like Fee and the rest of those randoms. You're
so much better than that, Bilal. You're one of the
good guys. You need a good girl. You want some
dinner? We're having lasagna."

"Sure." I nodded.

Dell playfully hit her on her butt as she walked
out of the room, and when she was gone, he
looked at me and said, "Told you she started
acting like she got some sense: cooking Daddy's
favorite meal and everything."

"You probably begged her to come back." I
laughed.

"Man, you know better than that. More like
the other way around. But, listen, I'm glad you
came through, because I got some business for
you. Somebody broke into Malik's crib. Got him
for seventeen G and a lot more."

"Damn, are you serious? When?" I frowned.
Malik was another friend of ours that we'd
known since high school. He was also a dealer.
He moved coke and guns across the country.

"Night before last. I told him when he moved into that spot to call you. I think it was an inside job."

"If he woulda called me when you told him to, he woulda had proof if it was."

"No doubt. But robbery or not, he better do something, because I need my money," Dell made sure to point out. Getting robbed was a part of the game, but even knowing that, Dell did not play about his money.

"I feel ya. Tell that brother to call me. I got him." I sighed.

"We can roll over there after we eat. You ain't got shit else to do, R. Kelly."

"You still got jokes, huh? Yeah, we can roll through."

"Dell, you want me to take this lasagna out of the oven, or you gonna come in here and finish it yourself?" Marlena yelled. "All you wanted me to make was the salad, remember?"

"Uh, I . . . what?"

"Well, while you were making it, you told me not to touch it, so I just wanna make sure."

Clearly busted, Dell jumped up and made a dash toward the kitchen, trying to avoid the teasing he knew was about to commence.

I never could confirm which one of them cooked dinner, but it was delicious, and I enjoyed it nonetheless. Based on the way they were making bedroom eyes at one another, I could tell Dell was glad to have Marlena home.

"Baby, I gotta make a run with B," he told her once we were finished eating.

"Dell," Marlena said in a warning voice, "we talked about this. You said no more late-night runs."

"It ain't that type of run, Lena. This is a business meeting," Dell said. "B gotta meet with a potential client. Tell her, B."

Marlena looked over at me for confirmation, and I nodded. "Yeah, it's a run for me."

"Fine, but Dell, you remember what I told you. You mess up one more time, and I'm gone for good."

"I got you, Lena." Dell groaned and gave her a kiss.

"Thanks for dinner, Lena. It was great."

"You know you're welcome here for dinner anytime, Bilal. Next time, bring your girl. You know I gotta make sure she's legit and give my approval."

"Will do," I promised and gave her a kiss on the cheek.

Dell and I drove over to Malik's home. As soon as we got out of my truck, a guy came out of nowhere with an assault rifle pointed at us.

"What the fuck?" I yelled when I spotted him.

"Man, Skeet, if you don't put that fucking thing down, I swear," Dell growled.

Recognizing Dell, the guy lowered his weapon, but he didn't put it away. "What's good, Dell? Malik ain't tell me you was coming."

"He ain't know we was coming. I gotta be fucking announced now?" Dell asked him.

"Naw, you can come on," Skeet said and led us inside. "Malik!"

We waited in the entryway, and I took a look at the door. There was a standard doorknob and a top lock. There was no indication whatsoever that there was any type of security system in place: no cameras, no motion sensors, no detectors.

"Who that?" Malik yelled back.

"It's Dell. I got Bilal wit' me!" Dell hollered before Skeet could announce us.

"What up, fellas?" Malik spoke as he walked down the steps. He was an average-sized dude with a bald head and full beard.

"'Sup, Malik?" Dell dapped him up.

"What's good, Malik?" I did the same.

Malik looked back over at Skeet and said, "You can get your ass back out and stand on post."

Skeet didn't respond. He just nodded at Dell and walked out the front door.

"You got armed guards out front now?" Dell asked.

"Shit, I shoulda had 'em before now. Then maybe I wouldn't be in the situation I'm in now," Malik said, rubbing his head.

"Man, I heard what happened. That's fucked up," I told him.

"Yeah, I shoulda listened to Dell when he told me to have you come through a little while ago, but I was thinking niggas wouldn't be dumb enough to hit my crib. Shit, I been pushing weight in these streets since eighth grade. I been in the game longer than some of these dudes been born, and they know I play no games. I'm a fucking legend. But that ain't stop them from coming into my crib and taking my shit."

"Man, Malik, you know ain't no loyalty out here. I don't trust nobody out here these days," Dell told him.

"You know who did this?" I asked.

"I got an idea, but I ain't sure." Malik shrugged.

"Well, Bilal here is gonna make sure if anything goes down again, you will be more than sure," Dell told him.

"I hope so, but I don't know if that's a good thing, because if there's a next time and there's proof, whoever it is is gonna end up dead, that's for sure," Malik said, his voice full of anger. "I want my shit to be harder to get into than the fucking White House, and I wanna be able to see shit even when I ain't here."

"No worries. I'm gonna make sure the entire spot is secure and you're able to see each and everything that goes on in this house at all times."

"That's what I'm talking about." Malik nodded. "Lemme show you around."

Malik gave us a full tour of his huge home. I made notes of each room and exactly what would be needed. It was going to be a huge job and cost him a pretty penny, but what he was getting would be way cheaper than everything he had just lost. We ended the tour in the great room of the house, where Malik and I were discussing how long I would need to finish the job. My best friend's attention was drawn to two women who happened to be sitting on the sofa, drinking wine and watching TV.

Dell wasted no time speaking. "How y'all doing?"

"We're fine." One of the women smiled back a little too eagerly.

"I'm Dell."

The eager girl introduced herself. "I'm Kareema, and this is Tey. You want a drink?"

"Naw, we're good. We just had wine with our lasagna. Right, Dell?" I gave him the side-eye and shook my head, hoping it would remind him of the fiancée he had waiting for him back at home.

"Oh, yeah." Dell gave me a disappointed look.

"That's a damn shame the police ain't go look for that girl when they called. Now look at what happened," Tey commented.

"I know. Seeing her mama cry like that made me wanna cry," Kareema said.

"I know that dude that's with her from somewhere." Tey pointed to the television. "Ain't that Tiesha baby daddy?"

"Oh, shit! B, look," Dell said.

I looked over at the television, and there was Uncle Patrick, standing beside a familiar woman, who was screaming about her missing daughter being found by the police.

"Yeah, he said something about being a spokesperson for some family," I mumbled. I tried to pinpoint why the woman was familiar to me. The camera panned out and zoomed in on the face of a teenage girl standing beside them that I instantly recognized. It was Kendra's little sister, one of the twins that I met when I picked her up for our date. The other woman had to be her mother, who I'd seen coming home just before I left.

Reading the headline running across the bottom of the screen, I turned to Malik and said, "I gotta dip. I'll come through tomorrow and we can finalize everything."

Dell gave me a strange look. "Man, what's wrong?"

"That's Kendra's mom and sister."

Diane

"Brighter Home Health Care, this is Adrienne."

I stepped outside the hospital to have some privacy as I dialed the number to my job. I made sure to call after they were closed so that I would speak to the after-hours receptionist, who I was cool with, to let them know I wasn't coming in for a couple of days. I didn't want to talk to anyone else, especially with everything that was going on now. Plus, I'd dodged their calls all day, because I damn sure wasn't going in to cover anyone's shift. Ironically, I now had to call in to make sure someone covered mine.

"Hey, girl, it's Diane. I ain't gonna be able to come in for the next few days, so someone's gonna need to cover for me."

"Hey, chick. What's going on with ya? You avoiding this place like everyone else?" Adrienne laughed. "They were blowing everyone up today to come in and take these piss tests. I'm glad I ain't smoked in a minute."

I was glad she couldn't see the horrified look on my face through the phone. It was a good thing I hadn't answered when my job called. There was no way I could pass a drug test, not today or any day soon.

"Oh, I didn't even know that's why they were calling. My daughter was in an accident, and she's in ICU at Granby West, girl. I don't know when I'm going to be able to come back."

Adrienne gasped. "What? Oh my goodness, Diane! I'm so sorry. Do you need anything? That's horrible."

"I know. I will be there to pick up my check on Friday, though." I looked up and saw someone walking toward me and said, "I have to go."

"I'll let the scheduling nurse know. And keep us updated on your daughter, Di."

"I will," I told her and ended the call.

"A'ight, so this is what I'm gonna need you to do. You and Avery have to come be at church Sunday," Patrick stated when we were standing face to face.

"Church? Oh, hell no," I said. "I don't do church."

We had been giving statements and interviews for the past hour and already had a few scheduled for the next morning. Things had gone from zero to one hundred in a matter of minutes, and I needed time to think.

"Well, you better start," Patrick warned. "You want this thing to work, then you gotta follow my lead."

Following Patrick Hurston's lead was going to be easier said than done. Once upon a time, we ran in the same circles, before he supposedly found the Lord, and if there was one thing I knew about him, it was that I trusted him about as much as I trusted the 45th President of the US. Even the way he popped up to be my family representative was shady. I had been standing outside the hospital, trying to convince Darnell to go to the liquor store for me when Patrick walked up.

"What the hell are you doing here?" was the first thing I asked when I saw him.

"Damn, Diane, it's like that? I thought we were cool. But to answer your question, Nikki called and told me about what happened to your daughter. I'm here to support the family in its time of need." Patrick smiled, then looked at Darnell. "Darnell, I see you're here holding her up too, huh? That's nice of you."

Darnell looked Patrick up and down then said, "Man, shut up. I'm going back upstairs, Di. You coming?"

"Yeah." I went to follow behind him, but Patrick stopped me.

"Diane, one sec. Lemme holla at you for a minute before you go."

"Go ahead," I told Darnell, then said, "What the hell do you want?"

"So, while I was over here, I got a call from one of the ministers from the church. He heard about what happened, and he was extremely concerned about the lackadaisical response from the local police department. He wanted me to let you know that they are just as disappointed as you are, and if you need anything, the church is there for you, as well as the community," he said.

"Uh, thanks?" I said blankly, making it more like a question than a statement.

"I'm sure, as a single mother whose child is laying in the hospital, you are going to need to rely on others to help your family get through this rough time, especially when it could have been prevented had it not been for the possible negligence of the police." He sighed.

"Listen, Patrick, I don't know what the hell you're getting at, but I got real shit to deal with right now. My kid is upstairs in ICU, and I just found out my job is about to give me a piss test that I ain't gonna pass, which means I'm probably gonna be fired too," I said. My mind was all over the place. I needed a drink, and Patrick was making me even more agitated. Darnell clearly wasn't going to the store like I asked, so I was going to have to sneak away and go myself or call Ronda and see if she would bring me something to calm my nerves.

"If you play your cards right, you won't even need to worry about that job." Patrick stared at me. "At least not for a while, anyway."

That statement made me stop and pay attention. I frowned and said, "What do you mean?"

Seeing my interest, he pulled me closer to him and said, "Come on, Di. You know you can spin this shit into a goldmine, right? With the right person by your side guiding you, of course."

"Lemme guess. You're the right person, huh?" I folded my arms and waited for his answer.

"I'm just saying, I got a homeboy who works security at the news station. They're always telling him to keep his ear to the streets so they can be the first on the scene for the good *hood* stories. Nikki already told me the police ain't start looking for your daughter when they were first called, and when they did find her, it was because someone spotted her laying in the ditch. Now, come on. You know folks will eat that shit up. Not only that, but they'll come out of their pockets. You remember when that little boy on the west end saved his sister and brother from that fire a couple months ago? You know how much they raised for his family? Forty-seven thousand dollars."

"What?" My eyes widened in surprise. Hell, I had even given a couple of dollars at the convenience store for that family one morning while I was buying my lottery tickets and cigarettes.

"Hell yeah. And the kicker is that his little ass was the one that started the fire," Patrick said smugly.

"Damn, I ain't know about that part," I said.

"Exactly, because they ain't let that little piece of info get out, and by the time it did, the money had already been raised. So, all I'm saying is I can make a phone call to my boy at the TV station and get the media down here. We can talk to them, and the next thing you know, the dollars will be coming in."

I knew Patrick well. What he was saying made a lot of damn sense, but he was and always would be a hustler. He wasn't willingly going to help; that was for sure. There would be some kind of catch.

"And what the fuck do you want out of all of this? Twenty percent?"

His eyes softened enough for me to almost believe the fake sincerity he was giving me, and he said, "Listen, I'm not an attorney or anything, Di. I'm just a friend offering assistance."

"Oh, so you gonna assist for free?"

"I ain't say that. And I don't want more than you would give the Lord. I only want a fifteen percent cut of whatever funds we raise for the cause." He smiled.

"Fifteen percent? That's more than the Lord. He only asks for ten percent. I may not do church, but I do know that much." I rolled my eyes.

"A tenth is the tithe. You still give him an offering. So, I figured that would be the extra five. But that's nothing considering we're gonna bring in at least fifty grand." He shrugged.

"There's no way we can bring in that much." I shook my head.

"Oh, but there is. We're not only gonna have the media on our side, but also the community and the church. I mean, we can do this, Di."

I thought about the possibility of having fifty thousand dollars—well, thirty-five after Patrick got his cut, which I was going to try my best to use my powers of persuasion to get him to lower. Either way, it was more money than I could ever imagine, and Lord knows I needed it. Hell, five hundred dollars would help me out tremendously.

"I don't know," I said, not wanting to seem too eager to accept his offer. "What makes you think I can't do this by myself and get just as much money?"

"You can't. Believe me, you need me. Because one, you need to focus on being the concerned mother and won't have time to deal with the calls, emails, and planning that will need to be made. Two, I'm a well-respected deacon of one of the largest churches in the city. Folks listen to me. Third, I'm still Pat from up the block, and niggas respect me. You may raise a few coins, but you won't be able to bring in the dollars I can. Now, what do you want me to do?"

I paused before finally saying, "Make the call. And take me to get a drink right quick, because I'm gonna need one."

He laughed and said, "No worries. I got a bottle in the car. Come on. Let's take a walk."

He made the call as we walked to his car. We had finished off the half bottle of Patrón he had hidden in his trunk, went back into the hospital, and ran into Kendra and Ashley. The reporter chick arrived, and we quickly gave our first press conference. The drink certainly had helped, but hearing that he wanted me to come to church was a whole other beast within itself.

"Hold on. Nikki is calling me," he said, answering his phone. "Hey, baby. Yeah, that was me. Naw, I was on my way up there to be with you when I ran into Diane, and then the news people were harassing her, so I did the Christian thing and stepped in. What? That's great news. We're on our way up there now. I just finished praying with her. See how quickly God works?"

"What? What happened?" Ashley asked.

"Come on. They're letting the family back to see Avery. I need for you to be ready, because now that everyone has seen us, this story is gonna spread like wildfire," Patrick told us.

"We gotta talk to more TV people?" Ashley whined. "I don't want to."

I snatched her by the collar and said, "You gonna talk to whoever I tell you to. Not only are we about to talk to more TV people, but we 'bout to share this with the whole damn world. We 'bout to get paid, and you are not gonna mess this up for me. Now, come on so we can go check on your sister."

Celia

Darnell stared at me, not saying anything. His silence gave me all the answers I needed. I couldn't believe this was happening to me. I had suspected that his ass was cheating, but never in a million years would I have thought he was sleeping with Diane. This was low, even for her skank ass. Tears of hurt and anger began stinging my eyes, and I tried to blink them away.

"Celia." Darnell had the nerve to look defeated, even though he was the one that caused the crippling damage in my heart. I turned and walked away, determined to get as far away from him as possible. I hadn't made it very far when I walked into Detective Donaldson, literally.

"Oh, sorry," I told him.

"No, it's my fault. Are you okay?"

"Yes, I'm fine." I nodded.

He reached into his pocket and handed me a handkerchief. I politely thanked him and dabbed at my eyes, embarrassed by my tears.

"Listen, I know it's a little overwhelming, but the doctors are very optimistic about Avery, and so am I. From what they say, she's a real fighter," he said.

I realized he thought my tears were due to my niece and not my trifling husband and slut of a sister.

"She is," I told him.

"Celia." Darnell's voice came from behind me.

I took a deep breath and said, "No, I'll check on her later. Thank you for all of your help, though."

"Are you sure everything's okay?" Detective Donaldson asked with a look of concern on his face.

"Yes, I'm sure." I nodded and walked away.

"Celia, wait," Darnell yelled, and I sped toward the elevator, which was a few feet away.

"Sir, can I speak with you for a moment?" I heard Detective Donaldson say.

"Naw, I need to catch my wife before she gets on that elevator," Darnell said.

"I don't think she wants to speak with you right now, sir," Detective Donaldson told him.

I pushed the elevator button several times, praying that the doors would open soon. I needed some air and to clear my head.

"Man, can you please move so I can talk to her?" Darnell asked.

I pushed the button again, and finally, the doors opened. I looked back once more before stepping on and seeing the tall police officer blocking Darnell. Had I not been so pissed, I would've been amused by the sight of them.

"Celia don't—"

The elevator doors closed before Darnell could finish his sentence. I leaned my head against the back of the elevator as it descended. My husband and my sister. My sister and my husband. The thought was nauseating. All I'd done for both of them was bust my ass. I busted my ass so that Darnell and I could live in a nice house and drive nice cars and go nice places. I busted my ass so that I could help take care of her fucking kids, the ones that she barely saw during the week because when she wasn't so-called working, she was either getting drunk with her friends or screwing some random-ass man—one of which happened to be my husband. Darnell was sleeping with Diane.

As soon as the elevator stopped, I ran off and rushed to the nearest bathroom, where I threw up and finally released the tears that I'd been holding in. Once I was all cried out, I washed my face and hands. I was about to walk out of the bathroom when Nikki called.

"Where are you? The doctors are looking for you. They're letting family members back to see Avery."

"Is she awake?"

"Well, no, but they're saying two people can go back two at a time for a few minutes."

"Nikki, I'm leaving."

"Leaving? Where the hell are you going? You can't leave. Is this because of Diane and Patrick?"

I shook my head in confusion. "What? Diane and Patrick? What the hell are you talking about?"

"They were just on TV, and she went off about the police not looking for Avery in time. Poor Ashley was standing there beside her, looking like a deer in headlights. You didn't see them?"

"No, I didn't," I said.

"Then why are you leaving? Look, I don't know what's going on, but you can't leave now. At least not until Avery wakes up. Where are you, Celia?"

"I'll call you later," I told her. "Do me a favor, Nik."

"Anything, girl. What is it?"

"I need you to stay here with the girls. Tell Kendra I'm not feeling well and I had to go."

"That's not a problem. But, Celia, please tell me what's going on."

"I just gotta go." I knew Nikki would have my back and make sure my nieces were good, even if she wasn't sure about what was going on. As much as I wanted to be at the hospital for Kendra, Ashley, and Avery, I couldn't. There was no telling what I would do when I came face to face with Diane, and it wasn't the time nor the place for me to issue the ass-whooping she had coming.

I walked out of the bathroom and out the front door of the hospital, where several news crews were setting up. My phone rang again, and Darnell's name came across the screen. I immediately ignored it and put him on Do Not Disturb.

"Celia, Celia!"

I turned around and was surprised to see Champ walking toward me.

"What's up, Champ? What are you doing here?" I asked.

"Well, Kendra called me earlier and told me Avery was missing. And then next thing I know, I see Diane on the news. I came to see what was going on," he said. "Is she all right?"

"I don't even know. Right now she's in a coma and in ICU," I told him.

"Are you serious? Damn, I don't believe this." He shook his head. "Where's Kendra?"

"Uh, she's upstairs, sixth floor waiting room. But, uh, I think she might be in Avery's room, because, uh, the doctors finally let the family in."

"Are you okay, Celia?" Champ was looking at me strangely.

I nodded. "I'm fine. I'm just worried about Avery."

"Naw, girl. You ain't fine. And it ain't just about Avery. What's going on?"

Again, tears began streaming down my face, and I began crying harder than I had in the bathroom minutes earlier. Champ looked confused for a moment, and then he pulled me into a supportive embrace, and I buried my head into his chest. I was an emotional wreck, and I was glad that he was there, even if it was just to awkwardly pat my back.

"I'm sorry," I said, embarrassed by my breakdown.

"It's okay." He smiled and hugged me again. "Now, what's going on?"

"Celia, what the hell are you doing?" Darnell's voice seemed to come out of nowhere.

"Darnell, leave me alone. I'm not about to do this with you. Not now and not here," I told him.

"What's good, Darnell?" Champ spoke, but Darnell just looked him up and down. Normally, the two of them got along really well. I could see that Champ was confused by his sudden discontent with him, but he shrugged it off.

"Celia, we need to talk about this."

"Not now, Darnell. Leave me alone," I warned.

"Hey, I don't know what's going on, but—"

"You're right. You don't know what's going on, so you need to stay out of it, Champ," Darnell told him.

"Celia—" Champ started, but Darnell interrupted him.

"Damn, Champ, leave us alone!"

"Who the hell you yelling at, son?" It was obvious that Champ was done trying to be pleasant about the situation.

"I'm yelling at you!" Darnell responded.

The two of them came face to face, and I could feel the tension building. My husband wasn't much of a fighter, and as bad as I would have loved to stand back and watch Champ kick his ass, I couldn't allow that to happen. I went to step between the two of them when Kendra came running.

"Daddy?"

"Hey, baby." Champ immediately stepped away and went to put his arm around his daughter. "How you holding up?"

"I don't even know."

"Kendra, how's Avery?" I asked. "Did you see her?"

"Yeah, Aunt Celia. Her face is all bruised and swollen, and her leg's in a cast, but it looks like she's just asleep." She was crying.

"It's gonna be okay, baby," Champ told her.

"Celia, listen . . ." Darnell started again.

"Kendra, listen, I gotta go, okay? But you call me if there's any change."

I expected Kendra to throw a fit, but instead, she looked from me to Darnell, then back to me and said, "Okay, I will."

"Don't worry, Celia. I got her." Champ hugged Kendra tighter. I knew that between him and Nikki, she and Ashley would be fine until I got myself together enough to be able to come back, if that happened.

"I love you," I said, kissing her cheek. Then I looked at Champ and said, "Thanks, Champ."

The two of them headed back into the hospital, leaving Darnell and me alone.

"Celia—"

"Darnell, I'm gonna tell you this one more time: leave me the fuck alone. I don't have anything to say to you right now, and I suggest you don't even come home tonight," I told him.

"Where the hell am I supposed to stay?" he asked.

"Don't know and don't care. Maybe you can stay wherever you were earlier when I was trying to reach you. I'm sure there's plenty of room in Diane's bed," I said and walked away.

Kendra

"What the hell is he doing here?"

I had hoped my dad and I would somehow miraculously avoid seeing my mother. Unfortunately, as soon as we walked into the waiting room, she walked in. As happy as I was that he was there for me, I knew she would go ape shit when she laid eyes on him. I had faith in my father, though. It didn't matter how bad my mother clowned; he was going to be pissed, but he wouldn't lose his cool.

"Hello, Di. I came to check on Kendra," he said simply.

"Well, as you can see, she's fine. You can leave."

"Where's Ashley?" I asked her.

"She's still in there with Avery," she answered, still staring at my father.

"How is she?" my father asked.

"In a fucking coma. How do you think she is?" Mama snapped at him then looked at me. "Where the hell did Celia and Darnell go?"

"They left," I answered, remembering the conversation I'd overheard and the look of hurt on Aunt Celia's face when she was in the parking lot. She finally knew about my mother and uncle. Had my sister not been in the ICU, I would've left with her. She was the last person I wanted to be around.

"What? Why would they leave when all of this is going on? Any other time she would be all up in my business, trying to dictate what should be going on with my children, and now she decides to dip out? This is that bullshit I'm talking about. But she loves y'all so much." Mama rolled her eyes at me.

"She had a valid reason to leave," I said flatly.

"Oh, really? What reason is valid enough to leave while her niece is laying in a coma in ICU?"

"Diane, you know Celia—"

"Why are you still here, Champ? I asked you to leave."

"I ain't going nowhere until I get ready, Diane. I told you, I'm here for Kendra," Daddy told her.

"You know what? I don't have time to argue with your ass right now," she said, then turned to walk out. "I'll be back later."

"Mama, where are you going? Don't you need to stay up here to talk to the doctors?" I asked.

"I need to go and handle my business; that's what I need to do. Champ, you better not be here when I get back. I don't want to have hospital security kick you out," she said before leaving.

"Unbelievable." I sighed and flopped down on the sofa. My dad came and sat beside me, rubbing my back as I leaned forward, holding my head in my hands.

"It's okay, Kendra," he whispered. "I know you're scared and your mother ain't making this no better, but it's gonna be okay."

"I hate her," I said.

"You don't hate her. You just don't like her, and for good reason. She's a hot mess," he said. He was trying to make me smile, but it didn't work. "Come on. Let's go check on your sister."

"You heard what she said? If she finds out, she's gonna be pissed," I warned him.

"Hell, it won't be the first time, and it won't be the last."

When we got to the nurse's station, she led us back, and I was surprised to see Ronda in the room.

"Okay, Ashley, move a little closer and kiss her cheek," she instructed my sister.

"Oh my God, what are you doing?" I demanded, realizing she was standing at the foot of the bed, taking pictures with her cell phone.

"Girl, chill out," Ronda told me. "Ashley, move closer!"

"But her tube," Ashley whined, looking like she was gonna cry. She was leaning close to Avery's bruised and swollen face, which was covered with medical tape that held a respirator in her mouth.

"Ashley, move," I said, pulling away.

"Ronda, put that damn phone away," my dad whispered.

"First of all, why the hell are you even here, Champ? And second, don't come in here telling me what to do. You must have me mixed up," Ronda snapped at him.

"Why would you even be in here doing this?" I asked her, feeling violated. "Why would you even want to take pictures of my sister like this?"

"Because her mama asked me to. She needs them." Ronda shrugged.

"Needs them for what?" my dad asked.

"None of your business. And again, why the hell are you here, Champ? This ain't your daughter, remember?" Ronda taunted. "The twins ain't yours, and you got the blood test to prove it."

Ashley looked down at the floor and started to cry. I felt horrible. Even though she never brought it up, she hated the fact that she didn't know who their father was. I walked over and put my arm around her.

"Ronda, can you please just leave?" Daddy asked her, his voice full of tension.

"Hold up. That's a good one." Ronda held the phone up again, facing it toward Ashley and me, and I heard the camera snapping. "Both of the sisters crying at Avery's bedside."

I walked over and reached to snatch the phone away, but she was too fast.

"What the hell are you doing, Kendra? Don't get fucked up in here. We're in the hospital, so the damn ER is right downstairs. I will send you there." Ronda stood so close to me that I could feel her stank breath on my face.

"Get the hell away from her," Daddy warned.

"Your mama told me you think you grown these days. I guess somebody need to show you that you ain't," Ronda said.

"I ain't scared of you," I told her.

"Kendra, step back," Daddy told me, his hand on my shoulder.

"You better listen to your daddy."

"Leave her alone," Ashley cried, pulling my arm. "Kendra, let's go."

"What's going on in here?" A nurse came in, confused by what was going on. I glanced from Ronda over to her. "In case you all don't realize, this is a hospital, and that young lady laying in that bed is in critical condition."

"I'm sorry." I apologized as I stepped back from Ronda. She went to step toward me again, but Daddy blocked her.

"Don't," he said.

"Get the fuck outta my face, Champ, before I whoop your ass and then whoop Kendra's ass too." Ronda's neck rolled as she spoke.

"Ronda, you and I both know that ain't happening," Daddy said calmly.

"That's it. I'm calling security." The nurse turned and left the room.

"Daddy, let's go back to the waiting room," I told him.

Daddy turned and looked at me, then backed away. My racing heart slowed down, and I took Ashley by the hand.

"Kendra!" she shrieked.

I turned to see Ronda aiming for me, but Daddy blocked her and pushed her before she could make contact with my face. Surprised by his actions, Ronda stumbled backward, and she grabbed the first thing she could to keep from falling—Avery's IV pole. It tumbled to the floor, and alarms began sounding. Within seconds, the nurse returned with two security guards, and behind them, my mother.

"What the—Oh my God, Ronda!" Mama rushed over to Ronda instead of Avery, who was being treated by the nurse.

"He pushed me down!" Ronda shrieked, pointing at Daddy.

"He did what?" Mama yelled. "Didn't I ask you to get the hell out of here, Champ?"

Ashley tried to explain. "Mama, that's not what—"

"Shut the hell up, Ashley!"

I walked over and stood beside my father. "Come on, Daddy."

"You better get him the hell out of here," Mama said.

"All of you need to leave. *Now!*" the nurse said.

"All right, everyone, let's go," the two security guards said.

"Thank you." Mama smirked.

"You too," the nurse told her.

"What? I ain't going nowhere," Mama told her.

"Security." The nurse gave them a look.

"Ma'am, I'm sorry. You need to leave. Let's go," one of the officers told her.

"This is my daughter's room. You can't kick me out."

"I can and I will," the officer told her. "You can either come now willingly, or I will not only take you out of this room, but out of this hospital."

"Don't worry, Di. I got it all right here," Ronda said, once again holding up her phone.

"Ma'am, I'm gonna ask you to put the phone away," the other security guard said.

"Keep filming, Ronda, so folks can see that this is the mistreatment I'm dealing with. First the city police officers, the hospital staff, and now the security. This is how they treat black women, and I'm sick of it," Mama said into the camera.

"Ma'am, please leave so we can take care of our patient," the nurse said again.

"That patient has a name!" Mama screamed "Justice for Avery! Justice for Avery!"

I grabbed Daddy and Ashley. I could no longer stomach the circus my mother was creating and starring in. We walked back down the hallway and into the waiting room.

"This is embarrassing," I said. "She's making this bad situation even worse than it already is."

"I know, baby. She just likes being the center of attention, that's all," Daddy told me.

The door opened, and Mama and Ronda walked in, escorted by the hospital security officers. This time, there was a city police officer with them.

"Now, we're gonna let you wait in here, but if there is any other disruption, you're gonna have to leave," the security officer said.

"I want him out of here!" Mama demanded, walking into the room and pointing at Daddy.

"Sir?" The city officer looked over at us.

"It's not a problem, officer. I can leave," Daddy told him.

"And I don't want him back here. He shouldn't be here in the first place," she said.

"I told you I'm here to support my daughter," Daddy explained.

"He's my father," I told them, holding Daddy's arm.

"It's okay, Kendra," he said.

"I want him gone, and I want him banned from this floor." Mama folded her arms. "As a matter of fact, I want him banned from this hospital."

"We really can't do that without some kind of order of protection in place. And that can only prevent him from being anywhere near you, not the hospital," the officer explained.

"Fine. I'll take out an order of protection," Mama told them.

"Really, Di? Is that necessary?" Daddy shook his head.

"Mama, you're being ridiculous." I sighed.

"I'm protecting my family," she said. "He assaulted my friend. He should be arrested."

"What?" Daddy frowned, now realizing the extremes that Mama was willing to go.

"Is this true, ma'am?" The city officer looked at Ronda.

Ronda looked over at my mother. She was hesitant to answer until Mama gave her a threatening look. "Yes, he pushed me to the floor. They saw the whole thing."

She pointed to Ashley and me.

"That's not exactly what happened," I said.

"Did he push her or not, Ashley? And you better not lie!" Mama yelled at my sister.

Ashley was so afraid that she was shaking. She looked from Mama to Daddy, to me, and then, finally to the officer and said, "Yes, he pushed her."

"Sir, we're gonna have to take you with us." The officer reached for the cuffs that were attached to his belt buckle and stepped toward Daddy.

"Please don't do this," I begged and cried, standing in front of Daddy. "She was trying to hit me, and he stopped her, that's all."

"I'm sorry, but you're gonna have to step aside, miss," the officer told me. "Or we're gonna have to take you downtown too."

"Kendra, let the man do his job," Daddy told me.

I watched in horror as my father was handcuffed and taken away, my mother and Ronda smiling the entire time.

"Daddy, I'll come downtown and get you," I told him.

"You ain't going no-fucking-where," Mama said. "I swear to God, if you leave here with him, I'll make sure you can never come back here to see Avery. Try me."

Ashley wrapped her arms around my waist and clung to me. "Kendra, please don't leave me. You can't leave me here by myself."

"Stay here with your sister, baby. I promise I'll be fine," Daddy said as the officer walked him out of the room.

"You're going to have to go to the magistrate to take out the protective order," the officer reminded my mother. He said to Ronda, "And you're gonna have to come down and file a report as well."

"Serves his ass right," Ronda said when they were gone.

"I told his ass a long time ago that I was going to get the last fucking laugh. Now, here we are." Mama giggled, then looked over at me. "Well, some of us are laughing. Kendra ain't."

"Kendra was about to get her ass whooped." Ronda glared at me. "That's why."

"Oh, really?" Mama asked.

"Hell yeah." Ronda nodded. "But, check it. Not only did I get the video of you going off on security, but I got some good pictures, too, just like you asked."

"For real? Good. Come on. We need to get these to Patrick so he can upload them," Mama said.

"Girl, you 'bout to be paid," Ronda told her.

Mama glanced back at me and said, "Exactly, and I damn sure won't be riding around here in nobody's hand-me-down Volvo."

"Mama, you don't have to do this. I told you, you can have the car," I told her.

"Fuck that car. I'm 'bout to have a new ride that's paid for. Again, I'm always gonna get the last laugh," she said, and they walked out.

I hugged Ashley tightly, and we cried together. I reached for my phone and tried calling Aunt Celia, but the phone went straight to voicemail. My sister was in a coma, my father was being taken to jail, my mother had lost her damn mind, and my aunt was nowhere to be found. I tried to comfort Ashley, encouraging her to go to sleep and telling her that everything was going to be fine, but I wasn't even sure if that was true. I was alone and afraid, with no one to turn to.

Thirty minutes later, she was snoring lightly as I covered her with a blanket that I got from one of the nurses. I was sitting with her head in my lap when I heard the waiting room door opening.

"Kendra?"

I eased Ashley's head off my lap and stood up. "Bilal?"

"Yeah, I came to check on you. I was worried. Are you all right?" he said, whispering when he noticed Ashley sleeping.

I walked over, and he immediately pulled me into his strong embrace, holding me tightly. I allowed myself to enjoy the strength of his arms and released all the emotions that I had been holding onto into his chest. He held me so tight and so long that it felt like his arms were created by God specifically to comfort me.

I tilted my head and stared into his eyes. "My life is falling apart. I don't know what I'm going to do," I told him.

"Don't worry. It's not gonna fall apart. I'm here to help you hold it together." He kissed me gently on the forehead, and in that moment, for the first time, I knew that I was in love.

Celia

"Are you sure?" Nikki asked as she sat on the side of my bed. "I know Diane is trifling in a lot of ways, but this is low, even for her."

"I'm sure, and the sad part is, I'm not even surprised by her. She's always been a messed-up individual. Darnell, on the other hand, is fucked up," I told her.

"Where is he? Have you talked to him about this?"

"He's not home, and I'm glad he had sense enough to listen to me when I told his ass not to come home. There's nothing to talk about. There's no explanation he can give me for fucking my sister." I shook my head, tears of anger once again forming in my eyes. I thought I was all cried out after spending all night wiping my tears, but sharing the situation with my best friend brought a whole new set of emotions. "I'm leaving his ass. He can go and be with her since he wanna sleep with her. Hell, they deserve one another."

"But did he say that he slept with her, Celia? He confessed when you asked him?"

"He didn't have to confess. I asked him, and I could tell by his reaction what the answer was." I sniffed, and she handed me a Kleenex out of the box on my nightstand.

"Celia, you may be upset for no reason. There was a lot going on yesterday, and everyone's actions and emotions were all over the place, including mine. We were all on edge. Avery was missing, and then she was found, and the police were there, then Diane was acting crazy."

"What are you saying, Nikki? That I should ignore this because of what happened to Avery?"

"That's not what I'm saying at all. I am saying that you need to talk to him, and her, and find out what the hell is going on. It could just be a coincidence that neither one of them answered their phones." Nikki shrugged.

"That's bullshit, and you know it. But let's say you're right. How the hell did Diane find out we were at the hospital? Who told her? And they just happened to show up at the same damn time?" I shook my head. I knew Nikki was naive when it came to Patrick, but there was no way she could believe what she was saying about Darnell and Diane.

"Maybe her job called, or the police finally reached her. You don't know, because you haven't talked to her, have you?"

I took a deep breath. "No, I haven't. I left the hospital without saying anything to her. I didn't wanna talk to her. Trust me, if I talked to her, I woulda knocked her the hell out, so it's best that I left when I did."

"It's kind of a good thing that you did leave, because shit got ridiculous and out of control."

"Oh, Lord. What happened?"

"I guess Ronda stepped to Kendra, and some kinda way, Champ got involved and pushed her down. Then security got called, and Champ was arrested. Diane took a restraining order out against him and everything," Nikki said.

"What? That's crazy!"

"Oh, and then there's a video of Diane going off in Avery's hospital room, screaming 'Justice for Avery' that's floating around, and these horrible pictures. It's a mess."

"Why am I not surprised by any of this?" I leaned back against the headboard and closed my eyes.

I felt so bad for my nieces. I had been ignoring Kendra's calls all night, the same way I'd been ignoring everyone else's. There was no telling how she was dealing with all of this.

"Celia, can I talk to you for a sec?" Darnell walked into the bedroom, looking like he'd lost his best friend. I wasn't moved at all by his pathetic demeanor.

Nikki immediately stood up and said, "I'll leave y'all alone."

"Nik, you don't have to leave. Just wait downstairs in the den, please?" I asked, wanting her within earshot in case I needed a witness of some sort.

"Okay," she said, giving me a nod.

"Celia, baby." Darnell sat in the same spot that Nikki had gotten up from and reached for my hand. I snatched away from him, and for the first time that morning, I got out of bed. I went into the bathroom and closed the door. As I sat on the commode, I thought about what Nikki said, and I convinced myself to at least hear him out. When I walked out, Darnell was still sitting there, waiting.

"Darnell, what do you want?" I rolled my eyes at him.

"Celia, you're really acting irrational, and I don't understand why. Where is all of this coming from?" He exhaled.

"It's coming from the fact that you're screwing Diane and I know it," I snapped, standing at the foot of the bed.

Darnell stood up and walked over to me. "Celia, why would you think that?"

"Darnell, shit between us hasn't been right for weeks. You're sleeping in the other room, and you barely touch me. All you do is walk around and complain."

"I'm telling you I'm not sleeping with Diane. I'm just under a lot of stress at work. And you know the doctors have me on blood pressure pills, and that fucks with my libido. I love you, Celia." He reached for me again, and I pulled back.

"Darnell, I don't believe you." I shook my head.

"What? Why would I lie?" he asked.

I was about to answer him when I heard the doorbell ring.

"I'll get it," Nikki yelled. A few seconds later, I heard her talking to a male. Then she reappeared in the doorway of my bedroom. "Celia, Detective Donaldson is here. He needs to speak with you."

I looked down at the oversized T-shirt I was wearing. "Tell him I'll be down in a few."

"Celia, we're not done talking," Darnell said.

"What the hell do you want me to do, Darnell? Tell the damn police officer I can't answer any questions right now because I have to listen to my husband?" I snapped, walking over to my dresser and taking out a pair of leggings, a sports bra, and a hoodie. I pulled my T-shirt over my head and slipped my clothes on. I could feel Darnell's eyes on me as I got dressed, and I cut my eyes at him. "Can you not?"

"Why can't I? You're my wife, aren't you?"

"Barely," I said as I slipped on my Nike slides and headed downstairs.

Nikki and the detective were seated in the living room. When I walked in, he stood up.

"How are you, Mrs. Baker?"

"Please, call me Celia," I told him.

"Celia." He smiled. "Sorry to come over unannounced, but my captain has the entire department working on your niece's case, and I need to go over some questions with you that we didn't get to yesterday."

"It's no problem. Can I get you something to drink?" I asked.

"No, I'm fine." He nodded and pulled out a small notepad and a pen from his pocket. I almost laughed, thinking how cliché it was, and wondering if all cops still used a pen and paper rather than something digital. He remained standing as I sat beside Nikki and answered the questions about Avery and my timeline from the day before. He wore an intense look on his face as he jotted down my answers.

Finally, he said, "That's all I need for now. I understand your sister is filing suit against the department regarding the handling of your niece's case, but I assure you, we did everything in our power to find her. It's just that there's a protocol to these things. I wouldn't have handled it any differently had it been my niece. I know this is quite an ordeal for your family and—"

"Well, she ain't your niece, and I don't think it's appropriate for you to come over here attempting to persuade our family into not filing suit," Darnell said as he walked into the living room.

"That's not what I was doing at all," Detective Donaldson told him.

"Darnell, that was uncalled for," I told him. "I apologize for his rude interruption, Detective Donaldson."

"Don't apologize for me. I'm a grown-ass man," Darnell said.

"Then act like it," I snapped.

"I'm gonna go ahead and leave," Detective Donaldson told me.

"I'll walk you out." I stood up and cut my eyes at Darnell as we passed him. We walked out of the front door, and when we got to the steps, he stopped and turned to me.

"Are you sure everything is okay between you and him?"

"Yeah, he can be a little intense, but trust me, his bark is worse than his bite. I'll be fine. But I do appreciate all of your help," I answered.

"Part of my job," he said. "You still have my card?"

"I do." I nodded.

"Feel free to call if you think of something or need anything else."

"Well, there is one small thing. I don't know if you'll be able to help, though," I told him.

"What's that?" He frowned.

"My brother-in-law—well, ex-brother-in-law. It seems he was arrested at the hospital last night for some craziness caused by my sister and her friend. If you could just check on him for me and let me know, I'd appreciate it. He's a decent guy, and my sister, well, you've already witnessed her." I shook my head.

"She's a piece of work. But I'll definitely check into it and let you know."

"Thanks, Detective."

"Sean," he said.

"Huh?"

"Sean. That's my first name."

"Oh, Sean." I smiled.

"I'll be in touch, Celia," he said and headed down the circular driveway.

I went back inside and was relieved that Darnell was nowhere in sight.

"What the hell was that about? Why is Darnell tripping so hard and snapping at the damn police?" Nikki asked.

"I don't know. He's acting out because he's guilty, probably." I shrugged.

"Did you ask him about Diane?"

"Yeah, and he denied it, of course. But I don't believe him."

"I don't know, Celia. So, you're just not gonna go back to the hospital to check on Avery? I know you wanna check on her and Kendra and Ashley," Nikki said.

"I don't know. I ain't trying to run into Diane."

"Don't worry about that. She's over at the church with Patrick, because they're planning some kind of rally for Avery. Maybe you can sneak over there now while she ain't there?"

"I don't know, Nikki." I shook my head.

"Well, let me know if you want me to go check on them a little later." Nikki gave me a hug.

"Thanks, Nik. I appreciate it."

When she was gone, I walked back upstairs. Darnell was in the shower. I grabbed my phone off the charger and hurried down the steps and out of the house, determined to be gone by the time he was finished.

I drove around for a few minutes, contemplating what I should do. My stomach began growling, and I pulled into the drive-thru at Panera. As I waited in line, I pulled up my Facebook page, and the first thing I saw was a picture of Avery, hooked up to IVs and machines in her hospital bed. There was a GoFundMe page linked to the post, with a goal of twenty-five thousand dollars. Already, more than nine thousand had been collected. I felt sick to my stomach as I realized my sister was using Avery as her cash cow.

"Can I take your order?" the voice came through the intercom for the second time since I'd been sitting there.

I thought about Kendra and Avery, who probably hadn't eaten all morning, and Diane, who most likely hadn't even thought about feeding them. I ordered enough food for all of us and headed back to the hospital, praying I wasn't making a mistake.

Diane

"So, now what?" I leaned over and whispered to Patrick. We were sitting in the conference room of Mount Hebron Baptist Church, waiting on the man who ran their outreach program. I'd been invited to discuss a rally they planned in support of Avery. It seemed like Patrick's little plan was working. Money was pouring in, I had done more news interviews than I could count, and had requests for more. We had used that fiasco in Avery's room with Champ to our advantage, and now not only was the police department kissing our ass, but the hospital too. The pictures and videos Ronda took were just the icing on the cake. My girl always came through for me.

"Well, the rally is Sunday night, so you, Kendra, and Ashley definitely need to be at church so folks can see your face and be inclined to come out. Plus, seeing you in person will make them more inclined to share the GoFundMe page on social media," Patrick mumbled.

"I told you I don't do church," I hissed.

"You gonna do what I tell you, and that's be here tomorrow morning for eleven a.m. service," Patrick said, no longer trying to whisper.

The door of the conference room opened, and a middle-aged guy came in and introduced himself as the director of outreach. I only half listened as he and Patrick went over the plans for the community gathering that would be held outside of Avery and Ashley's school.

My phone buzzed, and I looked down. It was Darnell, who had called me three times. Patrick gave me a dirty look.

"Um, I gotta take this," I said.

"Of course." The man nodded.

I stepped into the hallway and answered, "What do you want? I'm busy."

"Where the hell are you? Is Celia at the hospital?" Darnell asked.

"None of your damn business, and I ain't even at the hospital. I'm in a meeting," I said, suddenly enjoying how official I sounded.

"A meeting? With who?"

"Again, none of your damn business, Darnell. Why do you keep calling me?"

"Because I need to talk to you. Celia knows."

I paused for a second. "Knows what?"

"About us."

"And?"

"What do you mean *and*?" he snapped.

"I mean what I said: *and*?"

"I don't know why you're acting like you don't care."

"And I don't know why you're acting like you do. Hell, Darnell, if you cared about her, you damn sure wouldn't've been screwing me. Now, I gotta go." I hung up and went back inside.

"Is everything okay?" the outreach director asked.

"Yes, they were just updating me about some blood work. It's fine. But I do need to leave," I told him. Then I looked at Patrick and said, "I'll talk to you later. "

Patrick stood up. "I'll walk you to your car, Sister Diane."

When we got to the parking lot, he said, "Don't fuck this up, Diane. Everything's in place and moving exactly the way we need it. I need you and your girls here tomorrow morning. Get here early."

I sighed. "Fine. But I'm gonna need some money."

"Money for what?" He frowned.

"I damn sure don't have nothing in my closet that's appropriate for church. I need to go shopping," I told him. He reached into his pocket and handed me some folded bills. I counted them then asked, "What the hell am I supposed to do with sixty dollars, Patrick? Don't play me like I'm stupid. All that money we got sitting in that GoFundMe account and this is all I can get? I gotta get dresses and shoes for Kendra and Ashley too."

"First of all, that money stays in the account for a certain amount of time before they release it." He reached back into his pocket and handed me a few more dollars. "That's all I got."

"You need to get some more." I counted the money, which now totaled two hundred dollars. "Don't play with me, either."

"Fine. I'll call you in a little while, and we can meet up." He shook his head at me.

Satisfied that he understood that I meant what I said, I got into my car and headed out, waving as I drove out of the parking lot. I called Ronda and asked her if she wanted to go with me to the nail salon, deciding to treat her to a manicure and pedicure for all her help. She was more than happy to accept the invitation, and I promised to pick her up in thirty minutes after stopping by my house first. I hadn't been lying when I told Patrick that I needed something decent enough for church, but I wanted to double check in case there was something in the back of my closet I could wear.

I unlocked the door and stepped inside the house, nearly jumping out of my skin when I saw a strange man sitting in my living room.

"Who the fuck are you?" I yelled, fumbling in my purse for my blade.

"Oh, wow. I didn't mean to scare you. I'm Bilal, a friend of Kendra's," he said, standing up. He was tall, handsome, and fine as hell. I couldn't stop staring at him.

"Kendra? Where the hell is she?" I asked, relaxing a little.

"She's in the shower," he replied.

"Her ass is supposed to be at the hospital where I told her to stay. Why the hell is she home?"

"I convinced her to let me bring her home and take a shower and change right quick. She had a long night, and the doctors even said it was a good idea for her to get some air," he explained. "We're going right back."

"Well, aren't you a good friend. What did you say your name is again?" I asked him.

"Bilal."

"Bilal, you're just sitting here waiting, huh?" I eased closer to him. I swear, he had to be one of the best-looking men I'd ever seen.

"Yes, ma'am." He nodded.

"And how old are you?" I asked, moving even closer to him. By now, we were standing face to face. I was expecting him to be nervous, but he didn't seem to be, which turned me on even more.

"Twenty-two."

Damn, I thought, *the things I could do to his young ass.*

"I'll be ready in a few min—" Kendra stopped dead in her tracks when she saw me. Her bathrobe was tied tightly around her waist, and she was rubbing her wet hair with a towel. "Mama?"

I took a step back from him and turned around. "What the hell are you doing home, Kendra?"

"I came to shower and change," Kendra answered.

"You sure that's the only reason you up in here?" I looked Bilal up and down smugly. "You sure you ain't do anything else?"

"Oh my goodness! Yes, Mama. You know me better than that." Kendra's face turned beet red.

"I know you up in this house butt naked with a fine-ass man," I said. "Where is Ashley?"

"She's at the hospital. I told her I would bring her a change of clothes. She didn't wanna leave." Her eyes went from me to Bilal, then back to me.

"But I told you to stay there until I got back," I said. "Didn't I?"

"Yeah, but I didn't even know how long that was gonna be. You didn't come back at all last night, and you didn't even call to check on Avery." Kendra folded her arms.

"Because I was out taking care of business. I had to go to the police station, and by the time I was finished, it was late as hell, so I came home to get some sleep."

"The doctor was even surprised when you weren't there this morning," Bilal said.

"And how would you know what the doctor said?" I asked.

"Because I was there all night with Kendra and Ashley, and I was there this morning when he came in to do rounds," he answered.

I turned and frowned at him, preparing to cuss him out.

Kendra said, "Don't worry about it, Mama. I'm going back."

"Don't bother. I'll go back my damn self," I told her, suddenly becoming worried. If the hospital staff said anything to anybody about me not being there, I knew it would not be good—for me, or for the money I was trying to pull from folks.

I jumped in my car and told Ronda to be ready and waiting when I got there, because we had a stop to make before we could be free to enjoy the rest of our day.

"Miss Hughes?" The nurse at the desk seemed surprised to see me as Ronda and I got off the elevator.

"Yes, hello," I said, giving her a half wave as I walked past.

"The doctor was just about to have me call you and update you on Avery." She stood up.

"Why? What's wrong with her? My oldest daughter said she was fine. She's home taking a shower and resting. We figure it's easier to be here in shifts rather than all of us here at once," I told her.

She said, "Oh, okay. Well, there's no change in Avery's condition right now, but she is probably going to need surgery."

"Surgery?" I repeated.

"Yes, on her arm. The break is pretty bad."

"Oh, that's all." I sighed, wondering why the nurse made it seem like it was so serious.

"Well, thanks for the update," I said before continuing down the hall. I was almost to Avery's room when I stopped dead in my tracks. Coming toward me were Ashley and Celia.

"Ma," Ashley mumbled when she saw me standing in front of them.

"Ashley, I'm gonna go ahead and leave. I'll call you later, okay, sweetie?" Celia gave her a hug.

"Aunt Celia, please don't go." Ashley clung to her, and it made me cringe. I hated the way my children adored her like she was some kind of A-list celebrity.

"What the hell are you doing back here anyway?" I snapped.

Celia ignored me and looked at Ashley. "It's okay. I'm sure Kendra will be back in a little while. You and Avery won't be here by yourself for long, I'm sure."

"What the hell is that supposed to mean? I'm right here with her."

Again, Celia didn't respond. I replayed the conversation I'd had with Darnell in my head. My sister was so angry that she was pretending I wasn't there.

"Celia, you're being childish," I told her.

"You know what the doctor told us when he came in earlier?" Celia asked Ashley.

"Yes." Ashley nodded.

Celia hugged her and said, "Good. Remember that. I love you."

The longer I stood there watching her and Ashley, the more agitated I became.

"This is some bullshit," I commented.

"Di, come on. Let's just go in the room," Ronda said.

"Naw, yesterday she up and left and didn't give a damn about who was here. Now, this morning she done popped up acting all concerned, as usual, like they ain't got a mama. You're good for that, ain't you, Celia? Only wanna be bothered when it's convenient for you. But guess what? That ain't how life works. I'm their mother twenty-four seven, whether I'm here or not," I told her.

Oddly enough, Celia looked at me and smiled. Then she had the audacity to laugh.

"What's so damn funny?" I asked.

"You." She tried to walk past me, but I blocked her.

"Di, don't do this. Let her go, and let's go check on Avery so we can get up outta here," Ronda told me.

"Exactly." Celia nodded. "Go make a pit stop and take some more pics to post. Ain't that why you're here?"

"The question is why are you so angry with me all of a sudden, Celia?"

"I'm not gonna do this with you." Celia went to turn around and go the other way.

"Tell me. Is this about Darnell?" I asked innocently, and Celia stopped.

"Diane, not now, girl," Ronda pleaded with me, and I felt her hand on my arm. "And not in front of Ashley."

I pulled away and took a few more steps toward Celia. "Naw, I'm good. And she needs to understand why her devoted aunt is abandoning the family—because she's in her feelings over a man."

"Mama!"

I turned around to see Kendra standing behind Ronda, along with fine-ass Bilal.

"Well, well, well, perfect timing." I looked at her and said, "This is all your fault anyway."

"What are you talking about? What's my fault?" Kendra asked.

"That your aunt is pissed at me. But I can't say I didn't know this was coming. Hell, I'm surprised it took it this long to tell her about me and her trifling husband. I thought you woulda been told her. Truth is, I was doing her a favor. I told you, Celia, life ain't about doing shit when it's convenient for you."

Celia's stare went from me to Kendra. "So, it's true. You've been sleeping with my husband. Kendra, you knew?"

"Oh, shit," I said, realizing it was me who had let the cat out of the bag. Before I could say anything else, Celia's hand flew across my face, and I was knocked to the floor.

"Di!" Ronda reached out and helped me get to my feet.

No one else moved, which made me even angrier. I went to lunge at Celia, but the sudden appearance of hospital security stopped me.

"What's going on here?" the skinny white guy asked.

"This woman is harassing me, and I want her escorted out," I told him.

"Ma." Kendra finally spoke.

"Shut up!" I glared at her over my shoulder. "And I want her banned from my child's room. As a matter of fact, from this point on, anyone who tries to visit her must be approved by me. Family or not!"

"Ma'am, you need to leave," the security officer told Celia.

"Tuh. Gladly," Celia huffed.

"Aunt Celia, please . . ." Kendra called out as Celia turned away.

"I swear to God, if you go after her, I'll make sure you're banned right along with her," I threatened. She frowned at me, but I gave her a look to let her know that I wasn't bluffing, and she relented. "That's what I thought. Take your sister and your grown-ass boyfriend and go in the waiting room."

Kendra looked like she wanted to kill me, but she did exactly like I told her. Now that Celia, normally her saving grace, was pissed at her, she didn't have any other choice but to do what I said.

Ronda and I walked into Avery's room. The truth was that the reason I had stayed away from the hospital was that I didn't like seeing my daughter bruised and broken, hooked up to machines and IVs. She had always been my little shadow, my mini-me. I was scared. I touched her forehead softly, then leaned over and kissed her cheek.

"Wait, Di. Do that again. I missed it," Ronda said, reaching for her phone.

"No, don't." I stopped her.

"Huh?" Ronda frowned.

"I mean, just give me a second," I said, then touched Avery's cheek and whispered, "Shug Avery, I know you can hear me. Listen to your mama. I need you to hold on for me. You got a lot of folk rooting for you, including me, so you're gonna have to wake up soon. And I promise you, when you do, I'm gonna take you on a vacation, a real one, just you and me like we always talked about."

I smiled when I thought about the many times Avery had sneaked into my room and climbed into my bed. We would laugh and talk, and she promised that one day, when she got older, she would take me on a trip, just the two of us. Now, it looked like she wasn't going to be able to keep that promise.

"Okay, I'm ready," I said, blinking away the tears as I posed beside Avery.

Bilal

Throughout my twenty-two years on earth, I had run into more than my fair share of bitches, but Kendra's mom took the cake. Kendra had forewarned me that her mother was a bit of a drama queen, but the way that she behaved was horrible. I was taken aback by the way she carried on when she walked into her house while I was there, but it was nothing compared to how she showed her ass at the hospital. I was sitting in the waiting room, attempting to comfort Kendra when my uncle walked in.

"Nephew? What you doing up in here?" He smiled.

"'Sup, Uncle Pat." I sighed.

"Man, I was planning on calling you later this afternoon, and here you are, sitting up in here with these pretty ladies. How you doing, Kendra?"

"I'm fine." Kendra nodded.

"And what about you, Miss Ashley?" he asked.

"Fine," Ashley politely answered.

"That's good, that's good. And Miss Avery? How's she doing?" Patrick sounded sincere. I wondered if his interest was genuine, but only for a second. More likely, he was fishing to see how much longer he was going to be able to ride his latest cash cow.

"No changes," Kendra told him.

"Well, that's a good thing." He shrugged.

"How?" Ashley asked.

"Because even though she's not as well as we want her to be, the fact that she ain't any worse is something to be grateful for," he told her.

I had to admit, he was making sense.

"I guess that's true." Ashley went back to playing a game on her phone, something that she'd been doing since we got into the waiting room.

"What are you doing here, Uncle Pat?" I asked him.

"I came to check on Avery myself and pray with her."

"She's in a coma. She can't pray." Kendra looked at him strangely.

"Well, pray nonetheless." He glanced over and asked me, "So, tell me how you know this beautiful family, nephew."

"Kendra and I are friends," I said.

"Friends. Okay. That's nice, neph, real nice. She's a pretty friend to have, that's for sure, just like her mama." He winked.

"And like Miss Nikki. She's pretty too," Kendra reminded him.

"Uh, you're right about that." Patrick backed off a bit, then asked, "Speaking of your mother, where is she?"

"She's with my sister," Kendra answered.

"I'm right here," Diane walked in and announced. "Did you get the pictures we just sent?"

"Yeah, I got them. I'm gonna add them to the site in a few minutes," Patrick said.

"Good. And the other thing?" she asked him.

"I got that too." He handed her an envelope from his pocket. I noticed the church logo on the outside of it. "Courtesy of Mr. Simmons, the director of outreach."

"Cool," Diane said, taking it from him and putting it into her purse without looking inside.

"Nephew, can I speak to you outside for a second?" Patrick asked.

"Sure thing." I stood up, and we stepped outside the room. Then, he reached into his pocket and took out another envelope, bearing the same church logo as the one he had given Diane moments earlier. He passed it to me. I opened it and looked inside. It was the money he owed me.

"Told ya I was gonna get your money to you."
He grinned. "Didn't even take me the extra
days."

"Unc, what the hell are you doing?" I said,
almost giving him the envelope back.

"What do you mean? Paying you your money
back. Why? I know like hell Dell ain't tryna
charge interest, is he? See, this is why I told you
to let me pay him back my way."

"No, Unc, he ain't charging you no interest.
Which, by the way, I think he should, considering how long you've owed him. But I'ma tell you
like I told him: this is the last time y'all need to
do business together."

"I don't know why you're tripping. We're
family. That's why I went to him in the first
place. He's paid back in full, and that's the end
of that." Patrick acted as if he were the one doing
me a favor, instead of the total opposite.

"I'm asking what the hell are you and Diane
doing? This ain't right, and you know it," I whispered loudly. "That little girl is in there fighting
for her life."

"Don't you think I know that? That's exactly
why I'm getting the church and the community
to support her and her family. I'm doing my
duty as a deacon. The last thing Diane needs to
be worried about is how her bills are gonna get

paid, or how she's gonna be able to afford these medical bills that are piling up every day that Avery is in this hospital. What ain't right about that, nephew?"

I didn't have an answer. Had it been anyone else, I probably would've commended them for what they were doing. Hell, I probably would've joined the cause; but this was my uncle, who I'd known my entire life, and I knew he never did anything without it being beneficial for himself.

"If you say so," I told him. "I hope that's all this is."

"That's all it is." He clasped his hand over my shoulder. "Now, let me go on and get out of here."

"I thought you came by here to pray for Avery, Unc. You ain't even go and see her," I commented.

"Oh, yeah. You know, she's got enough visitors right now. I'll just make sure to lift her name and include it on our sick and shut-in list," he said as we walked back into the waiting room. "Well, I'm gonna go ahead and head on out of here. I got some running around to do to get ready for tomorrow's service. Diane, Kendra, Ashley, I'll see y'all in the morning at church." Patrick turned to me and said, "Nephew, you're more than welcome to come as well."

"Naw, I'm good, Unc." I shook my head.

"We'll be there. What time again?" Diane asked him.

"Service starts at eleven. But you need to be there by ten, because I wanna introduce you to Pastor and First Lady," Patrick answered. "See you in the morning."

When he was gone, Kendra looked at her mother and said, "Mama, I'm not going to church tomorrow. I'm staying here with Avery."

"You gonna go where the hell I say you're gonna go. Just because you're fucking a grown-ass man doesn't make you grown." Diane rolled her eyes at Kendra, who looked like she wished the floor would swallow her up just to get away. "Now, that damn pastor and congregation are expecting the three of us to be in service tomorrow, and all three of us are gonna be there."

Kendra glanced over at me, then back to her mother, and said, "I'm not going. You can go, but I'm staying here with my sister. Why would you even want her to be here alone?"

"She won't be here alone. Shit, Ronda will be here with her," Diane answered. "You listen to me and listen to me good, Kendra. I ain't gonna let you fuck this up for me. You're gonna have your ass at church tomorrow at ten o'clock. I swear, if you don't, not only will I block your ass from being able to see Avery, but I'm gonna kick your ass out of my house. Do you understand me? You know what? Don't even worry about coming tomorrow, and you can go ahead and leave now. Go to the house and get your shit."

"But Mama—"

"You heard what the fuck I said. I want you out of my house and out of this hospital. I don't know why motherfuckers keep trying me."

"Mama, please," Kendra pleaded. "Fine. I'll get out, but don't make me leave here. What about Ashley? She can't be here by herself."

For a split second, it seemed as if Kendra's mom had forgotten all about her other daughter. She paused for a second and said, "I'm gonna allow you to visit with your sister, but I want your ass outta my house. I mean that. Come on, Ronda," she said, and the two of them walked out the door. Ashley slid closer to Kendra and leaned on her, and Kendra affectionately rubbed her back.

"If you go, Kendra, I'm going too," Ashley whispered. The two of them were clearly used to leaning on one another.

"I'll be right back," I said. I wanted to do something to help the situation if that was possible.

I caught up with Diane and Ronda just as they were getting on the elevator. "Hold that."

The look Diane gave me as she stuck her arm out to stop the doors from closing almost made me say never mind. It was a look that I'd seen plenty of times before from women who clearly wanted me to know that I could have what they were offering without asking for it. It was the last look I wanted to get from her, because I already knew how much trouble she could cause. But I had to do something. I took a deep breath and stepped onto the elevator.

"Thanks," I told her.

"No, thank you. It's nice to have a fine-ass man escorting us down and making sure we're safe." Diane rubbed her hand along my arm, and I eased it away.

"Yes, it is." Ronda looked me up and down and licked her lips at me. I ignored her actions as well.

"Ma'am . . ." I started.

"Ma'am? Boy, please. I ain't old enough for you to be calling me that. Call me Diane."

"Uh, okay, Diane, no disrespect, but I think you're not being fair to Kendra," I said. "It took everything to get her to leave the hospital this morning just to take a shower. Neither she nor Ashley wants to leave Avery's side, and I don't blame them. I know if my sister was in this situation, I wouldn't want to leave either."

"Oh, really." She smirked briefly, then frowned. "Well, let me first say I don't really give a damn what you think. Now, I know you're her new so-called friend, and I know why you're posted up beside my daughter and being so—what's the word I'm looking for? Oh, I know: *supportive.*"

"Mm-hmmm." Ronda nodded. "Real supportive."

The elevator stopped, and a few other people got on. Putting our conversation on hold, it allowed me a few minutes to think. I gladly put some space between me and Diane for the other people to get on. As soon as we reached the lobby and stepped off, a couple of news reporters waved their arms at Diane, who seemed pleased with the attention and eager to go see them. I knew if I was going to say something, it needed to be now.

"Diane, I don't have any ulterior motives by being here with Kendra. You're right; I am her friend, and I care about her a lot. But I don't expect anything from her. All I'm asking is that you give her a break and be reasonable. That's not too much to ask, is it?" I said.

She turned and faced me. "You say you don't want nothing from my daughter?"

"No, nothing at all," I replied. "Like I said, I'm just here for support, and I'm also trying to understand why you're doing this to her."

"You're a damn fool if you think I believe that. No man does shit for a woman and expects nothing in return, including you. Now, you ain't doing shit for me, so I don't owe you nothing, not even an explanation, but if you truly care about my daughter like you say that you do, you'll encourage her to do what the hell I tell her to do in the future, because now it looks like you'll be supporting her ass while she's living on the street."

"Look, you don't have to do this." I shook my head.

"Oh, I know I don't. But, you see, Kendra, my sister Celia, and everyone else has been treating me like what I say doesn't mean shit. All I asked her to do was play her position and go to church tomorrow, and she couldn't even do that. Now the time has come for me to show them better than I can tell them."

In that moment, I knew that no matter what I said, it wouldn't matter. This woman was on a mission, and whatever it was, she wasn't going to back down until she had what she wanted. She was willing to do whatever it took to get it.

Kendra

"So, you mean to tell me your mother really kicked you out?" Sierra asked.

"Yep, she did," I told her as we stood outside of Cell City. I had come to talk to Dante before the store opened, to discuss me taking a few days off to care for my family. I had also emailed my professors. Most of them had heard about Avery's accident either on the news or through social media and were understanding.

"So, where are you staying? Do you want to come and stay with me? You know my mama won't care, and we have a pullout sofa in the den. Or you can sleep on the air mattress," she offered.

"No, I'm fine. Most of the time I'm at the hospital anyway," I told her.

"You're sleeping there? That can't be good."

"No, I leave at around ten at night when they kick me out," I said.

"Don't tell me you're sleeping in your car, Kendra." Sierra frowned.

"No, I'm not sleeping in my car, Sierra." I exhaled and then looked down shyly.

"So, where the hell have you been staying?"

"With Bilal."

"What? Oh my God! And you're just now telling me this?" She grabbed my arm and pulled me into the back hallway. "I've texted you damn near every day. I know you said he was checking on you, but you damn sure ain't mention sleeping at his crib."

"I know, I know. I kinda wanted to tell you face to face." I shrugged.

"Damn! So, tell me. Is his place nice? Where the hell does he live? Does he live by himself? Is this a permanent situation? I need details." She asked all the questions at once. "And make it quick, because you know Dante is about to come waltzing in here giving orders in a few."

"His place is nice. He lives downtown in one of those renovated office buildings that they turned into lofts. His is Waterman's Towers. And yes, he lives alone, and hell no, this ain't permanent," I told her, making sure to answer everything she'd asked.

"Waterman's Towers? Those are nice—and expensive. I definitely wouldn't expect a street dealer to be living there, that's for sure," she said.

"He doesn't sell dope, Sierra." I laughed.

"What? Are you sure? Because I coulda swore—"

"Yes, I'm sure. He owns his own business. A legitimate one," I said, reaching into my pocket and handing her one of the business cards that he had given me.

"Select Security Firm? Girl, you living with the ADT man?" Sierra teased.

"Shut up, Sierra." I tried not to smile. "He is not the ADT man."

"I know, I know. But I gotta say, this makes me a little relieved." She passed the card back to me. "The thought of you living with a dope boy—I don't care how fine he is—made me kind of nervous. I guess he's the real deal, huh?"

Calling Bilal the real deal was a true understatement. From the moment he'd arrived at the hospital, he had been nothing but supportive. After my mother kicked me out, he insisted that I could stay at his house until things calmed down and I figured things out. At first, I was hesitant, because after all, I had only known him a few weeks. My plan was to just stay at the hospital as long as possible until my mother calmed down. She had totally ignored me when she came to pick up Ashley, so I figured it was probably going to take a few days before she would be over it. But on Sunday morning, when I went home to shower and change, I found all my belongings in garbage bags on the front porch. She sent me a text, instructing me to leave my key under the mat. I had thought that she was bluffing, as she had done several times before when she threatened to kick me out. This time, she had put some action behind her words. I picked up the bags and put what would fit into the trunk of my car, and the remaining bags into the back seat, then sat in front of the house for a few seconds, trying to figure out where to go. After I couldn't reach Aunt Celia, I called my father.

"Hey, baby girl. How's Avery?"

"She's improving, Daddy. They say she'll make a full recovery," I told him.

"That's good. I'm glad she's doing better."

"Champ, you want these pork chops fried or smothered?" I heard a female voice ask.

"Don't matter to me," Daddy answered. "I'm sorry, baby girl. Doreen in there cooking dinner, and you know she don't do that very often."

Doreen was his on again, off again girlfriend. She didn't really care for me that much, and the feeling was mutual. Her cooking dinner was a clear indication that they were on again, which meant staying with him wasn't an option.

"Well, I didn't want anything, Daddy. I was just calling," I told him.

"I'm glad you called. Give Avery a big hug for me, and tell her I asked about her. And Ashley too," he said.

"Champ, I need you in here to light this stove for me."

"Okay, be there in a minute," Daddy yelled.

Doreen's voice was full of attitude and suddenly closer. "I need it lit now."

"It's okay, Daddy. I'll talk to you later," I said, hitting the END button without even saying goodbye. I checked my bank account to see how long I would be able to afford a motel room, because a hotel was definitely out of the question. Then, my phone rang, and it was Bilal.

"Hey, I'm just checking on you," he said.

"I'm okay," I lied.

"Are you sure?"

"Yeah, I'm sure."

"Well, I wanted to go to breakfast before heading back to the hospital, if you'd like."

"Bilal, you don't have to come back up there. I know you have a life. I appreciate everything you've done so far, but I'm fine, really," I told him, not wanting him to see that I was wearing the same clothes from the day before.

"Nonsense, Kendra. Meet me at Brutti's in twenty minutes."

"Brutti's? I'm not dressed for that place," I said, thinking about the fancy, popular brunch spot that I had been wanting to try for months. "I'm fine. You go ahead."

"You don't want Brutti's, that's cool, but I'm not going anywhere to eat without you. You haven't eaten, and neither have I. As a matter of fact, I'll meet you at your house, and then we can decide."

"No, wait, listen. I'm still getting ready. I'll call you when I'm done, and we can meet up."

"Okay, I'll talk to you then," he said then hung up.

I debated on whether I should avoid him altogether until I figured out my living situation, or just face him. I closed my eyes and began to pray, something that I'd become quite used to doing these days, despite not wanting to go to church. If I ever needed God, it was definitely now, especially since I didn't seem to have anyone else. I asked Him to forgive me for not going to church but hoped he understood my reasoning behind it, and I also asked that He heal my sister, and my Aunt Celia's broken heart. Then, I asked that He look out for me.

Beep. Beep. The sound of the horn caused me to jump, and I looked into my rearview mirror. I looked at the time on my phone and realized almost thirty minutes had passed. I had fallen asleep while praying, and not only had Bilal pulled up behind me, but he had gotten out and was walking up to my car. I turned around and tried to think of a way to hide the bags in the back seat, but it was too late. He had already seen them. I opened the door and stepped out.

He gave me a concerned look and reached for my hand. "Kendra."

"It's cool, Bilal. She's just being overdramatic right now. I'm good. If I can't reach my Aunt Celia, then I'm gonna stay at a motel for a couple of days until she calms down." I feigned a smile.

"What? Absolutely not." He frowned. "You're not staying in a hotel. I can't believe she did this. I'll talk to her."

"No!" I said a little louder than I'd intended. "Don't do that. You'll only make it worse."

"I gotta do something, and it's either I talk to her and you move back in, or—" He stopped.

"Or what?" I asked.

"You stay with me." His voice was as soft as his fingers that now touched my face.

"I can't do that, Bilal." I shook my head.

"You can, and you will. Now, get in the car and follow me."

I didn't bother protesting, because deep down, I had been hoping that he would offer me a place to stay. I didn't have enough money to afford a hotel room—well, at least one located someplace safe. Spending a night or two with him would give me time to figure out what to do. I told myself that going to his place was a sound, practical business decision, even though I knew it had more to do with the fact that the more time I spent with him, the more I liked him.

I did as instructed and followed him to the building he lived in and parked in the parking space he directed me to. He waited while I went through the bags and found some basic toiletries and a change of clothes, then he took my hand, and we went upstairs to his apartment. He opened the door and let me walk in first.

"It's a bit messy, but give me a few, and I can straighten—"

"It's fine," I said, looking around the spacious loft. Everything was modern, from the sleek hardwood floors that shone like they had just been buffed to the stainless steel appliances that I saw as we passed the entryway to the kitchen. The mess that he was talking about was a pillow and blanket that were on the sofa, and a pile of mail sitting on the coffee table beside a pizza box and a half-empty glass of what appeared to be red Kool-Aid. He grabbed the box and glass and took them away after pushing the pillow and blanket aside so that I could sit.

"You want anything to drink? I have juice, water, soda, and wine," he called from the kitchen.

"Isn't it too early for wine?" I asked.

"After the morning you've had, you probably need a glass of wine." He laughed. A few seconds later, he returned, handing me a wine glass.

"Oh my God, I don't want that," I said, staring at it.

"Relax, it's just cranberry juice. I just wanted to make you feel special."

I took the glass from him and took a sip. Sure enough, it was juice. "Not funny, but thanks."

"You're welcome." He smiled and pulled me to him after sitting beside me. "You're gonna be okay, Kendra. You can stay here as long as you need to, you know."

"It will only be a night or so, Bilal."

"Well, a couple of nights, a couple of weeks, a couple of years, I got you. Whatever you need." He kissed the tip of my nose.

"Thanks, but right now, I need a shower." I smiled.

Bilal's loft had two master suites, one that was his bedroom, and the other that he used as a makeshift office. He insisted that I stayed in his bedroom and gave me some towels and a washcloth. I took one of the longest showers of my life. When I was finished, I got dressed and sat on the bed. I decided to lay back for a few minutes and close my eyes.

When I opened them, I was covered with a soft blanket, and it was hours later. I jumped up, and for a second, I didn't know where I was. I walked through the house, calling his name, but Bilal was nowhere to be found. He walked into the apartment a little while later carrying bags of groceries.

"Why didn't you wake me up?" I asked him.

"Because you needed some sleep. Did you know you snore?"

I felt my face turning red. "Only when I'm tired."

"Well, you were really, really tired then." He laughed.

"I gotta get back over to the hospital," I told him.

"Don't worry. We'll head back over there after you've eaten. Now, go relax."

He made a breakfast big enough for a king, and I enjoyed every bit of it. Then, as promised, we went to the hospital, where we stayed most of the night, until the nurse told me that we needed to leave and promised to call if there were any changes. When we got back to Bilal's apartment, we watched TV on his sofa, where I cuddled on his chest until we both fell asleep. He had been a perfect gentleman. He even offered to cancel some appointments he had scheduled on Monday, but I assured him that I would be fine and agreed to come back to his place by midnight.

"Sierra, I know this is gonna sound crazy, but he's perfect." I sighed.

"You're just saying that because you're *dickmatized* right now. All girls think the first guys they have sex with are perfect," Sierra said as we headed back toward the front of the store.

"I'm not *dickmatized*. We haven't even had sex," I told her.

Once again, she pulled me back into the hallway. "What? You haven't given up the goods? Why not? You just said he was the real deal and perfect."

"He is. He's been like a knight in shining armor during this whole mess. I kinda feel bad, because if you look at it, he's not even my boyfriend, for real. We've only been on like two dates, and then *this*," I explained.

"Yo, that is crazy. Well hell, Kendra, do you want to sleep with him? Are you ready?" She leaned back against the wall.

"I like him. I know that. Honestly, I more than like him. He's smart and funny, and it's like, when I'm with him, I'm safe, and I wouldn't wanna be anywhere else."

"But, do you wanna fuck him? You can like someone and not be ready to have sex with them. You know how many smart dudes I know that can crack jokes? That don't mean I wanna sleep with them, Kendra."

"I do wanna sleep with him. Well, I think I do. I mean, I don't know, Sierra. Sex is the last thing I'm thinking about right now, and he hasn't even brought it up." I shook my head in confusion.

"You know what, girl? You're right. And I'm sorry. With everything going on with your family, I'm sure it hasn't crossed your mind, even with that tall, sexy-ass might-be boyfriend by your side these past few days. But seriously, how's your sister? I saw your mom's interview with the news on my Facebook page this morning. She's pissed at the police, but that GoFundMe is popping," Sierra said. "She's raised over eleven thousand dollars so far."

I was in the middle of updating her on Avery's medical status when Dante finally arrived. He

gave me a hug and listened as I finished telling
Sierra about Avery's injuries. Then, to both mine
and Sierra's surprise, he offered me the rest
of the week off, with pay, something that was
unheard of. I thanked him and promised Sierra I
would call her later.

I was headed back to the hospital when I
took a chance and stopped by the accounting
firm where Aunt Celia worked. The receptionist
greeted me with a big hug.

"Oh, Kendra baby, how are you? How's Avery?
My prayer circle was at the neighborhood prayer
vigil with your mama and sister the other night
at Mount Hebron."

"Thanks, Mrs. Bertha." I tried to breathe while
she squeezed me. "She's hanging in there. Is Aunt
Celia in her office?"

"Girl, no. She called yesterday and said she'd
be out for the rest of the week, if not longer.
She's not at the hospital?" She frowned.

"Uh, okay. I'm actually on my way there now,
so I'll see her," I said, turning to leave.

"Okay, darling. We'll keep y'all in prayer. Oh,
and the firm is gonna be making a donation for
your sister's fund. That poor baby. Don't worry;
God's got her," Mrs. Bertha called out.

"Thank you. I'll speak with you soon." I waved
as I walked out the door.

I tried calling Aunt Celia again, but she didn't answer. I spent the rest of the day hoping that she would show up at the hospital, but she didn't. It was after ten o'clock when the nurse convinced me it was okay to leave. Instead of driving to Bilal's loft, I drove to her house, hoping she would talk to me. When I got there, her car wasn't in the driveway where it was normally parked. Still, I hopped out and rang the doorbell. There was no answer, so I returned to the only place I had to go.

Later that night, I was tossing and turning in Bilal's bed, unable to sleep. I looked at my phone and saw that it was almost two in the morning. Realizing I was thirsty, I got up and headed to get something to drink. When I walked into the dark kitchen, I gasped and stared. Standing in front of the fridge, drinking a bottle of water was Bilal, wearing only a towel.

"Oh, did I wake you? I'm sorry," he said, putting the cap back on the bottle. I didn't respond. I was too busy staring at his chest, which looked as if it had been chiseled perfectly. My eyes continued to travel along his muscled torso down to where the towel was wrapped around his waist. My eyes widened as I noticed the slight bulge.

"Kendra, you okay?"

"Huh?" I blinked, quickly returning my gaze to his face.

"I asked if you were okay." He looked at me strangely.

"Oh, I'm uh . . ." My voice cracked, and I cleared my throat. "I'm fine. And no, you didn't wake me. I was thirsty."

His eyes looked me up and down, and I was suddenly aware of the heat that was rising between my legs as I stared at him. He took a step closer to me, handing me the bottle of water he was holding, but I didn't take it. Instead, I reached out and touched his chest, running my fingers across the ridges of his muscled torso. He lifted them, putting them to his lips and kissing them softly. I inhaled his scent and wrapped my free hand around his neck. His mouth pressed against mine gently, then harder, as my lips parted and my tongue met his. I gasped as his hands slipped under my shirt and cupped my breasts. He teased my hardened nipples.

Then, I felt it: a firmness pressing against my thigh. I reached for the towel and tugged slightly, causing it to fall to the floor. My hands slowly eased down until I reached his thick penis. It took everything for me not to pull away because of its size and thickness, and it wasn't even fully erect. My emotions were all over the place. This was really about to happen. I was going to have sex. Despite being anxious and nervous, I was still turned on.

Bilal smiled, then lifted me off the floor, and I wrapped my legs around his waist as he carried me into his bedroom. We fell onto the bed, and after slipping my shirt and panties off, he began exploring every inch of my body with his tongue, starting with my toes. He sucked each one, then nibbled the inside of my ankles all the way to my inner thigh, which he bit softly. His fingers slipped into my wetness, and I moaned in ecstasy and opened my legs wider. Bilal put his mouth where his fingers had been moments before, causing me to squirm and grip the headboard of the bed. I felt myself about to lose control, and I was torn between begging him to stop or demanding more. I reached for his head to ease back, but he grasped my wrists and pushed me away just as he put my legs over his shoulders and licked deeper.

"Mmmm," he groaned, making me even wetter than I already was. His tongue glided back and forth along my swollen clit, and my legs began shaking.

"Oh . . . God . . . Bilal," I whined between gasps. "You've . . . got . . . to . . . stop."

He ignored my pleas and continued pleasuring me until I climaxed. As I was lying breathless, he eased off the bed and walked away. I was confused, until he returned seconds later, holding a small packet in his hands that he tore open. After slipping the condom on his now fully hardened manhood, he climbed in front of me.

"Bilal, wait." I put my hand against his chest.

"What's wrong?" He frowned.

"I . . . it's just . . ." I tried to find the right words to explain my hesitation.

"Are you a virgin, Kendra?" he whispered.

"Yes." I nodded.

He pulled back slightly as he stared into my eyes, then said, "We don't have to do this if you're not ready. It's okay."

His sincerity instantly made my desire for him increase. As I stared back at him, I knew that I was ready. I wanted to be with him, but I was still nervous.

"No, I want to do this, but . . ."

"But what? Tell me."

My eyes glanced down to his crotch, and I said, "I don't think it'll fit."

"It will fit; I promise." Bilal laughed, then kissed me. "I promise I'll take it slow."

I relaxed a bit, enjoying the feel of his lips on my skin as he kissed my neck, then shoulder, and down to my breasts. By the time I felt the swollen tip of his hardness between my legs, I was wet and inviting. I gasped loudly from the slight pain when he inserted his shaft into my tight crevice.

He paused and looked down at me. "You okay?"

I nodded as I bit my bottom lip, enjoying the feel of him inside of me. He took his time, starting with slow, intense strokes, which became deeper and rhythmic. My nails scratched his back as he pressed my legs back and continued nibbling my collarbone.

"Damn, Kendra."

My hands eased across his shoulders, and I called out as his shaft plunged into me. "Bilal . . . I'm . . . about . . . to . . ."

Before I could even tell him, he kissed me long and hard, and I climaxed over and over again, and then, so did he. A blissful feeling came over me. I'd never been so satiated in my life. I immediately came to the conclusion that sex was something I definitely enjoyed.

Bilal rolled over and exhaled loudly. "Whoo!"

"What does that mean?" I giggled.

He raised an eyebrow at me and said, "It means that was fucking amazing, no pun intended. Are you okay?"

"I'm great," I told him.

"Are you sure? I tried to make sure not to hurt you."

"I'm sure, and it was incredible. Thank you."

"And you thought it wouldn't fit." He reached over and playfully hit my thigh, then pulled me up off the bed and into the bathroom. After showering together, we returned to the bed and both fell into a deep slumber.

The sound of my phone vibrating caused me to open my eyes. Bilal rubbed his hand along my back as I eased off his chest. "Where do you think you're going?" he whispered, kissing the top of my head.

"My phone," I told him as I stretched toward the nightstand. Seeing that I couldn't reach it, he slid over to the nightstand and took the phone off the charger, passing it to me just as it stopped. Seeing the number on the screen, I sat completely up and tried dialing the number back.

"What? What's wrong?" he asked.

My heart was pounding, and I tried to breathe as I answered him. "It's the hospital."

Celia

I listened to the latest messages from Kendra.
She had been calling and texting nonstop, and I
continued to ignore her. I knew that what happened between her mother and Darnell wasn't
her fault, but I wasn't at a place where I could
talk to her. I was dealing with the aftermath of
my emotions. I wasn't surprised by my sister's
actions at all. I had learned years ago that she
was who she was and didn't give a damn about
anybody who was hurt by her actions. I was
angry at her, but most of my anger was directed
toward Darnell, who had not only slept with my
trifling sister but lied about it when I confronted
him. His lying just added fuel to an already
burning fire of fury, and I wanted to kill him.
Luckily, his life was saved, because he wasn't
home when I arrived after leaving the hospital.
I still lost it, breaking pictures and vases and
throwing anything I could get my hands on.
I was enraged, and even after destroying my

living room, hallway, and den, I was still pissed. Perspiration that had formed on my forehead eased down the side of my face and mixed with my tears. I looked around the mess I'd created and decided the last place I needed to be was in that house. I packed my bags and left.

My phone rang again. This time, it was Nikki, so I answered.

"Cele, where are you? I'm worried," she said.

"I'm fine, Nikki. I just needed to get away. How's Avery?" I asked. Although I was tempted to leave town and go far away, I didn't. I still wanted to be near my niece, even though her dumb-ass mother had prevented me from seeing her. Instead, I drove to one of my favorite resort spas and checked into a suite, hoping to clear my head and find some peace of mind.

"That's why I'm calling so early."

"What happened? Is she okay?" I sat up in a panic.

"She spiked a fever, and they ended up doing emergency surgery the other day," Nikki explained. "She's fine now."

"This is so messed up." I sighed. "But I'm glad they got it. So, now what?"

"The doctors are still just watching her closely." Nikki sighed.

"I know Kendra is a wreck with all of this."

"Yeah, she is. I told her to just give you some space right now, but, Cele, she's a mess, especially since Di kicked her out."

"What? When did Di kick her out?" All the anxiety that I had released over the past two days slowly returned.

"The same day she kicked you out of the hospital. Kendra said she was trying to make her go to the church service at Mount Hebron, and when Kendra said no, Di lost it and kicked her out. She even threatened to block Kendra from being able to see Avery, but she changed her mind. Hell, she would probably kick me out of there, too, but we haven't run into one another, thank God. I know when she's going up there, because Patrick tells me," Nikki told me.

"Don't tell me you're still letting him be around her, Nikki. You can't be that gullible." I sighed.

"He's not around her like that. I told you he's just acting as her PR person while all of this is going on and keeping her reigned in. And really, he's not doing it for Diane. His only interest is Avery and making sure she's good."

I closed my eyes and tried not to snap on my best friend. A blind man could see that Patrick had dollar signs in his eyes every time he talked about Avery and the accident in front of the news cameras and on social media. The last

time I'd gone against my better judgment and
checked the GoFundMe campaign, it had over
ten thousand dollars and counting. And I didn't
care what Nikki said; there was no doubt in my
mind it wasn't going in any kind of trust fund for
my niece. It was going to her man and my sister.

"I guess," was all that I said then went back
to a more pressing issue. "So, if Diane kicked
Kendra out, where the hell is she staying? With
Champ?"

"Nope, with her boyfriend," Nikki answered.

"What boyfriend?"

"Bilal."

"Bilal? Since when? I know I saw him at the
hospital, but I ain't realize they were a thing."

"How long? That part I don't know. But they
are together. He's been the absolute sweetest.
He's truly been looking out for her, Celia," Nikki
gushed.

I thought about how Kendra had reacted when
we ran into Bilal at the car wash and I coaxed her
to give him a chance. My gut instinct had turned
out to be right. I knew that he would be good for
her, and hearing that he'd been there for Kendra
gave me a little relief. Still, I wasn't too thrilled
to hear that she was staying with him. Maybe I
had been a little too hasty in rushing off. Then, I
thought about why I left and the fact that Kendra,

who I had treated like my own child since before she was born, had known all along and hadn't said anything to me. A wave of hurt overcame me all over again.

"Well, I'm glad she found somewhere to go," I told her.

The phone got quiet until finally, Nikki spoke. "Celia, I know all of this is killing you. Talk to me."

"Nikki, listen, I don't want to talk about it. All I wanna say is you need to be mindful about your man. I'm not just saying that as your best friend. I'm saying that as Diane's sister."

"I get what you're saying, but trust me, I ain't worried about him and Di. Now, that heffa Tiesha, on the other hand. She's gonna make me go off. Ever since she saw Patrick on the news, she's been tripping. She actually had the nerve to show up at the vigil the other night. Patrick was so embarrassed."

"I'm sure he was." I was glad she couldn't see my eyes rolling through the phone.

"Cele, when are you coming home? You have to come and face the music eventually," Nikki reminded me.

"I know. I just need a break from everyone and everything."

"Have you talked to Darnell?"

"Not since he called and flipped out about me breaking shit up and leaving the house a mess," I said simply as if it were no big deal, which to me, it wasn't. I'd ignored Darnell for a day and a half until finally, I called him. He had the nerve to try and snap on me, until I shut his ass down and told him to get the hell out by the time I got back.

"Then he had the nerve to say 'Celia, I'm not going anywhere. You need to bring your ass home so we can talk about this.' And I told him, 'Fine. You don't wanna leave, then I will, and you can just talk to my attorney.'"

"Wait, you got a lawyer?" Nikki gasped.

"Not yet, but I'm getting one. You really don't think I'm gonna stay with his lying, cheating ass, do you?"

"I guess not." Nikki sounded sad. "This is just a mess."

"Oh, it's a fucked-up situation all the way around."

"I'm gonna keep you in prayer, girl. Anything you want me to tell Kendra?"

"Nope, just kiss Avery for me and keep me posted." I sighed.

"Will do. I'll talk to you later."

After hanging up, I called downstairs and ordered breakfast from room service. I took a quick shower and had just put my clothes on when there was a knock at the door. Thinking it was my food, I opened it without asking who it was. Stunned, I blinked for a second.

"Detective Donaldson?"

"Hey, Celia. Are we disturbing you?" he asked, pointing at his partner, who was standing beside him.

"Uh, no. I was expecting room service. Come on in." I opened the door, and they walked into my room.

"You remember my partner, Detective Perkins."

"How are you, ma'am?" Perkins asked.

"I'm fine. Um, what—how—" I tried to understand why they were there.

"Well, we've been trying to reach you for the past few days, and when we couldn't, we tracked you down," he said. "I was concerned, especially since the last time I saw you at your home, I could sense something was wrong. Went to your house, the hospital, your job and you seemed to kinda vanish, so I became even more suspicious."

"Oh," I said, feeling a little important, even though I knew he was only doing his job. "I needed to get away for a couple of days, that's all. Is something wrong?"

"Well, we're working on your niece's case and getting witness statements and additional information. Is there a reason why you left town, especially in the middle of a family crisis? It seems kind of odd." Perkins stared at me. "You were one of the first people to report your niece missing and at the hospital making sure she was taken care of. And then, you left and haven't returned. Is there a reason you're avoiding—"

"What are you asking?" I started to become offended with his line of questioning. "And the reason I haven't returned to the hospital is because I've been banned by Avery's mother. Did she nor the hospital tell you that?"

"No, she didn't," Perkins replied.

"Well, I'm sure she'll confirm when you ask." I folded my arms and was about to sit on the side of the bed when there was a knock at the door. "That's my food. Excuse me while I get it—unless you're afraid I'll leave here too."

"No, it's not a problem. Go ahead." Detective Donaldson nodded.

"Thank you." Cutting my eyes at Perkins as I passed him, I opened the door, and a guy from room service wheeled in a cart with my food. I signed for it without even making sure it was right, then pushed the cart to the side and walked back to continue my conversation. "So, now that you see that I'm alive and understand why I haven't been to see my niece, is there anything else you need from me?"

Perkins' phone began to ring. "Excuse me. I need to take this call."

"Go ahead," Detective Donaldson told him. Once we were alone in the room, he sighed and said, "Celia, first of all, I'm glad you're okay. Like I said, I tried calling you several times and couldn't reach you. It was as if you disappeared, and I became worried."

"I haven't really been having my phone on the past couple of days. I told you, I needed some time away," I explained.

"Are you sure everything is okay?" he asked softly.

I stared into his handsome face, noticing that his beard was a little shorter and neater than the last time I saw him at my house. I then realized that he had gotten a fresh haircut.

"I'm fine." I nodded. "Do you have any more information about who did this to Avery?"

"We actually got video footage from the parking lot of her school, and it looks like whoever did this targeted her," he told me.

"What? Someone did this on purpose? Who would do something like this?" I asked.

"That's what we're trying to find out. We've talked with her sisters, and they can't think of anyone who would want to hurt her, but clearly, she was approached by a car and was then followed. The video only shows so much, but we're working around the clock on this," he said. "Are you sure you haven't noticed any strangers hanging around your sister's house or neighborhood?"

"I'm not there very often," I told him. "But Avery is a sweetheart. All of my nieces are. Have you asked Diane?"

"See, that's another issue that we're having. She's refusing to talk to us or cooperate with our investigation. She's also claiming to have hired an attorney, because she's seeking damages from the city regarding your niece's disappearance and our handling of this. But we did everything by the book and handled it properly. You would think she would be more helpful in trying to find who did this, but she's not—which is a red flag." He became very still, and his stare was intense.

"She didn't have anything to do with this," I told him.

"How can you be certain?" he asked.

"My sister is a whole lot of things, bad things, but she loves those girls in her own way, especially Avery. She didn't do this."

"You don't know that for sure."

"I do." I nodded. "My sister's avoidance has nothing to do with what happened to Avery. It has to do with money. She's gonna do any and everything to get every single dime out of this horrible accident. If that means fundraisers, lawsuits, media blitzes, whatever, she's gonna do it. But I can assure you she didn't hurt Avery."

"But you haven't explained how you know."

"Because at the time when all of this was going down, my sister was somewhere fucking my husband. And that, Detective Donaldson, is why I had to get the hell away." I tried to remain stoic.

"I'm so sorry, Celia." He shook his head and then, as if he sensed my breaking down, he took a step toward me and hugged me close as I cried in his arms. I enjoyed the warmth of his embrace for a few moments, until the light tapping on the door caused me to pull away.

"Shit. I'm so sorry, Detective Donaldson," I told him, embarrassed as I regained my composure.

"Please stop calling me that." He laughed as he walked toward the door to open it. "It's Sean."

"Okay, Sean," I said. "I need a few minutes to get myself together."

I went into the bathroom and washed my face. When I looked at my reflection in the mirror, I saw that my hair was coming out from the already messy ponytail that I had made right before their arrival. My heart was racing, and although I told myself it was from the emotional breakdown I'd had moments earlier, I knew that wasn't the reason. I knew from the moment I saw Sean that there was a slight attraction, and now, there was no doubt that is was more than slight. But he was there to do a job, and I was still a married woman.

Whatever you're thinking about thinking about, don't, I told myself. *The last thing you need in your life right now is to be feeling someone else. You know better than anyone else: before you go trying to open a new door, you better make sure the old one is closed, locked, and the key is thrown away. Besides, that man is just doing his job, and you're feeling some type of way about your cheating-ass husband. Get it together.*

I opened the bathroom door and walked back into the room, where Sean and his partner were waiting.

"Did you guys need anything else?" I asked.

"No, I think we're done here. I did confirm with hospital security that your sister did ask that you not be allowed to see your niece. They didn't explain why. I'm sorry about that," Perkins told me. "But they also told us something else."

"What's that?" I asked.

"Celia," Sean said, "Avery woke up about twenty minutes ago."

Diane

"How is she?" Patrick whispered as he walked into the hospital room and stood on the other side of Avery's bed. "I thought they said she's awake."

"She has been opening her eyes. She's just asleep right now. They still got her on all kinds of meds," I told him. "Did you give a statement yet?"

"Yeah, I let folks know that she's regained consciousness but still not out of the woods," he answered.

"Yeah, because if people think she's better, the donations will slow down, huh?"

"Don't worry. We'll keep the momentum going," Patrick told me.

I realized that I had said the words out loud without planning to. I didn't want him to think that I was some kind of heartless monster who didn't give a damn about her child. I was elated when they called and told me that Avery had opened her eyes, and I didn't waste any time getting to the hospital. As soon as Ronda and I finished eating our lunch, we left in such a hurry that we didn't even take time to pay the bill. Coming into the room and seeing my child's eyes opened after being closed for a whole week brought me a sense of relief. She was only awake for about ten minutes at a time before drifting off, but clearly, her condition was improving.

"That's not what I meant," I said. "I'm just trying to see what's next, that's all."

"Well, what's your plan?" Patrick asked.

I didn't really have a plan. The donations had steadily been coming in online, and the total was well over fifteen thousand dollars. In addition, Mount Hebron had taken up an offering on the Sunday Ashley and I attended, in addition to taking up money at the vigil they held that night. Patrick said the amount was another four thousand that we had coming. Even after his cut, that was way more money than I'd anticipated. My original goal was to get enough to buy me a decent car and maintain my bills for a couple of months until I got another job. Now, the possibilities seemed endless.

"Did you talk to your lawyer friend? What did he say about filing a lawsuit against the police department?" I asked.

"He's working on it. But we need to sit down with him and sign some paperwork and pay a retainer," Patrick explained.

"A retainer? Avery's story has been everywhere, and this case is a goddamn goldmine. The city is gonna hurry up and settle. Fuck a retainer," I hissed.

"I'll see what I can do. In the meantime, we let folks know that Avery has mounting medical bills and a long road ahead of her to recovery. She's gonna have to have physical therapy, not to mention the mental anguish that all this has caused her, the emotional trauma, et cetera."

"I need that lawyer. The police have been on my ass, and I don't wanna talk to them until after that lawsuit is filed." I sat back in the chair and folded my arms.

"Just talk to them, Di. There's no harm in giving a statement."

"I ain't telling them shit. And when the hell am I getting my share of the money?" I glared at him. "It's been a whole fucking week, and you and these little nickel-and-dime payments ain't helping."

"The first deposit drops tomorrow, and I'll get your money over to you. Hell, I been waiting my damn self. I got moves to make."

"What kind of moves?" I asked.

"I decided to use my money and make a short-term investment." He grinned. I wasn't amused or impressed by his answer until he added, "I'm buying bricks."

"Of what?" My eyes widened.

"Don't act like you don't know. I damn sure ain't about to build a house with them, that's for sure."

Avery's body jerked a little, and she let out a slight moan. I rubbed her cheek and then hit the call button. When the nurse came in, I motioned for him to follow me out into the hallway, and we walked a little farther past the nurses' station, where no one could hear us talking.

"Now, tell me what the fuck you're talking about."

"I just decided now would be the right time to make a power move with my share of the money," he explained.

"So, you mean to tell me you're taking your cut and becoming a dope boy." I smirked.

"Hell no! I'm too old for that street bullshit. You can make street moves without touching product. You do know that, right? The dope game is very much like the stock market."

"You're flipping it." I thought about how much money my share had the potential to make. "With who?"

"A guy I know. He's actually my fam. I'm going holla at him to work out the details."

"I want in," I told him.

"What?" He sounded surprised.

"I wanna flip my share too. I want in."

"Nah, that ain't a good idea." He shook his head.

"Why not? I thought we were partners, Patrick. Haven't we made a good team up until now? Now you wanna be selfish?" I stepped closer to him.

"I don't know if he's gonna be willing. . . ." His nervousness started to show, and I almost laughed.

"I'm going with you to this meeting," I said matter-of-factly. "And I ain't taking no for an answer."

"Ms. Hughes?" The nurse waved at me from where she was standing outside of Avery's room. "She's awake again."

I glanced at Patrick then back at her and said, "Her big sister is around here somewhere trying to avoid me. You can find her and let her know that I'm gone, and she can sit with her for a while. I have a meeting I have to go to right quick."

"What up, nephew?" Patrick walked up to a guy sitting in the back of Chubby's, a greasy hole in the wall that served burgers and chicken wings.

"'Sup, Unc?" The guy looked up from the basket of wings and fries he was eating and nodded at Patrick, then me.

"Everything is everything." Patrick smiled, then said, "I see you still eating good."

"No doubt." The guy seemed unbothered by our presence, and I wasn't in the mood to listen to Patrick's usual conversational bullshit. I decided to speed things up so we could get down to our reason for being there.

"What's up? I'm Di." I introduced myself.

"I know who you are," the guy said, looking me up and down.

"Oh, really?" I smiled as I slid across from him in the booth. He was younger than what I usually went for, but he was legal, sexy, and from what Patrick told me, he had money. I figured if I played my cards right, I might be able to do this without Patrick's help.

"So, you've seen me around?"

"Kinda hard not to. You and Pat been all over everywhere about what happened to your little girl."

"Oh, yeah," I said, slightly disappointed.

"That's right, nephew. This is Avery's mom. Di, this is my nephew Dell." Patrick motioned for me to slide over so he could sit. "We need to holla at you, nephew, about some business," Patrick told him.

"Now, Unc, you know that ain't happening. Not after what happened the last time we tried to do business. I can make a donation for your little girl, but I can't loan you nothing," Dell told us.

"What?" I gave him a confused look. "A loan?"

"Naw, nephew, we ain't looking for a loan. We got money." Patrick leaned across the table and picked up one of Dell's fries. "We trying to give you money."

From the look on Dell's face, I could see that he was surprised by Patrick's statement. He pushed the basket of food closer to Patrick and said, "What are you talking about?"

"We wanna make a business investment of sorts." Patrick continued eating the fries and then turned to me and asked, "You want some?"

"Nah, I'm good," I told him. Then I said to Dell, "Patrick tells me you have a successful business, and I've recently come into an influx of capital."

Dell looked from me to Patrick, then said, "Is that right? How much capital we talking about?"

"Ten grand," I said.

Dell's eyes widened in surprise, and he sat up in his seat. "Ten grand?"

"That's right, nephew. I told you Unc wasn't bullshitting you. We here to do real business." Patrick smirked.

"And where is this ten grand coming from? Because it just took your ass damn near three months to pay me back three stacks." Dell glanced at Patrick.

"Come on now, Dell. Don't be like that. You know I paid you back and—"

"You paid me back?" Dell raised his eyebrows at Patrick.

"The point is that you got your money. There was a slight little hiccup in getting it back to you, and I'm sorry about that. But—"

"Don't worry. We're good for the money. I—I mean we—got it. Now, you tryna do business or what?" I said, becoming more and more frustrated.

"And just where did this ten grand come from?" He directed the question at me.

"It came from—" Patrick went to answer, but I stopped him.

"Doesn't matter where it came from. We got it, cash. Do you ask all of your business associates this many questions?"

"I do." He shrugged. "So, what are you trying to get for this investment?"

"A good return on our money, within a reasonable timeframe, of course. Let's say three or four weeks?" Patrick told him.

Dell reached and pulled the wing basket back across the table and said, "Three of four weeks? You want me to flip ten grand in less than a month?"

"Yeah, is that not possible?" I asked.

"Real talk, for me, it's not. Unc, you know better than I do that I ain't in the dope game like that no more. I'm trying to go legit. I got my hand in some shit, but not like that," Dell answered.

"Come on, man. This can be your last big hurrah. You know you got that wedding you planning. This can take care of that and the honeymoon if you handle it right," Patrick told him.

I could see the wheels in Dell's head turning. He took a few moments before he finally responded and said, "Lemme make a few calls and see what I can come up with."

"That's good enough for me," Patrick told him.

"I'ma tell you right now: if I find out this is some bullshit, it won't be good," Dell said.

"I don't deal in bullshit," I responded. "How long is it gonna take for you to make your calls?"

"A day or so. You in a rush?" he asked me.

"I'm just about my business, that's all. And if we ain't doing business with you, then Unc, as you call him, and I need to take our business elsewhere. I'm sure you understand that." I shrugged. "Come on, Unc. I got other shit to do."

"Oh, well, a'ight then. I guess we'll talk later, nephew." Patrick stood up and gave Dell a pound with his fist.

"Sure thing. Nice meeting you, Di. Again, I'm sorry to hear about your little girl," Dell told me.

"Thanks," I said and held my hand out to him. He stared at it for a second and then went to shake it, but I snatched it back then held it out again. "You said you were gonna give a donation for her."

"Oh, damn. You serious?" he asked.

"Damn right," I told him.

He reached in his pocket and handed me a twenty-dollar bill. "Here you go."

I took the money and tucked it inside my bra, making sure to give him a nice view of my cleavage, which I knew was popping in one of the new sixty-dollar Victoria's Secret bras that I bought when Ronda and I went shopping. "We appreciate your support."

Patrick and I walked out, and when we got into the car, he said, "Well, that didn't go exactly the way I thought it would, but it ain't go all the way left, so that's good."

"So, now what?" I asked him.

"We wait for him to call me," Patrick said.

"And if he doesn't?"

"Then I'll call him." Patrick shrugged.

I thought about everything Dell had just said. "Why the hell do we have to wait on his call? Why can't we just find someone else to flip it for us?"

"Because he's fam and I trust him. It ain't like we can google 'reliable drug dealer' and come up with a list."

"Shut the fuck up, smart ass. I know that. But didn't you used to be in the game?"

"Yeah, shit, I was the one who put Dell's ass on, to be honest. But that was before I cleaned up my act and found the Lord."

"Cut out that Lord bullshit, Patrick. You don't have to front for me." I shook my head.

"Front how?" He had the nerve to act like he didn't know what I was talking about.

"Well, for starters, you may work for the church part-time, but don't front like you don't be gambling down at Chubby's and at the poker games with the big boys around town. That's how you make money for real."

"I minister to the guys at Chubby's. That's called ministry."

"And say what you want about being in love with Nikki. That damn sure ain't stopped you from checkin' out my ass and titties every time you see me."

He put the car in park and turned around in his seat so that we were face to face, then gave me a lust-filled look. "So what? I'm a man. What do you expect me to do? Especially when you have your ass and titties out on display for me to look at."

"I expect for you to boss the fuck up," I said.

"And do what?" He reached out and ran his finger along the side of my breast, causing my nipples to harden.

Patrick was corny as hell, but he was a good-looking man. I didn't know if it was because I hadn't had any good dick since fucking Terry to get my car fixed, or what, but he was start-ing to turn me on. I eased my hand on his crotch to see what he was working with and was pleas-antly surprised. But we still had some business to deal with, and for me, that came first.

"Your nephew said he was making some calls, right?"

"Yeah." His hand slipped under my shirt.

I pulled his head to mine and whispered. "Why don't you call whoever the fuck he's calling instead, and make shit happen for us?"

Bilal

"Now, if you click right here, you can get a full view of the other camera," I said, showing Malik how to navigate the computer and use the new state of the art security system I had installed. I had done just as he asked and made sure he had the best system money could buy. He had video surveillance in every room of his house, none of which anyone could detect. People would never know they were being watched both inside and outside of his house.

"Damn, B, this is sweet as hell. Look at this shit." He smiled as he looked at Tey and Kareema on the screen. They were in one of the bedrooms, half dressed, laughing while doing their hair in the mirror. "Can I zoom in?"

"You sure can." I showed him how to zoom.

"That's what I'm talking about. Look at that." He wasted no time focusing on Kareema's naked breasts.

"Yeah, the picture quality is amazing," I said, reaching and turning to another camera angle.

"That ain't what I was talking about, but yeah, that shit is clear as hell." He laughed.

"A'ight, I'm gonna tell you this one more time, Malik. If you record certain stuff without their knowing and that shit gets out, you can go to jail. And you can end up with more time than doing other shit. They ain't playing out here about this digital consent stuff, bruh," I told him.

"I know, I know. I ain't gonna do no revenge porn. Don't worry." He laughed.

"If I were you, I'd put up a sign just to be safe," I suggested.

"A sign? What the hell?"

"It can be a small one somewhere outside the front of the house."

"A'ight, but that shit's gonna be damn near microscopic."

"Hey, as long as you got something up that says *video surveillance in progress*, you're good," I told him.

"Bet, that's what's up. Now, how you want your money, in big bills or what?" Malik got up and walked over to a safe in the corner of the office.

"Well, I would prefer a check made out to my business, but cash is fine." I sighed. This was the downside to doing business with my friends whose professions were illegal in nature. They paid me exceptionally well, but I couldn't count it as legitimate income to establish my business credibility, which was why I tried to maintain a balance between my clients.

"I really appreciate this, bruh. I ain't felt safe since those motherfuckers came in here and took my shit."

"Even with Skeet out front?" I took the stack of money he held out and put it into my work-bag. I knew I didn't have to count it, and it was probably more than I quoted him.

"Hell yeah."

Malik took one last glance at the screen where Tey was putting lotion on Kareema's back. "Damn, I shoulda listened to Dell and had you come hook this shit up a long time ago."

I stopped at the bank and was headed home to take a quick shower before heading over to the hospital when Dell called.

"What up, D?" I answered.

"Chilling. Where you at?"

"Just finished getting Malik's crib straight and I'm heading home right quick. What's good with you?"

"Nothing, man. I been meaning to catch up with you to tell you who rolled up on me the other day."

"Please don't tell me it was one of your good ol' blasts from the past. You don't need that type of drama in your life right now, and neither do I." I laughed.

"Naw, I told you I'm on the straight and narrow for right now."

"That's good to hear. So, who was it?"

"Unc."

"Oh, Lord. Don't you give him no more damn money, D. If you do, I'm out of it this time," I said. "I told him last time that y'all don't need to do business no more."

"Get this: he ain't ask for no money. He wanted to talk business, and he wasn't alone."

"What kind of business, and who the hell was he with?" I really didn't want to know about my uncle and whatever misdeeds he was trying to involve Dell in. I had warned both of them, and I was officially out of it.

"He was with Diane, old girl's mother. And you were right. She is a fucking trip. She actually came on to me, but I shut that shit down," he told me.

"What? Diane? Are you sure?" The fact that my uncle was hanging out with Diane was not surprising, but I was shocked that she was talking to Dell about business. They were both birds of a feather, I guess.

"Hell yeah, I'm sure. They came talking about they had ten grand and wanted me to flip it for them."

"Where the hell did they get—shit, the donations for Avery." I answered my own question.

"Bingo, bruh. I can't believe the two of them."

"So, what did you tell them? I hope you ain't gonna do it." I frowned.

"Hell naw, I ain't gonna do it. I ain't no religious man, but I do believe in karma, and what they're doing is dead-ass wrong on a whole other level, taking that girl's money while she's still recovering. I told him I was in the process of leaving the streets and I would make some calls and get back with him. Old girl had the nerve to ask me for a donation for the cause before she left." He sighed.

"That's ridiculous, man. I don't know who's worse: her for doing all this shit, or Patrick's ass for helping her. I hope they know if they get caught using that money for stuff that it ain't intended for, they're both getting locked up," I told him.

"Man, don't I know it. That's why I ain't touching it with a ten-foot pole. I just thought you

should know, though. You gonna tell Kendra?"
he asked.

I thought about the emotional roller coaster
and stress that Kendra was already dealing with.
The last thing she needed to be bothered with
was this. "Nah, I'm gonna handle it myself. But
I appreciate you telling me, though, D. Good
looking out."

"Hey, you know how we do. But for real,
Marlena been hounding me about having y'all
come through for dinner so we can meet her.
What's up with you and her for real? I mean, she
got a lot going on, and you know how you feel
about chicks with drama."

Dell was right. Drama was something I avoided
at all costs, especially when it came to women.
Although Kendra had a lot going on right now
with her sisters and mom, it wasn't through any
fault of her own. I liked her—actually, more than
liked her. It was like she filled an empty space in
my life that I hadn't even realized was there. It
wasn't just that I wanted to be with her; I needed
to be. I felt like I had to protect her, even against
whatever her mother and my uncle had going
on.

"I'm really feeling her," I admitted.

"Word?"

"Yeah, I am." I found myself smiling.

"Let me find out you in love and shit." Dell laughed. When I didn't protest or deny his accusation, he added, "Oh, damn, B. You are!"

"Whatever," I told him.

"Well, then we def gotta make this dinner happen soon. I gotta find out what this woman is all about. But you need to get a hold of Unc and see what they're up to."

"No doubt. And, D, thanks again."

"Holla at me later."

I hung up the phone and dialed my uncle's number. As usual, he didn't answer. I decided to call the one person who could track him down.

"Hello," Fatima answered my mother's phone.

"Hey, where's Ma?" I asked.

"Where's my phone, Bilal?" she asked.

"Look, I don't have time for this right now. I need to talk to Ma."

"For what?"

"Because I'm looking for Uncle Pat."

"Oh, he was just over here a little while ago. Had some woman with him, and it wasn't Aunt Nikki either," Fatima stated.

"Why was he there?"

"Came to bring Ma some money for her to give Tiesha's nagging ass. But I heard the lady telling him to hurry up so they could stop by her house and handle business."

"A'ight, bet. That's all I needed."

"What about the phone, Bilal?" Fatima whined.

"I got you."

"You keep saying that."

"I know, but I really do," I promised, then made an illegal U-turn and drove toward Diane's house.

When I pulled up to the house, Uncle Patrick's car was parked in the driveway like he lived there. I got out, walked to the front door, and rang the bell. I had to stop my uncle from getting into some shit that I wasn't going to be able to dig him out of. The street life wasn't like it was back in the day when he was a small-time hustler. These days, dudes would shoot you if they thought you were short-changing them a dollar, and they wouldn't think nothing of it.

I waited a few moments before ringing the bell again. I could hear music coming from inside, so I knew someone was there. I was about to ring a third time when the door opened. Diane stood there, smiling at me with a joint in her hand.

"Well, damn. Look who's here." She took a pull from the lit cigarillo and blew into my face.

I tried not to stare at her naked body, which was clearly visible under the open silk kimono she was wearing. Her body was tight and sexy, just like Kendra's.

"I'm looking for my uncle," I told her. "I need to talk to him."

"Well, he's a little unavailable right now, if you know what I mean. You wanna join us?" She winked and reached her hand out to touch me, but I stepped back.

"Make him available. I need to holler at both of y'all, as a matter of fact," I told her. "So, go get him."

"What the hell do you need to talk to me for? If this is about your little girlfriend, you can go ahead and save it. Kendra made her choice, so now she gotta deal with it. She wanted to be a grown-ass woman, so now she is."

"This ain't got nothing to do with her. This is about your little plan to steal Avery's money and what you're trying to do with it. It ain't happening. So, go get my uncle, and put some clothes on while you're at it."

She frowned at me for a second, then said, "I don't know who the fuck you think you are, but this is my house. You don't run shit here. I don't have to do shit. As a matter of fact, you can get the fuck off my property."

"Look, I ain't tryna argue—"

"Then leave now," she said. "As a matter of fact, I'll leave. What the fuck I look like, standing here talking to you anyway when I got some

perfectly good dick waiting for me in my room?
I'll let your uncle know you're looking for him."

She shut the door in my face, and I heard the
locks click. The thought of banging on the door
crossed my mind, but I knew it was a lost cause.
I turned and slowly walked back to my truck. I
was getting in when I heard the door open again,
and I looked up to see Diane standing on the
porch, robe hanging open as she waved goodbye.
I started my engine and drove off so fast that my
tires spun.

Kendra

For the first time since getting the call that my sister was missing, I was able to breathe. Avery was finally awake, and it seemed as if the worst was over. At first, she would drift in and out of sleep for a few minutes at a time, but now, she was finally fully awake and talking. She had improved to the point that the doctors had given the okay for her to be moved from ICU and into a regular room. I was elated. Even though her hospital room was full of stuffed animals that people had sent along with their good wishes, one of the first things she asked me for was Tubby, a stuffed whale which had been her favorite since before she could walk.

"I'll go home and get Tubby for you, Avery," I promised her.

"And some ice cream too?" she asked with a smile. Her face was still bruised and swollen, but she was getting back to normal.

"I didn't say all that. We have to ask the doctors," I told her.

"Okay," she said. "Kendra, is Mama mad at me?"

"What? No, she's not mad at you. Why would you ask that?" I held her hand.

"Because Ashley said the police were looking for me and found me. And she said if we made the police come to her house, she was . . ." Avery's eyes were filled with pain as her voice drifted off.

"No, she's not mad at you, Avery." I shook my head.

"Is Aunt Celia mad?"

"No, she's not mad either."

"I lost my phone that day, and she's upset. Mama said that's why she's not here and hasn't been to see me." The fear that had been in my sister's eyes moments before was now replaced with hurt. I didn't know what to do. I couldn't tell her that the reason Aunt Celia wasn't there was because Mama wouldn't let her be there. Hell, I barely had visitation privileges myself, and if I shared that information, I would be banned too.

"No, Avery, she's not mad. And she has been here. She was here the moment they brought you in here," I explained in an effort to make her feel better.

"She was?" Avery blinked away her tears and turned to look at Ashley, who was sitting quietly on the other side of the bed.

I gave Ashley a nod, and she said, "Yeah, Avery. She was here before."

"Yes, she was. And I'm sure once you get moved and settled in your new room, she'll be back."

"And you're gonna go get Tubby for me?" she asked.

"Yes, Avery, I'll go and get Tubby for you." I laughed.

"You sound like a three-year-old," Ashley teased. "You gonna go and get Tubby for me?"

"Shut up, Ashley. How does that sound?" Avery snapped.

I couldn't help but laugh. My sister was definitely on the mend. The doctor and a nurse came in and said that they were ready. They gave Ashley and me the room number where she was going to be moved, and we began packing up her things while they were transporting her down.

"Kendra?" Ashley asked.

"Yeah?"

"Here." I looked up and saw her holding out her set of house keys. "So you can go and get Tubby for Avery."

"I was just going to tell you to bring Tubby when you came back tomorrow," I told her.

"No, she really wants him, and I want her to have him. Can you please just go now?" she begged.

"I don't know about all that. What if Mama's home?"

"I'll call and see where she's at." Ashley took out her cell phone and made the call. "Hey, Ma. Yeah. They're moving her now. Me and Kendra are moving her stuff down there. Yeah. No. Room four ten. Uh-uh. Ma, what time are you coming back? I'm hungry, and Avery wants some ice cream. Okay. Yes, ma'am. Bye."

"What did she say?" I asked.

"She is out with Mr. Patrick taking care of some business, and they'll be back before nine." She held the keys out again. "But she did say she ain't bringing me nothing back to eat, so can you get me and Avery some McDonald's?"

Bilal sent a text saying he was finishing up with a client and would meet me at the hospital in a few. I sent him a quick response, telling him I had an errand to run, and I asked if he'd stop by McDonald's on the way to grab some food.

Then, I took the keys and told Ashley, "Fine. Aunt Nikki will be here in a few minutes. Tell her and Avery I went to go get Tubby and I'll be back in a little while."

I thought I was seeing things when I saw Bilal walking away from my house. I blew my horn to get his attention, but he sped off. I glanced over to the front porch and saw my mother standing in the doorway, waving at him, and my heart sank. She had on her familiar silk robe, and I could see her naked body from where I was. As soon as Bilal pulled off, I parked the car in front of the house and jumped out.

"What the hell are you doing here?" she said, a surprised look on her face.

I could hear the sounds of Bobby Brown's "Tenderoni," and the scent of marijuana hit me.

"Why, Mama? Why would you do this? You already kicked me out, but you had to go and do this?" I cried.

"Kendra, what the fuck are you talking about?"

"Bilal, Mama? You had to have him, huh? You have to have everybody's man, don't you? Aunt Celia's, mine . . . Is it because you can't keep your own man? Is that what it is?" Tears streamed down my face.

"You're out here acting crazy about your little boyfriend? I knew you were fucking him. Poor thing." She laughed and went to turn around, but I grabbed her by the arm. "Kendra, if you don't get your fucking hands off me, I swear—"

"You swear what, Mama?" I said angrily.

She snatched away and said, "Don't act like I won't whip your ass out here, Kendra."

We stared at one another briefly, as if we were each daring the other to make the first move. And then, I laughed. "You know what? You are pathetic. Look at you, around here too busy fucking dudes my age to spend time with your daughter, who's awake and talking for the first time in days. It's sad, really, that you have to stoop to this level to prove something. But to who? Not me. You didn't have to do this to show me how low you'd go to hurt me. I already knew that when you kicked me out in the street. You want Bilal, you can have him—and any other man you need to screw to get ahead in life. I hate you."

From the look on my mother's face, I could see that my words stung. She stepped back and pulled the flowing robe around her. I braced myself for what she was about to say, but she didn't speak at first. Instead, she simply smiled, then turned and opened the door. But just as she closed it, she said, "Stay the fuck away from me and my children. If you come anywhere near

me or your sisters again, I'll have you arrested.
Don't believe it? Try me."

I stood on the porch, sobbing as I listened
to the door being locked. The woman who had
given me life had somehow now taken everything I loved away from me, and I wanted to die.

Celia

"Hey, Auntie!" Seeing Avery's face on my phone and hearing her voice was like heaven to me. My prayers had been answered, and she was going to be okay.

"Hey, Avery Boo. How is my baby doing?" I gushed at her. "It's so good to talk to you. You feeling better?"

"Yeah, my leg and my side hurts, but I feel okay," she told me.

"That's great, and I know your leg and side are gonna get better really soon," I said.

"Auntie, I'm sorry." Her face was full of sincerity.

I was confused. "Sorry for what? Why are you saying that?"

"You're mad at me because I lost my phone. I didn't mean to lose it, Aunt Celia. I promise. You don't even have to get me another one. Ashley said she'll just share her phone with me," Avery told me.

"Yes, Auntie, we can just share one phone." Ashley's face appeared beside her sister's. "Don't be mad."

"I'm not mad at her. What are y'all talking about?" I shook my head in confusion. "Who told you that?"

"Mama," Ashley said before Avery could answer. "Because she lost her phone in the ditch."

"You're not? So, you'll come and see me?" Avery asked, ignoring her sister.

"I'm gonna try, sweetie. But listen, I am *not* mad at all. I'm very proud of you, and I'm going to have Aunt Nikki bring you something special from me. I promise," I told her.

"Okay." Avery seemed slightly disappointed. She asked, "Are you mad at Mama?"

"Avery, no one is mad at anyone. Everyone is just happy that you're better. Now, give Aunt Nikki the phone. I love you. Kisses." I blew a kiss at her, and she blew one back.

"Love you, Aunt Celiaaaaaa," Ashley called out.

"Love you too, Ashley." I laughed.

"Hey, girl." Nikki's face replaced Avery's on the screen. She looked like she was exhausted, and I felt bad. Not only had she worked a double shift, but instead of going home, she stopped by the hospital so that I could FaceTime with Avery. I didn't dare call Ashley's phone, even though I was the one who paid the bill. I didn't want to take the chance of Diane seeing my number and taking it out on her.

"Thanks so much, Nikki. I know you're tired, so go ahead and go home. Call me in the morning," I told her.

"I'm fine. I'm gonna hang out here for a few."

"Di still not around?" I shook my head.

"No, they said she was here earlier, but she doesn't stay around for long. Told the nurses she had a meeting and would be back," Nikki said.

"She's probably still avoiding talking to the police." I lowered my voice so the girls wouldn't hear me.

"What's up with that? I heard Patrick talking to some lawyer about taking her case. This whole thing is getting crazy," Nikki said.

While standing in the kitchen, I heard the front door open, followed by the sound of keys being placed in the bowl on the table in my foyer. Darnell was home. I had found a way to avoid him most of the time by either not being home or locking myself in our bedroom or the upstairs study, where I was temporarily working from home.

"Listen, I gotta go. I'll call you back in a little while," I told her and hung up. I looked at the sandwich I was halfway finished making and contemplated throwing it in the trash, but I was starving. I inhaled deeply and decided to finish doing what I was doing.

"Hey," Darnell said when he walked in and saw me standing there.

I glanced up at him and paused before finally saying, "Hey."

"How was your day?"

"Fine," I said, cutting my finally finished sandwich in half.

"That's good. So, you making one of those for me?" he said with a weak smile.

My fingers tightened around the knife I was holding, and I looked at him like he was crazy. "You really do have a death wish, huh? Did you really just ask me that while I'm holding a knife?"

"I'm just trying to break the tension in here, Celia. Hell, it's so thick you can use that knife to cut it. I know that sounds cliché, but it's true. You've been home for three days and haven't said a word to me." He leaned against the island and folded his arms.

"I don't have shit to say to you, Darnell. You'd better be glad that we're having this brief conversation, which is now over." I tossed the knife into the sink and picked up the plate holding my sandwich.

"So, we're just not gonna talk about this at all. We're gonna walk around here like total strangers who happen to live together in this big-ass house?" He frowned.

"That's pretty much how we've been living for the past few months anyway, isn't it? At least now I know why. For months, I asked you what was wrong, and you lied. I don't do well with liars, especially ones who are fucking my sister. So, excuse me if I don't feel like talking right now," I snapped.

"I get it, Celia. I fucked up, and I'm sorry. I don't even have a lame-ass excuse for doing what I did, except I was selfish. But I need for us to figure this out and move past it. I'll do whatever it takes—counseling, therapy, whatever. Just tell me what you need from me, and I'll do it," he pleaded.

"What I need from you is some space, Darnell. Guess it's a good thing that we live in this big-ass house, huh?" I rolled my eyes and went upstairs to my bedroom. As hungry as I had been while I was in the kitchen, somehow, I no longer had an appetite. I put the sandwich on my nightstand and wiped away my tears, grateful that they hadn't started falling until I was alone. Darnell sounded sincere with his apology, but I wasn't ready to accept it. I was still mad as hell, and just because he said sorry, that did not mean I was ready to forgive him anytime soon.

I grabbed the remote and tried to find some drama-filled, ratchet reality TV show to distract me from my own problems. I didn't even realize I had fallen asleep until I heard my cell phone ringing. I sat up and saw that it was Nikki.

"What's up?" I answered, clearing my throat because I sounded like a man.

"Have you talked to Kendra?" she asked.

"No, why?"

"Cele, Bilal just called me from the hospital."

"Is something wrong with Avery? What happened?"

"No, it's not Avery. Kendra's missing," Nikki said.

"Missing? What do you mean, missing?"

"She left the hospital earlier, and no one's seen or heard from her since. She texted Bilal and asked him to bring food to the girls, and they were supposed to meet up here. But she hasn't shown. He's called, Ashley's called, but she's not answering," Nikki told me. "He went home, thinking she'd be there, but she's not. We're worried."

I looked at the time and saw that it was almost ten o'clock. "Okay, let me see if I can reach her. I'll call you back."

I dialed Kendra's number, but her phone went straight to voicemail. I sent her a text, asking her to call me ASAP. Then, I called Bilal.

"What's going on?" I asked. "Where's Kendra? When's the last time you talked to her, and what did you say?"

"I—she—I talked to her last around noon. I told her I was doing a system install for a client. She was excited because Avery was awake, and the nurses told her Diane asked her to sit with her this afternoon. You know she's been tripping about when Kendra could be in the room. She sent me a text a little later, saying she had somewhere to go right quick, and I haven't heard from her since. I don't know where she is. She never came back to the hospital. She's not at my apartment, and she's not answering her phone." Bilal sounded nervous, which made me anxious.

"What errand did she have to run? Did she say where she was going?" I stood up and started pacing back and forth.

"Celia, that's the thing. She was going home to get something for Avery," he told me.

"Home? Her home?" I slipped on my sneakers and grabbed a hoodie from my closet.

"Yeah, her home."

I hung up before Bilal could say anything else and headed out to find my niece.

I kept calling Kendra's phone over and over, but it was either dead, or she had turned it off. I became overwhelmed with guilt for not being there when she needed me the most. I knew how unstable and psychotic my sister was, and I was the only reliable person she had, but I got too caught up in my own issues to even be concerned with everything she was dealing with. I was just as selfish as Darnell.

I made it to Diane's house in record time. The house was completely dark when I got there. I sat in front for a few seconds and tried to think. Then I called Champ.

"Hey, Celia. Everything okay?" he asked.

"Have you talked to or heard from Kendra?" I asked.

"No, not since yesterday when she called to tell me Avery was awake. Why? What's going on?"

I didn't know if telling him Kendra was missing was premature. I didn't want to cause a panic if there was no need. I decided that I wouldn't alarm him just yet. "I've just been trying to call her, and she's not answering."

"Oh, okay." He got quiet for a second and said, "She told me what happened, Celia. About Di and Darnell. I'm sorry. It's a bad situation, and she feels bad. She was just caught in the middle and couldn't figure out what to do. Her mom put her in a position that she never should have been in. Kendra loves you. You know that."

"I know she does, Champ. And I was wrong for abandoning her when she needed me. But I'm gonna fix it," I told him.

"I know you are. But hey, I'm working overnight tonight, and I gotta get back. If I talk to baby girl before you do, I'll let her know you're looking for her," he said.

"Thanks, Champ," I said.

I sat outside the house, waiting for another half hour, then I drove to the one place I figured my sister would be. As I drove through Crossways Projects, a lifetime of memories came flooding back to me. It was the neighborhood where Diane and I had grown up, and the place where we vowed we would move away from and never look back. It seemed as if I was the only one who had done so. Even though she no longer lived there, my sister still hung in Crossways like it was home sweet home.

I took a deep breath as I parked my car and got out, praying that it would still be there when I came out. I walked up to Ronda's door and knocked hard so I could be heard over the music that was blasting.

"Who is it?" Ronda yelled.

"It's Cele!" I yelled.

"Who?"

"Cele, Ronda."

"What the hell do you want?" she asked, opening the door slightly. I glanced past her and saw several people sitting in the small living room area, but I didn't see Diane.

"I'm looking for Di," I told her.

"She ain't here." Ronda gave me an ugly look, which wasn't hard, considering how unattractive she already was.

"Aunt Celia!" Ashley came running to the door and gave me a hug. I kissed the top of her forehead and said, "Hey there."

"What are you doing here? Is Kendra with you? Did y'all come to get me?" she said in a pleading voice.

"No, baby, Kendra's not with me. I'm here to see your mom," I told her.

"She's in the back room," Ashley said. "I'm not allowed back there."

"That's probably a good thing," I said, then looked at Ronda. "Can you go get Di, please?"

Ronda rolled her eyes again and said, "You wait out here."

"Aunt Celia, I don't know where Kendra is. She didn't come back to the hospital at all. She was supposed to go and come right back, but something happened when she got there. I heard Mama telling Ronda she and Kendra had a fight," Ashley whispered. "I don't wanna stay here. Please take me with you."

"I don't think your mom's gonna let me, Ashley, but if anything happens, you call me, you understand?"

"But you said if Mama found out I called—"

"Don't worry about what I said. You call me." I hugged her close to me.

A few seconds later, Diane appeared in the doorway. "Go get your ass inside, Ashley."

Ashley looked from her mother to me, and I nodded.

"Go ahead inside. Remember what I told you."

Ashley hugged me one more time and then ran back into the apartment. When we were alone, Diane asked, "This must be hella important for you to bring your ass here to find me. I'm surprised you knew how to get here."

"Di, where's Kendra?"

"What? How the hell should I know where the hell she is?" She frowned.

"Because you were the last person to see her, and now we can't find her, that's why," I said, trying my best to remain calm.

"How you figure?"

"Di, don't play dumb. You had some kind of fight at your house while she was there. Now, what happened to her?"

"We ain't have no fight. It was more like a misunderstanding." Diane smirked.

"What kind of misunderstanding?" I demanded.

"She saw her little boyfriend leaving my house, and she flipped out. Said I was a whore who stole everybody's man, including yours."

"You slept with Bilal?" I screamed. I couldn't believe my sister, especially after what she had just done to me. My heart broke for my niece, because I knew exactly how she felt. It took everything within me not to strangle Diane.

"Did I say I slept with him?"

I paused then said, "But she thinks you slept with him. And you let her believe that? Why would you let her think that?"

"I don't give a damn what she thinks, and I don't know where the fuck she is. I told her to stay away from me and the twins, and she left. That's the last time I saw her."

"What is wrong with you, Diane? Why would you push away the one person who was always there for you? That's your daughter, your first born, and you hurt her to the point of no return?" I asked.

"You should've heard the things she said to me. She was the one who hurt me, over a dude who is only using her and is gonna eventually throw her ass away for the next piece of ass he comes into contact with. She would rather be loyal to him and not me."

"How do you know he's going to do that?"

"Because, Cele, that's what men do, and the sooner she learns that lesson, the better off she'll be. What I did today helped her. I taught her a lesson she'll never forget."

"What lesson? How not to trust men?"

"Exactly. You trusted Darnell, and look at what he did. They're all the same. Even if I didn't fuck Bilal, I did her a favor by letting her think I did. Now, is there anything else?" Diane asked. "Because I have somebody waiting for me inside."

I realized that my sister was damaged beyond repair and emotionally scarred to the point that she could no longer feel human emotions. The only thing she cared about was attention from men. She had always been that way, even as a child. She was a daddy's girl, no doubt. Our father loved us both, but there was something special about Diane. When he would come home from work, she would climb in his lap and tell him all about her day, and he would laugh. On those occasions when he would have his friends over at the house, he would call Diane to come into the living room and perform for them.

"Di, show them that dance you were doing the other day," he would yell, turning up the radio.

Diane would smile as she effortlessly moved her body to whatever song was playing and showed off her dance moves. "This one, Daddy?"

"Yeah, baby girl. That's what I'm talking about. Look at my baby, y'all. She got some moves!" Daddy would brag.

"You right, Nelson. That girl can dance, and she's pretty, too," his friends would comment.

I would stand in the doorway, unnoticed, watching this group of grown men leering at my baby sister, whose innocent moves seemed to have them in some kind of trance. Diane loved being the center of attention. It wasn't until I got much older that I realized Daddy was objectifying my sister without even realizing it, and in actuality, he had created a monster.

As I stood there in the hallway, staring at Diane, who was more concerned about whatever man she had waiting inside than her missing daughter, I cringed.

"Yeah, there is," I said.

"What?"

"I want to take Ashley with me. Avery's awake, and you don't need her for your little prop anymore. Besides, now that Kendra's not around to babysit, what are you going to do?" I waited for her to think about what I said.

She turned around and opened the door, going back inside without saying goodbye. I walked back to my truck and was about to get in when Ashley came running toward me.

"Aunt Celia, wait!" she yelled.

"What are you doing?" I asked.

She walked to the passenger side of the truck and got in. "Mama told me to get the hell out and go with you. And she said you can go see Avery now too."

Even though my sister was a cold-hearted, evil bitch, she still cared enough to release Ashley to go with me. There was probably some underlying ultimatum in her doing so, but I didn't care. And now I could finally go see Avery at the hospital. Once we were both buckled in, I hauled ass out of the Crossways, determined never to come back again. I called Bilal and told him what Diane had done and asked if he had heard from Kendra, but he hadn't. I promised to let him know as soon as I heard anything.

"Aunt Celia, how are we gonna find Kendra?" Ashley said, bringing our pressing issue back to the forefront of my mind.

"I don't know, baby. We're gonna need some help," I told her.

"From who?"

I thought of the only person I knew that could help me, and I called. After several rings, he finally picked up, and I said, "I need your help. My niece Kendra is missing."

Diane

I watched Ashley get into Celia's truck, and they drove away. For a second, I wondered where the hell Kendra could be, and I wondered if she was okay. Then, I told myself I didn't have time to be distracted by her little disappearing act because her feelings were hurt. I had more important things to deal with. I had let it slip to Ronda what Patrick planned to do. She was concerned that even though Patrick seemed to be on the up and up, maybe I should talk to someone who had experience in the drug game that could offer some insight. That person turned out to be her cousin, Junie, who had done time for selling dope and considered himself an expert.

I walked back into Ronda's back bedroom, where he was lying across the bed, blazing up while he finished giving me a lesson in Street Hustling 101.

"Now, the good thing is you got a lot of free capital to work with. You use that shit to your advantage. So, what exactly are y'all trying to buy?" Junie asked, trying to feel me up when I sat on the bed.

"I don't really know now. We had a more solid plan when we were gonna deal with his nephew. Now things are a little up in the air. All I know is I ain't getting ready to be selling drugs outta my house or on no street corner. That's for damn sure."

"Well, the return on powder would be high, but so is the risk. Weed has a lower return, but it's safer. Definitely stay away from heroin. It's too much fucking work. You gotta cook it and shit."

"You make a great point." I nodded.

"I can't believe y'all was tryna fuck with whack-ass Dell anyway. That dude ain't got no ten grand worth of product, not even weed. Dell small-time now. He ain't running these streets like folks think he is."

"Sounds like you're hating." I laughed.

"Nah, just stating facts." He shrugged and put his hand on my leg.

I pushed it away and said, "Well, we ain't dealing with him anymore. We 'bout to go meet another dude in a few minutes. Patrick's on his way to pick me up."

"Who?" Junie sat up.

"I don't know. Some guy that Dell deals with."
I shrugged, taking the blunt from him and taking
a pull.

"Dell sent y'all to this dude?"

"Nah, Dell don't even know we going to see
him." My phone vibrated and displayed a text
from Patrick saying he was waiting outside.
"Well, I'm out. Thanks for the info."

"No doubt. Hey, if shit don't work out, hit me
up. I got a guy that can make it happen for you,"
he told me.

"I'll let you know," I said, taking one last toke
and passing the blunt back to him.

"So, who is this we're about to go see?" I asked
Patrick when I got into his car.

"This cat named Malik. He's a solid dude, and
I know Dell does business with him quite often,"
Patrick said.

"I can't believe Nikki let your ass out this late.
You know how she keeps your ass on a short
leash." I laughed.

"Don't play with me. I ain't got no kind of leash.
I make sure I take care of home, and I don't have
no issues when I ain't there, unlike Darnell's ass.
See, had he made sure his woman was happy, he
wouldn't've got caught," Patrick said.

"Yeah, right. So, where does she think you're at now?"

"At a business meeting. I ain't lie."

"And she knows you're with me?" I smirked.

"I ain't tell her all that."

"Why not?"

"Because she don't need to know all the details. The less she knows, the better," he said.

"Yeah, I bet." I laughed.

Fifteen minutes later, we were pulling up to a large, two-story house in the back of an older neighborhood. The house reminded me of the one on *The Brady Bunch*, but there was a fence around it. Patrick parked the car out front, and we got out. He was about to reach to open the fence when suddenly, we heard the cock of a gun and a man's voice.

"Stop right there. I don't know where you think you're going, but it ain't in here."

"Whoa, whoa, whoa. It's all good, young gun. We ain't armed or dangerous. We just came to see if we could speak to Malik for a few minutes, that's all," Patrick said with his arms raised.

"And who the fuck are you?" the guy asked, his gun still pointed at us.

"Dell sent us over here," Patrick told him.

They guy looked at me, and I said, "I'm with him."

"Well, Malik ain't here, so y'all can turn your asses right around and leave."

"Bullshit. I know he's here. Just tell him we need to holler at him for fifteen minutes, that's all," Patrick said.

"Man, you got fifteen seconds to get the fuck off this property before I bust a cap in your ass." The dude took a step toward us.

I grabbed Patrick by the arm and said, "Man, come on. We don't have to stand out here begging nobody to see us. Junie already said if Malik don't want our business, he got somebody who does. Fuck this clown and his midget-ass fake security."

"Bitch, you take your thot ass on somewhere before I shoot you instead of him," the guy said.

Patrick and I walked back to the car and drove off.

"Well, it was a longshot," he said. "I can't believe that dude tried to handle us like that."

"Fuck that dude. Like I said, I already got a backup plan in motion. I shoulda been the one handling this shit in the first place. You just make sure you have that cash ready tomorrow so I can make shit happen," I told him as I took out my phone and called Ronda.

"Hey, where's Junie? He still there?" I asked.

"Yeah, in the same spot where you left him."
She laughed.

"Put him on the phone," I told her. I held on
while she went into the room.

"Yo," he said.

"Hey, you know what we were talking about
earlier and the connect you have?"

"Yeah."

"Hook it up," I told him.

"You sure? This man ain't about to play no
games."

"I ain't playing none either."

"Bet. Oh, and another thing," Junie said.

"What?"

"I want my finder's fee."

"Fine." I sighed, thinking about how I had no
intention of giving him anything.

"Cash, up front. Be ready when I call tomorrow—by yourself."

I glanced over at Patrick, knowing there was
no way he was going to let me do this without
him. "Okay, no doubt."

"So, what's the deal?" Patrick asked when I
ended the call.

"He's setting it up for tomorrow. I told him I
would bring the cash, so make sure you go make
a withdrawal and bring it to me," I said.

"You're not doing this by yourself. You don't even know this dude. How do we even know we can trust him like that? This ain't no chump change. This is ten thousand fucking dollars," he snapped at me.

"I know how much it is, and I do know him. I've known him since he was a kid. It's my best friend's cousin, and we're from the same neighborhood. I trusted you when you nearly got us shot going to see some fucking dude who didn't even wanna talk to us. What's the difference?" I demanded.

"The difference is I knew who we were meeting. You don't even know who this dude Junie is taking you to see. He could be setting you up to rob your ass. I don't think this is a good idea at all." Patrick shook his head.

"Fine. You don't wanna partner on this deal, that's fine. I'll do it by my damn self. Just make sure you bring me my half of the fucking money first thing tomorrow," I told him.

"Di, listen to me," he said as he pulled into the front of Ronda's building. It was after midnight, but folks were still hanging out like it was six in the evening.

"No, you listen to me. Bring me my cash by noon tomorrow," I said and got out of the car. "Don't make me come and find you."

Bilal

I had been up all night, worrying as I paced the floor, hoping that Kendra would come home or at least call, but she didn't. I couldn't believe Diane told her that we slept together. If it had been anybody other than Kendra, I would've been pissed that they believed the story without even talking to me first. But given Diane's history and the behavior I'd witnessed over the past few weeks, I understood why Kendra took what she said and ran. If only I could talk to her and explain, but it was like she had vanished into thin air. I tried everything to find her, using every technical and computer skill I had, from tracking her phone to hacking into her mobile banking information to see where she'd last spent money, but I couldn't find anything. I was starting to fear that she was somewhere hurt, or worse, dead.

I decided to go back out and drive around, hoping to find her somewhere. I grabbed a jacket and was heading out the door when I got a call from Malik. It was only seven o'clock in the morning, so I knew something had to be wrong.

"What's up, Malik?"

"Yo, B, I know it's mad early, but I need you to come through. I got something to show you right quick."

"Man, right now? I was just about to go out and take care of something," I told him, not in the mood to go see whatever sexual act between Kareema and Tey that Malik happened to catch on video and was so eager to show me.

"I'm sure whatever it is you need to take care of can wait. I'll see you in fifteen. Dell is already over here. We waiting," he said and hung up.

Now I knew that whatever it was, it was more serious than homemade porn. Dell never went anywhere to do anything before ten in the morning. I got into my truck and made the twenty-five-minute drive to his house within fifteen minutes as he'd instructed. I expected Skeet to be posted up outside, but he wasn't, so I went straight to the front door and rang the bell. It was Dell who opened it and let me in.

"You ain't gonna believe this," Dell said.

"Man, what the hell is going on?" I asked as I followed him up the steps and into Malik's office. There was Malik, sitting at the desk, staring at the security camera footage. Sitting in a chair nearby was Skeet. They were so engrossed in what they were looking at that they didn't even see me walk in.

I looked at the screen, and the first image I saw was a naked Kareema, lying in bed. I cleared my throat to signal that I was there.

"Oh, damn. 'Sup, B?" Malik said, turning around and holding out his fist for me to pound.

"What's going on? What you got to show me?" I said, anxious to see what he had.

"So, check it. Last night, this man and this chick roll up to the crib, saying they need to holler at me about some business. Now, you know that shit ain't happen, because first of all, they was unannounced, and I don't play that," Malik told me.

"I'm sure Skeet ain't let that happen." I looked over at Skeet.

"You know it. They ain't have a chance," Skeet said with pride.

"So, they ain't get in," I said.

"Nope, but I wasn't even home anyway when they rolled up. But when I got in this morning, Skeet told me what happened. Said the dude told him Dell sent him. So, you know me. I call D and ask why the fuck he sending clowns to my crib without giving me the heads up first."

"Yeah, he woke me up with this bullshit, knowing damn well I wouldn't do that." Dell looked as irritated as I was. "So, now I'm pissed, and so is Lena, who starts bitching at me because my phone was going off at six in the morning and she's thinking it's some random. And I'm telling her that it's Malik—"

Malik interrupted him. "So, he comes over and we pull the fucking tape."

"Who was it?" I asked, turning my attention to the screen.

"Check this bullshit out." Dell folded his arms, and we all watched.

I leaned down to get a closer look, making sure my eyes weren't playing tricks on me. "What the hell? Is that—"

"Hell yeah, that's them." Dell nodded. "But it gets crazier."

My mind became filled with thoughts of what they were about to say, and I prayed it didn't involve them doing something to Kendra. If it did, I was prepared to kill both of them.

"Tell them what they said, Skeet." Malik sat back in his chair.

"After I told them to get the fuck on, the chick starts talking about how they were gonna take their business to Junie's guy," Skeet told me.

"Junie?" I asked.

"Hell yeah, Junie's lightweight ass."

"Dell said they told him they got ten grand. Junie ain't got no guy around here that's got that kinda weight. Shit, the only real cat Junie deal wit' is D-Lo, and he was getting his shit from me until I got ro—"

It was as if we all thought the same thing at the same time.

"Oh, shit," Dell said.

"Aw, damn." Skeet sat up.

"I'm gonna fuck somebody up." Malik stood up.

"Man, I told Uncle Pat—" I started.

"Wait, this clown is really your uncle?" Malik said.

"Yeah, he is, but I can tell you right now, he don't deal with Junie, and he's out of his element with all of this. He probably don't even know who Junie is, for real. This ain't him." I stared at my uncle's face on the screen, then looked at the woman beside him. "This is that bitch right there. I gotta go, but I'll call you in an hour."

"B, wait," Dell called after me, but I ignored him and headed out the door.

I left Malik's crib and drove to Diane's house. She wasn't there, and neither was her car. I went to Nikki's and didn't even bother ringing the doorbell. I banged on the door until finally, I heard Uncle Pat's voice.

"Who is it?" he yelled.

"Open the door!" I yelled back.

"Bilal, what the hell? What's wrong with you coming over here this early, knocking on the door like you're the police? You ain't even call first," he grumbled sleepily as he opened the door, dressed in a burgundy robe and slippers.

"Like you ain't call when you showed your ass up at Malik's crib last night?" I replied.

He quickly looked over his shoulder before slipping through the door and stepping outside. "Lower your voice, nephew. You're gonna wake Nikki. What are you talking about?"

"I know all about you and Diane popping up at Malik's last night. You're playing with fire, Unc. You better be glad Skeet ain't shoot your ass on sight, because he has been known to do that. What the hell is wrong with you?" I asked.

"Calm down. We just went to talk to the man, that's all. He wasn't available, so we left." He acted like he hadn't had a gun pointed in his face a few hours ago. "How the hell did you find out, anyway?"

"It don't matter. Now, where the fuck is Diane? Because by the time I get my hands on her, she's gonna wish Skeet had bust a cap in her ass. I swear, I'm gonna fuck her up."

"Can you please lower your voice? I don't know where she is. What is wrong with you, Bilal?"

My uncle never called me by my first name. I paused and stared at him before saying, "Uncle Pat, you've got to leave this chick alone. She's crazy, and she's gonna get you killed."

"Listen, I know she's got issues, but I ain't new to this, and I know what I'm doing."

"It ain't like it used to be back in the day out here, Uncle Pat. She's about to have you involved in some shit that I ain't gonna be able to get you out of. Listen to me," I warned him.

"I appreciate you trying to look out for me, but I got this. Your uncle been around a long time. I know how to handle women like Diane. Trust me." He winked, and from the look on his face, I knew my uncle was not only scheming with Diane, but he was sexing her too.

"Man, please don't tell me you're smashing her. You're smarter than this, Uncle Pat." I threw my hands up in frustration.

"Hey, she offered, and I accepted. What was I supposed to do?" He shrugged.

"Tell her skank ass no, maybe? You know what? I don't even care. But I'm telling you right now, you need to cut your losses and stay away from her, because it's about to get real. Junie ain't no good, and unlike you, he ain't got nothing to lose," I told him.

My phone rang, and it was Celia. I prayed she had some information about Kendra.

"Hello."

"Hey, Bilal, any word?" she asked.

"Nah, nothing. I was hoping you were calling me with some good news," I told her.

"Not yet, but Detective Donaldson is on his way now to help us expedite a missing person's report. Can you come over?" she asked.

"Yeah, I'm on my way," I told her, then turned to my uncle and said, "I gotta go. Whatever you and her got planned, cancel it. I'm telling you it ain't gonna end well."

"I hear ya, nephew," he said and went back inside the house.

"So, you mean to tell me they're planning on using the money they've collected to buy drugs? What the fuck is wrong with them? I don't believe this. Wait. Yes, I can. Nothing my sister does shocks me anymore. But I thought Patrick had more sense than to do something as stupid and dangerous as this," Celia said as we sat on the sofa in her living room. While we were waiting on the detectives to arrive, I filled her in on everything I'd learned.

"Hopefully, my uncle will take heed and listen to what I told him. He's a smart guy," I said.

She gave me a sarcastic look and said, "Really?"

"Okay, maybe smart isn't the right word. He's a reasonable guy. My point is, he knows better than this. I told him this cat Junie is reckless," I said.

"Yeah, well, so is Diane, so I don't know how this is gonna play out."

"Hey, I'm gone to work."

I looked up and saw Celia's husband, Darnell, who we didn't realize had been standing in the doorway.

"What's up, Darnell," I spoke.

"Hey, Bilal. Any word on Kendra?" he asked.

"Not yet," I told him.

"I can hang around if you need me to, Cele," he offered.

"No, go ahead. We've got things covered," she said coldly.

The doorbell rang, and she jumped up to answer it. "That must be Sean."

"Who the hell is Sean?" he asked me.

"I don't know," I told him.

Celia returned to the living room, followed by the same detective I'd seen several times at the hospital. From the grimace on Darnell's face, he wasn't too pleased to see him.

"Good morning. How is everyone?" the detective asked as he walked in.

"I'm good," I answered. Darnell remained silent.

"Thanks so much for coming," Celia said with a half-smile. Then she looked over at Darnell and said, "I thought you were leaving."

I watched as Darnell stared at the detective a few moments longer, then walked out. I heard the sound of the front door opening and closing a few seconds later.

The detective began asking Celia and me questions about Kendra and where she could have gone. We both told him as much as we could, including what had happened with Diane.

"So, she told her you slept together, but you didn't?" he asked me.

"No, sir, I've never touched that woman. She lied," I told him.

"She said it to hurt my niece," Celia explained.

"Do you think she would do anything to physically harm her?" he asked.

I looked at Celia and waited for her to answer. Personally, I wouldn't have put anything past Diane's crazy ass.

"No, I don't think she would have," Celia said. "But I don't know. She's got so much bullshit going on right now."

"Such as?" the detective asked.

Celia looked over at me, and I gave a slight flinch, hoping she'd get the hint and wouldn't mention anything about Diane and Patrick's plans for the money. I didn't mind the police helping with the search for Kendra, but there were some things I just wasn't gonna talk about. I would let the streets handle those things.

"Aunt Celia?"

I was surprised when Ashley walked in.

"Yes, baby?" Celia said.

"Oh, hey, y'all," she said. "Did you all find Kendra?"

"We're working on it now. You remember the detective who is working on finding out who hurt Avery? He's helping with this too," she said.

"Yes." Ashley nodded.

"Hello, Ashley, it's nice to see you again. I've been wanting to talk to you for a while, but we haven't had the chance. I have some pictures I need you to look at if that's okay?" He turned and asked Celia.

"Yeah, it's fine," Celia told him.

He opened the folder he had been holding and took out a grainy still image from a video

and passed it to Ashley. "This is the car that was
following your sister. Have you seen this car
before?"

"No, I don't think so," Ashley said, looking at
the picture.

The detective took out another picture and
passed it to her. "Okay, this is the man that was
driving the car. Have you ever seen him?"

Ashley took the picture and held it close to her
face. "It's blurry."

"I know it is, sweetheart. Try looking at this
one." He handed her another one, which really
wasn't any clearer.

"It's blurry too," she whined.

"Yeah, that's the problem. They're all kinda
blurry." He handed her a couple more pictures,
and as she looked through them, he said to
Celia and me, "These pictures are the only real
lead we have. This is the car that witnesses said
approached Avery while she was walking in
the parking lot, and it's the car that was seen
following her."

"You can't see the image of the tag?" I asked
him, thinking how much better the quality would
be if it had been some of my equipment.

"No, we tried."

"Maybe, but in this one," Ashley said as she
held up one of the pictures.

"You recognize the man?" Celia said.

"I think I do. It kinda looks like my mom's old boyfriend a little," Ashley said, passing the picture to Celia. "Look, Aunt Celia."

"Oh shit," Celia said. "She's right."

"Who is it?" I asked.

"It's Terry, one of the guys Diane was dating a couple of months ago."

"Yeah, he's the guy that Mommy robbed and Avery shot at."

I closed my eyes and hoped this guy hadn't found Kendra and did to her what he had tried to do with Avery.

Kendra

I woke up to the smell of pancakes and bacon. My eyes fluttered open, and I smiled as I saw the floral wallpaper of the bedroom where I was sleeping. I remembered how as a child, I always wanted flowered wallpaper, but my mother never let me get it. I pulled the comfy quilted bedspread tighter around me and looked around the room: the family photos on the wall, the shiny gold jewelry box on the dresser. I sat up in the bed and stretched, enjoying the warmth of the sun that was streaming through the blinds. After lying in bed a few minutes longer, I finally got up and ventured down the hallway.

"Well, good morning." A loud voice greeted me when I walked into the kitchen.

I smiled and said, "Good morning."

"About time you woke up to eat. Your breakfast been waiting on you," said the older woman sitting at the kitchen table reading the newspaper.

"I'm not all that hungry," I told her as I sat in the empty chair across from her.

"Nonsense. I know you're hungry. You ain't hardly touch your food last night," she said, standing up and going over to the stove. The food that she was speaking of was the plate of baked chicken, cabbage, macaroni and cheese, rice and gravy, and cornbread that she cooked for me when I showed up on her doorstep, crying uncontrollably. I had only been to Sierra's house, where she lived with Gran, her grandmother, once or twice, but I remembered exactly how to get there, and when Gran opened the door, she ushered me right inside. We sat on her sofa, and she rocked me in her lap while I told her everything and was all cried out. Then, she left the room and came back holding a handkerchief and a glass of something that she told me to drink. I took it from her, took a swig, and nearly choked.

"I thought this was tea, Gran." I coughed.

"No, it's probably Wild Turkey." Sierra snickered.

"It's good for your nerves and your mind. Helps you think," Gran told me.

I tipped the glass to my lips again, this time taking a slow sip. The liquid burned as it went down my throat, but for some reason, I liked it. The tension that was in my head lessened.

"See, you feel better already, don't you?" Gran asked me.

I nodded. Gran then had us follow her into the kitchen, where Sierra and I sat while she cooked and talked to us for hours. By the time dinner was done, I was exhausted emotionally and physically and had no energy to eat. I was also a little tipsy. She insisted that I spend the night, and I immediately accepted the invitation.

"Come on. I'll show you where the extra bedroom is," Sierra said. We walked out to my car so I could grab my stuff.

"Thanks, girl. I'm sorry I popped up like this, but I didn't have anywhere . . . and Bilal . . ." I said, feeling embarrassed and guilty at the same time.

"What the hell are you apologizing for? I told you from the jump you could come and stay here. You're my best friend. Although I'm mad Bilal turned out to be a fuck boy. I know how much you liked him." Sierra sighed.

At the mention of Bilal's name, I felt a lump in my throat. I was tired of crying and just wanted to sleep. "I did. But at least he showed me his true colors sooner rather than later. I don't wanna talk about him anymore."

"I understand."

I gave her a hug and said, "Thanks, Sierra. I appreciate this."

"Nonsense," she said. "That's what besties are for. Now, come on so you can go to bed, and I'm gonna go in here and help Gran put this food up before she starts screaming my name."

"Sierraaaaaaa!" Gran yelled, and we hurried back inside.

I took a shower and had the most peaceful night's sleep I'd had in weeks, with no thoughts of my mother, Bilal, Aunt Celia, or my sisters. Gran had been right: Wild Turkey was good for my nerves and my mind. My heart was still aching, but I felt a little better.

"Here you go." Gran set a plate holding pancakes that were so big, there wasn't enough room for the bacon on the plate, so she just laid the slices on top. "Now, you want some juice or milk?"

"Gran, I can't eat all of this," I said.

"Juice or milk?" she asked again, leaning into the open refrigerator.

"Juice," I answered.

"Apple, orange, or cranberry? You been cuddled up with that boy, so we're gonna give you cranberry to clean you out," she said.

"Gran, really?" Sierra shook her head, then mouthed the word *sorry* to me.

"Oh my God, Gran." I began blushing, wondering if, during my emotional breakdown, I had shared a little more than I should have. "I guess as long as it ain't Wild Turkey."

"Here you go." She put the glass of cranberry juice in front of me, along with a bottle of syrup.

"Thanks again, Gran," I said, biting into a piece of bacon.

"Stop thanking me, girl." She picked up the paper and went back to reading.

"But I really appreciate you. I didn't have anywhere else to go. I should've came here when she first kicked me out when Sierra told me, instead of going to Bilal's. It's just that he was so supportive." I sighed.

"You know, when I was growing up, my mother was the same way," Gran said, her face still hidden behind the newspaper.

"She was?" I asked.

"Yep, couldn't stand me and treated me real bad. Used to cuss me out and embarrass me all the time, put her hands on me for no reason."

"Her mama tried to kill her," Sierra added.

"What" I gasped.

"Yeah, she stabbed me." Gran sighed. "She hated me. But I learned why."

I put my fork down and paused before I asked, "Why?"

"My mama was jealous of me. That was her problem. From the moment I was born, she took issue with me. She couldn't stand the way my daddy's attention went from her to me, the way he doted on me and loved me. She couldn't handle it. Had somehow made up in her mind that he loved me more than her, and she turned cold toward him. Eventually, she drove him away, and once he was gone, she got even madder at me."

I thought about how my mother always teased me about my looks. When I was small, she would call me "Light Bright," and not in a good way. I grew up hating my lighter complexion and curly hair, and especially my eyes, because she called me a green-eyed monster countless times. But, the strange thing was that I resembled her. I never understood why she disliked me so much, and now I was starting to understand.

"My mother has always hated me," I said.

"Listen to me." Gran put the paper down and looked at me. "That ain't got nothing to do with you. It's got to do with her. Those are her issues, not yours. You're smart and beautiful—"

"She's smart and beautiful too," I said, wondering why I felt the need to defend the woman who I had just admitted hated me my entire life. It made no damn sense. I wanted to hate her as much as she hated me. She deserved it. But for some reason, I couldn't.

"But unlike her, you have your entire life ahead of you, and a chance to have everything she's ever wanted and didn't have. And that makes her jealous, which is her issue, and not yours. She's your mother, and I know you still love her the same way I loved mine even after she tried to kill me, but you're at a point in your life where you're going to have to learn the same way I did. You're gonna have to love yourself more. You've gotta get out of that toxic environment and that toxic relationship that you have with her. It ain't good for you," Gran told me.

"She's right, Kendra. You can't keep living like that." Sierra reached over and grabbed my hand.

"But it's not really about her. It's about my little sisters, too," I explained.

"You can still be there for them," Gran told me.

"How?" I said, using my napkin to wipe the corners of my eyes, where fresh tears were forming.

"By creating a better life for yourself. Now, eat up before that food gets cold." Gran went back to reading her paper, and I dug into the plate in front of me.

Diane

"Di, I'm telling you, don't do this. We can come up with another plan," Patrick said after handing me the duffle bag of cash.

"We already got a plan, and it's a good one. You're just punking out, and I ain't." I took the bag from him and put it in the trunk of my car.

"This Junie dude is bad news. The people he's dealing with ain't legit. I don't wanna see you hurt."

"There's no such thing as legit in the drug game, Patrick. And I'll be fine. I know how to handle myself. Now, I gotta go. You already got me looking stupid because I ain't got all the fucking money I said I was gonna have. But I'll make it work," I said, not wanting to waste any more time listening to him try to convince me not to go through with this.

"Listen, I have a guy at the church who—"

"I'll call you later to get the rest of my money and figure the rest of this shit out. Oh, and make sure you contact that lawyer, because the police have been blowing my phone up, and we need to file that lawsuit against the police department. That's really gonna be my next come up," I said, opening my car door and climbing in.

"Diane—"

I left him standing in the parking lot of the neighborhood grocery store where we had met. I called Junie and told him the amount of cash I had, and he promised to call me back in an hour. This was finally about to be it. My chance to finally have something I'd never had: real money.

Since becoming a mother at seventeen, I had struggled. Even after Champ and I got married, it was still a struggle. I'd never had the finer things like Celia had. I couldn't buy my children the latest cell phone or get them tickets to concerts, but she could. Once this was handled, she wouldn't be the queen bitch that she thought she was; it would finally be me.

I decided to wait for Junie's call at the hospital and was almost there when Darnell called. I ignored it twice, but when he called a third time, I answered.

"What do you want?" I asked, making sure he heard the attitude in my voice. The last time we talked, he was cussing me out about Celia, and I wasn't trying to hear him whining about her.

"That's how you answer the phone now?"

"It's my damn phone. I answer it the way I wanna answer it. Now, what the hell do you want?"

"I wanna see you. Where are you?"

"I'm at home, and I'm not alone," I said.

"You're lying. I'm sitting outside of your house, and your ass ain't there."

"What the hell are you doing? Stalking me? I got shit to do today, so I don't have time to give you no ass, if that's what you're trying to do. You're gonna just have to—"

"Damn it, Di, I'm not trying to fuck you. I'm trying to talk to you. I need to talk to somebody, and yeah, we have a good time in bed, but I thought we were friends." His tone was serious, and I was stunned. Clearly, something was wrong.

I looked at the time. I hadn't been to the hospital and needed to go see Avery. Then again, chances were that Celia was already there anyway, so she was fine. I would go and sit with her later instead.

"Fine. Where are you, Darnell?"

"Can you meet me at Crawford Park in twenty minutes?"

"Yeah," I agreed.

Twenty minutes later, I pulled up next to him. He was standing beside his car. "You getting in, or am I getting out?"

"I'll get in," he said. As he walked around the front of my car, I saw that he was dressed in a shirt and tie. Whatever was bothering him had him so messed up that he hadn't gone into work.

"What's going on?" I asked when he got in.

"You tell me," he said.

"Nothing's going on with me, Darnell," I told him. "You're the one acting all suicidal and shit."

"I can't tell. What's up with you and Patrick?"

"Nothing's up with us. He's helping me straighten some things out, that's all. I told you that before when you asked me about him." I sighed.

"Don't lie to me, Di. Something's up with y'all. I saw him going into your house the other day. You fucked him, didn't you?" His stare was intense as he waited for my answer.

"Is that what you wanted to talk to me about? Oh, hell naw. Get the hell out of my car, Darnell," I said as I reached over to open the door for him.

He grabbed my wrist and held it. I tried to pull away, but his grip tightened. "What is wrong with you? Why do you keep doing this?"

"Doing what? What the hell is wrong with you, Darnell?" I finally yanked away from him.

"It's over, Di. I'm leaving Celia," he said.

I was stunned by his words. My mouth opened to say something, but nothing came out. I didn't know what to say. His hand remained on my wrist, and I slid my hand up so that my fingers were now intertwined with his.

"Darnell." I finally managed to speak.

"I don't want to be with her anymore. I'm done."

"But . . . I don't understand why." I couldn't believe it. Darnell and Celia had been together forever. And although I had been sleeping with him and we had been caught, I didn't think they would break up. Hell, men cheated all the time and stayed married, so I didn't think they would be any different.

"Because I'm not happy, that's why. I think that's why I was with you, honestly, because you were different. I felt alive and just . . . free." He sighed.

"Yeah, I am way different." I laughed half-heartedly.

He smiled, but he said, "You are. And I want to still be with you, Di."

"What?" I gasped.

"I'm in love with you, Di. That's why I need to know what's up with you and Patrick." He touched my face with his free hand, and my

stomach fluttered. I hadn't had a man tell me he
was in love with me since Champ. I suddenly felt
strange.

"Darnell . . ."

"Di, don't you love me too?"

I looked into his eyes, and I wondered if I
really did love him. I no longer even knew what
love felt like. It never mattered to me. I only
cared about getting what I could get from guys
and leaving them alone before they could get
close enough to break my heart. Men were just
the means to an end, and love was never part
of the equation. At least, I didn't think it was.

"I don't know, Darnell."

"If you don't, then that's fine. You go and be
with whoever the fuck you wanna be with. But
I'm leaving Celia, and I want to be with you. I
want to build a life with you, but I also need to be
able to trust you."

I thought about the possibility of being with
Darnell and having everything Celia had, except
with my kids. Life would be so different, and
the struggle would finally be over. Darnell made
good money. I could go back to school and
become a nurse, or a cosmetologist. or any other
dream I used to have before I got knocked up
and my life fell apart. Darnell had at least been
somewhat consistent, and he was right. We did

have fun when we hung out. I enjoyed being with him. Maybe I did love him.

"Yes, Darnell. I love you." I nodded and kissed him. His mouth was warm, and his tongue seduced mine until the car became so hot that the windows fogged up.

When the kiss ended, he said, "Good. And Patrick?"

"There's nothing between Patrick and me, Darnell. You're right, we had sex, but it wasn't even good sex. It's just business at this point, and after today, I won't even need him anymore anyway."

"What do you mean?" He frowned.

"We were supposed to use both shares of our money and flip it in the streets, but he punked out, so I had to go another route," I told him. "I got the cash in the trunk of the car right now."

"So, you mean to tell me you're using the money from Avery's GoFundMe and other contributions to buy drugs, Diane? That's crazy, not to mention illegal. That money is supposed to be used for her," he said, shaking his head at me.

"It's not. It's like investing in the stock market and using the money to make more money. Same thing, like one of those 529 college plans. At the end of the day, Avery's gonna benefit, trust me. She's gonna have plenty of money. I've hired a lawyer to file a lawsuit against the city and the police department. I'm even making sure to avoid them so they can't get no statements from anyone so I can prove that they're dragging their feet on solving the case. It's all good, Darnell. I've got it all worked out," I assured him. "And now, I've got the icing for the cake that's already baking, baby."

"What's that?"

"I've got you."

"Yeah, you're right. You do," he said and kissed me again.

My phone vibrated and showed that I had a text from Junie, telling me he had everything set up and giving a time and place to meet up.

"Listen, I gotta go," I said.

"Who's that?" Darnell asked, trying to look at my phone.

"That is the bat signal. I will call you later."

"Are you sure about this, Di?" he asked.

"I've never been more sure about anything else in my life."

He kissed me one more time before getting out of the car, and I could see him watching as I drove away. I couldn't believe everything was working out better than I ever imagined. I was about to have it all: the car, the house, the money, and even a man. Then, I remembered that it was my sister's man. I knew that as happy as I was, she was going to be heartbroken. She loved Darnell; and now, Darnell loved me. As much as I hated Celia, she didn't deserve this. Or did she? If she really loved him, she would've made sure he was happy with her the way he was with me.

My nerves were all over the place, and I suddenly became so nauseous that I had to pull over and throw up. I told myself to calm down before I met up with Junie and the connect, because Darnell or no Darnell, I wasn't about to fuck this opportunity up.

The directions Junie gave me were to a house that looked like it should have been condemned. The siding was worn and hanging, and so were the shutters. The lawn, if that's what you wanted to call the dead grass out front, looked like it hadn't been watered in years. I considered turning around and leaving; then, someone tapped on my car window, causing me to jump.

"You getting out or what?" Junie seemed to appear out of nowhere.

"Yeah. I was waiting on you. I wasn't about to go in there by myself," I yelled through the closed window.

"A'ight, well, I'm here. Let's do this," he said.

I reached into the glove compartment of my car and took out a .22 caliber pistol and tucked it into my shirt, then zipped up the oversized jacket I wore. I grabbed the miniature bottle of Grey Goose that was stashed in the car console and drank it, hoping it would help me calm down. Finally, I stepped out of the car.

"You scared the shit out of me," I told Junie. "Where the fuck did you even come from?"

"I was over there on the other side of the porch, talking to my man. I don't know why you ain't see me," he said.

I looked in the direction he was pointing and didn't see anyone. Patrick's voice played in my head, warning that this could be a setup for a robbery, and I became hesitant. "Are you sure about this?"

"Girl, bring your ass—and the cash. I hope you got it," he said.

"Yeah, I got it." I nodded, reaching into the back seat and taking out a duffle bag.

"And my fee?" he asked.

"Got that too." I reached inside the bag and handed him an envelope containing ten hundred-dollar bills.

He grinned as he counted it. "A'ight, let's go."

I followed him toward the house. He opened the door without even knocking. Inside, there were several guys sitting on a raggedy sofa, playing video games. A girl was sitting on the other side of the room, painting her fingernails. No one even looked up when we walked in.

"Hey, hold tight for a sec. Lemme go let my man know you're here."

"What?" I said, clutching the duffle bag tighter.

"It's cool. Ain't nobody finna do nothing to you. Chill," Junie said and walked out.

When he was gone, the girl stood up. Looking me up and down, she said, "Ain't you a little old to be fucking wit' Junie?"

"First of all, I ain't fucking with him. And it ain't got nothing to do with his age. I don't fuck wit' broke-ass boys. Second, what I ain't is too old to whoop your ass if you don't get outta my face," I said, letting her know that I was not about to be intimidated by her lanky, ugly self.

"Whatever," she said.

One of the guys on the sofa said, "Fee, sit your skinny ass down before Junie come out here and stomp you. He already told you he was bringing a broad through to talk business." She backed off.

"A'ight, Di. You can come on back," Junie called from the hallway.

I walked down the small hallway, and Junie led me into a back room, where an oversized, frog-looking guy wearing sunglasses smiled at me.

"How you doing, sexy lady?"

I stared at him, thinking he looked more like the character on the Sugar Smacks box than a drug dealer. "I'm good."

"D-Lo, this is my cousin I was telling you about," Junie told him.

"So, you tryna buy some wholesale product, huh?" D-Lo asked.

"Yeah, you got some you tryna get rid of?"

"Depends on what you tryna get." D-Lo walked over and took out a key to unlock the closet door. My mouth dropped at the contents. There were shelves that held guns, powder, weed—you name it, he had it. "Now, what you tryna do?"

"Well, before I do anything, we need to discuss a few things," I told him.

"We can discuss whatever you want as long as you got the cash Junie says you got," D-Lo said. He gave Junie a slight nod. Junie walked over and closed the door then locked it.

"I got it. But I . . ." I gripped the bag tighter and took a few steps back, trying to figure out how I was going to reach my gun.

"Relax, Di," Junie said, walking up on me so close that I could feel his breath on my neck.

"Listen, I don't think this is gonna work," I said. My heart was racing, and the same nausea I felt earlier was creeping back in. "As a matter of fact, I need to leave, because I'm gonna be sick."

"Damn, you sexy as fuck." D-Lo stood up and licked his lips at me. Not only was I about to be robbed, but I was about to be raped as well.

"You ain't going no-fucking-where." Junie went to grab me from behind, and I doubled over and vomited on the floor.

"What the fuck?" D-Lo screamed.

I reached under my shirt between heaves and pulled out the gun. Junie was confused by what was going on until I turned around and pointed the gun at him.

"Bitch, are you crazy?" He laughed and went to lunge at me. I pulled the trigger, and the gun went off.

"Oh, shit!" Junie fell to the floor.

I heard a loud crash and screams coming from outside the room. D-Lo ran to the closet and pulled out an assault rifle and snatched the door open. More gunshots rang out, and I began gagging as the room filled with smoke. I was terrorized and in a frenzy, and I couldn't see anything.

"Metro police department! Everybody put your hands up now!"

Those were the last words I heard before I passed out and fell into the pool of vomit on the floor.

Kendra

"All these people, Kendra. Look!" Avery stared out of the pink Hummer limo that we were riding in. We had just turned onto our street, where we were welcomed by a crowd of people holding signs and clapping. My heart leaped as I saw the reaction in my little sister's face.

"I know, and they're all here for you, girl!" I hugged her body against mine.

"Wow," Ashley said, sitting on the other side of her.

"They're here to welcome you home, Avery." Aunt Celia smiled.

The limo had been a pleasant surprise for all of us when Avery was discharged. We had wheeled her out of the hospital, and the limo was waiting for her, along with a full police escort. People had been so supportive, including the police department, who wasted no time in arresting Terry for a long list of crimes for what he did to my sister.

"I can't believe this." Avery smiled and squeezed my hand.

Our motorcade slowed and came to a halt in front of our house. A huge WELCOME HOME sign was hanging across the front, and people were shouting and clapping. I scanned the faces and noticed Sierra standing near the front door, along with Nikki and a few other neighbors.

"You guys ready?" Aunt Celia asked.

"Yes, let's go!" Ashley nodded.

The driver got out and opened the door for us. I climbed out first, waving at the crowd. Aunt Celia got out next, then Ashley, who took her time and helped Avery ease over to the door.

We all looked over to see Detective Donaldson, or Detective Sean, as we now called him. He walked over to the limo and took Avery into his arms, then carried her all the way to the front of the house, gently placing her down. Aunt Celia gave a brief thank-you speech to the crowd, on behalf of Avery and the family, as people yelled out "We love you, Avery" and "Welcome home, baby girl." Avery gave one final wave, then Sean picked her up again and carried her inside. Sierra and Nikki followed us into the house.

"Something smells good," Sierra said.

"We have so much food that people have brought over. Every restaurant in town has delivered something, seems like," I told her.

"Officer Sean, you can put her down now. She can walk," Ashley said when they made it into the living room.

"Stop being a hater," Avery said.

"Stop being lazy," Ashley fired back.

"Hey, how about both of you ladies chill out?" Aunt Celia told them.

"Well, I guess things are gonna be back to normal sooner than I thought." I laughed.

Sean put Avery on the sofa, and she looked around the room. Once we'd gotten the word that Avery would be coming home, Ashley and I spent three days cleaning the house from top to bottom. We'd rearranged the furniture and organized all the cards and gifts that had been sent over. The room somehow seemed bigger and brighter.

Nikki went straight into nurse mode and made sure Avery was adjusted on the couch and her arm, still in a cast, was supported properly on the pillows.

"You good?" Sean asked her.

"Yes, thanks." Avery nodded.

I looked over and noticed her smile fading. Immediately concerned, I asked, "What's wrong? Is something hurting?"

She shook her head. "No, but I was hoping Mama was gonna be here when I came home."

Aunt Celia, Sean, Ashley, and I all looked at one another, waiting for someone to speak. Avery knew what had happened to our mom; hell, the entire city did. The drug bust and her arrest had been all over the news. Some of the people crowded out front were probably there just to be nosy and see if my mother was going to be here. But she wasn't. Diane Hughes was still very much in jail. We hadn't heard from or spoken to her at all. She'd refused all visitors except for her attorney, who assured us that she was fine. On the one hand, I was hurt; on the other, I was glad. Not having her around made things easier for all of us in some ways. I was able to come back to the house and, for the first time in my life, live in a stress-free environment. I made sure Ashley got back and forth to school, and we both spent a lot of time at the hospital, where the staff was able to help Avery recover a little faster without my mother giving demands and making scenes or threatening everyone with lawsuits. But I could see my younger sister's disappointment in not having our mother there to welcome her.

"Hey, even though she's not here, she's glad you're home," I told her.

"That's right. And if she finds out you were in here pouting, you know she would be giving you something to cry for." Ashley went and sat beside her.

"I ain't pouting." Avery perked up a bit. "I just miss her a little, that's all."

"I know you do, and that's fine. It's okay to miss her," I said. "But you have all of these people here that love and support you, so you can continue to get better."

"And you have all of those gifts over there that people sent that you need to open." Ashley pointed.

"Those are all for me?" Avery asked, clearly no longer thinking about our mother.

"Yep, they're all for you." Aunt Celia walked over and picked up a few of the wrapped boxes and brought them over to Avery. We spent the next hour watching Avery open her gifts, then indulged in the smorgasbord of food in the kitchen.

"I'm sleepy," Avery announced.

"Come on. We got Mama's room set up for you to sleep in for now," Ashley told her.

Avery hesitated. "What? Won't she be mad?"

"No, she won't be. I wanted you to be able to have your own bathroom without having to walk down the hall. It's just for a little while," I explained.

"You want me to carry you?" Sean offered.

"No, I think I got it. Ashley can help," Avery told him.

I expected Ashley to protest about Avery volunteering her assistance without asking first, but she didn't. She helped Avery to her feet and back down the hallway to the room.

"I'll go help her get settled," Nikki said. "I wanna make sure she keeps that arm elevated."

Sean stood and announced, "Well, I guess I'll get out of here too."

"I'll walk you out," Aunt Celia said.

I gave Sierra a look so she could confirm the vibe between them that I had noticed.

Sierra nodded. "I think you're right. He's feeling her."

"I told you," I said.

"I think she's feeling him too, though."

"Could be," I said. "I mean, he is fine, and he's really been there for us and making sure we're good. You see he ain't waste no time having that asshole Terry picked up and arraigned."

"I'm glad he did."

"Me too. This whole thing has been crazy for all of us."

"You sure you and your sisters are gonna be okay here? You know y'all are more than welcome to come and stay with me and Gran. She would love to have y'all," Sierra said.

"We're fine. And I know she would. I miss her."

"She misses you too. It's a pan of mac and cheese and yams in the fridge that she made for y'all, though. A big pan."

I laughed. "Good looking out, Gran."

"I'm surprised Bilal isn't here." Sierra raised an eyebrow at me.

I glanced down at the floor and said, "I guess."

"You guess what? You can't still be mad at him, Kendra. Even your aunt told you he didn't do what you thought he did."

"It's not about that." I sighed. "And I know he didn't."

"Then what the hell?"

"I don't know. I think I just fell too hard too fast, and right now, I have too much to deal with. My mom is in jail, and now I gotta take care of Ashley and Avery, and I have so much school work to catch up on, and I gotta figure out when I'm coming back to work before Dante fires me."

"Bullshit," Sierra snapped.

"What?" I frowned.

"Everything you just said is bullshit. First of all, you know Dante's ass ain't firing you. He may talk shit, but you know he loves you, and when you're ready to come back, your job will be there. Second, you're smart as hell, and it ain't gonna take that much time to catch up on that little bit of schoolwork you're talking about. And you have a support system to help you out with your sisters, including me. Hell, truth be told, you were damn near raising them by yourself before your mom got locked up." Sierra shook her head at me.

Her words were brutally honest, and I knew they came from a place of love.

"You made up all those excuses because you're scared," she said.

She was right. I was beyond scared. I was terrified. My already upside-down world was flip-ped around even more when my mother told me she'd slept with Bilal. I was crushed, and my heart was broken. I was relieved when Aunt Celia explained how it was all a lie and Bilal had done nothing wrong, but I realized the reason I had been so devastated was because I was in love with him. I also discovered that being in love with him gave him a place of power in my life. I enjoyed the euphoric feeling I had when things were good between us, but I never wanted to feel the pain I felt when things went bad.

"I can't . . . he just . . . what happens if he hurts me again?" I asked her.

"He hasn't hurt you, Kendra. Your mother did. She's always hurt you. Being in pain is your comfort zone. That's why you want to stay there and not resolve this issue with him. I know you and Bilal weren't together that long, but he made you happy. And now you're scared to feel that again, because you don't know how long or if that feeling is gonna last."

"You're right." I stood up and shrugged. "So why even take a chance right now when I have all of this other stuff going on? I just need to get some of it off my plate, and then I'll be able to deal with Bilal and all that comes along with him."

"You sound crazy, and I'm telling you right now, you're fucking up. You're an amazing woman, Kendra. Any man would be lucky to have you. You deserve a good man—one that makes you happy—like Bilal. You're worried about everything you've got going on, when there isn't a perfect time for love. You can't schedule it. It happens, and when it does, you work hard to keep it. That's what love is. It's work, it's communication, and it's trust. It takes all of those, even with the right person."

"She's right," Aunt Celia said. Sierra and I both looked up and saw her standing in the doorway of the kitchen.

"I don't know." I sighed.

"You can't push Bilal out of your life, Kendra. Now, if he'd done something wrong, that would be different, but he didn't. You're running away from a good man because you're scared," Sierra said. "You can have it all, Kendra. You can be a great sister and have a good man. You don't have to choose."

"Why do you think you have to choose?" Aunt Celia asked.

"Because I have to take care of them while Mama's away," I told her.

"No, you don't. I'm going to take care of them. It's time for you to go and enjoy life. The only reason I thought it was a good idea for Avery to come back here instead of my house was because I wanted her to see the community rally around her and welcome her back. I wanted her to see that although Diane wasn't here for her, she still has people that will celebrate her victories. But your sisters will be coming to live with me. I'm seeking custody of them." Aunt Celia walked over and put her arm around me.

"You don't have to do that. I can take care of them," I said.

"I know I don't have to. I want to. The same way I've always wanted to take care of you, but Diane wouldn't let me. You girls are the most important people in the world to me. And you need your freedom."

"But what about you and Unc—I mean Darnell?"

"I don't think there will be a me and Darnell anymore. It's time to put that thing to rest, too," she said. "I deserve to be happy the same way you do, and being with him no longer makes me happy."

"Wow," was the only thing I could say. My aunt and uncle had been together for a long time. They were the only example of a marriage that I had in my life. But my aunt definitely deserved better than him. I was glad she had made her decision to leave him.

"So, Aunt Celia, let me ask you a question," Sierra said.

"What's that?"

"You think that fine-ass Detective Sean might be able to make you happy?" Sierra winked.

Aunt Celia blushed and said, "I could definitely see him putting a smile on my face."

It was almost ten o'clock when everyone finally left, including the media that had been camped outside most of the day. After taking a shower and getting dressed for bed, I opened the door to my mother's room and peeked inside. Ashley was curled up in the bed right next to Avery, and they both were fast asleep. I walked over and kissed them both on the forehead and made sure Avery's arm was elevated the way

Nikki had instructed, then I softly closed the door behind me. I went into the kitchen, looking in the fridge for something sweet to nibble on.

I heard someone knocking on the front door. I went to see who it was, thinking maybe another reporter had come by trying to get an interview. My heart jumped when I peeked out and saw Bilal standing under the porch light.

"What are you doing here?" I asked, stepping back so he could come in.

He smelled as good as he looked in jeans, white Nikes, and a denim jacket. His hair was shorter than the last time I saw him, and I wondered if he had just gotten it cut.

"Sorry it's so late, but I wanted to check on you guys," he said. "I knew Avery was coming home today, and I wanted to make sure you were good."

"You could've called and done that," I told him.

"You wouldn't have answered."

"How do you know?" I said, locking the door behind him.

"You haven't been answering my calls."

"I've had a lot going on." I shrugged.

"Well, I'm glad you let me in. You look good." He smiled.

I looked down at my oversized shirt and leggings, then put my hand on the well-worn silk scarf that was tied around my head. "You're a liar, and a funny one," I said with a smirk.

"No, I'm not. I'm telling the truth, and I'm serious. You do look good."

I couldn't help smiling back at him. "Thanks, I guess."

"So, how did today go? Avery okay? I can't believe those news people stayed out there so long. They just left like fifteen minutes ago. I saw your aunt and Nikki leave, and your friend, Sierra." He sat on the sofa and leaned forward.

Instead of sitting beside him, I opted to sit on the love seat across the room. I didn't want to be tempted to touch him, because I really wanted to.

"How do you know when they left? How long have you been outside?" I asked.

"A minute. Well, maybe more than a minute. A couple of hours, really," he admitted.

"Bilal, why didn't you just come—"

"Because I didn't know how you were going to react, and I knew how important this day was for Avery. I didn't wanna chance having you be upset and cussing me out. And I guess I kind of felt like I was partly to blame because of my uncle. . . ."

"I wouldn't have done that. And I can't hold you responsible for your uncle's actions any more than you can blame me for my mother's. They're both grown-ass people who made the decision to do something stupid. This wasn't your fault. Honestly, I mean, you were really there for me when this all happened. You deserved to be here to celebrate her homecoming, and I'm mad that me being selfish didn't allow that. I'm sorry." I swallowed the lump in my throat. "This has all been a lot, and my mind and emotions have been all over the place."

"You don't have to apologize, Kendra. It has been a lot, and that's why I've tried to give you your space. But I've been worried, and I miss you."

I glanced over at him and said, "I miss you too."

He walked over and sat beside me. I tried to wipe my tears before he saw them, but it was too late. He brushed them away from my cheek and said, "Kendra, you know your mother lied, right?"

"I do." I nodded.

"I would never do anything like that. I would never hurt you, ever," he said. "I love you."

He loved me. After everything, he still loved me. My heart pounded, and I felt the fear begin to enter my chest. I remembered what my aunt and best friend said, and instead of pushing Bilal away, I inhaled deeply and said, "I love you too."

He covered my mouth with his, and I savored the taste that I'd been missing. I put my arms around his neck, and he pulled me tighter to him. The fear that was in my chest moments earlier was now replaced with joy. The heat between us increased, and when his mouth went to my neck and I found myself reaching under his shirt, I stopped and pulled back.

"What's wrong?" he asked, confused.

By this time, I was panting, and so was he. There was no doubt in my mind that these weeks without seeing one another had left both of us just as frustrated sexually as it had emotionally.

"We can't . . . do this," I said between breaths. I pointed to the hallway. "Girls . . . asleep."

Bilal smiled at me and nodded. "Oh, okay." Then, with a naughty grin, he reached for me and said, "We can be real quiet."

"Stop." I giggled and tried to get away from him, but I was too slow, and his grip around my waist was too tight.

Soon, we were kissing again, and I was so aroused that I was just about to pull him into my bedroom. Then, I thought about my mother and the different men she'd brought into our home that my sisters had already seen. Although they knew Bilal and they liked him, I didn't want them to think that he was just another man. I wanted to show them something different.

I stopped Bilal again and pulled away. "We can't do this."

He nodded his head and said, "I get it. It's cool."

"Thanks for coming by to check on us, though. I appreciate you. I really do," I said, then added, "Let me walk you out."

He stood and readjusted himself. I looked down at the bulge in his pants and laughed.

"Oh, that's funny, huh?" he said.

"I'll make it up to you, I promise," I told him, grabbing his hand.

"Well, I know Avery just got home and you're still getting settled, but do you think you'll be free sometime, so I can take you to dinner?"

I smiled. "I would like that, and I think I can make myself available."

Bilal was a good man, and I deserved to be happy. I realized that I could be the role model for the twins and show them what a right relationship with the right person looked like. Despite the drama my mother had caused, I was determined to go after every good thing I wanted and have it all.

Two Months Later

Diane

"How are you feeling?" Marty Goldstein, my attorney, asked me. He was a short Jewish man that had been appointed by the court. He didn't seem too thrilled to be representing me, mainly because I wasn't a very cooperative client, but I didn't care.

Hell, there wasn't much I cared about these days except getting the fuck out of jail. I was miserable. Surprisingly, I missed my girls and wanted to get home to them. The day Avery was released from the hospital, I watched her homecoming on the news and cried. I was so glad that she had gotten better. Unfortunately, the story of her homecoming was immediately followed by the updates of my pending trial, which included talk of whack-ass Patrick making a plea deal with the district attorney. Now, I had finally come up with a plan of my own.

"Is he here?" I said, leaning back in the chair and glaring at him.

"He should be here in a few minutes. I talked to him earlier, and he stated he would be here." He glanced down at his watch.

"He'd better show," I said.

"Look, Diane, I think we need to discuss—"

"I don't want to fucking discuss anything right now. I don't even wanna talk to you. I asked you to do one thing, and that was call and get his ass here. Now, that's all we need to discuss," I snapped at him so loud that the guard posted outside the door of the small conference room peeked in. I flipped the bird at him, and he frowned and turned back around.

Marty's cell began to beep, and he looked down at it, then back at me. "He's here."

I closed my eyes and breathed deeply. I had been planning this meeting for days, and now that he was here, I was suddenly anxious. I told myself to calm down and get it together. I needed to be confident and assertive if this was going to work.

A few seconds later, the door opened, and Darnell walked in, looking fine in a suit and tie. He also looked nervous as hell. I found it quite amusing.

"Well, hello there." I smiled.

"Hi," he said.

"You can have a seat." I motioned to the chair across from me; then I said, "Marty, leave us alone for a few."

"That can't happen. This is a legal visit, so as your attorney, I can't leave the room." Marty sighed. "I already explained that."

"Well, damn it, go over there in the corner and wait while my brother-in-law and I have a nice chat, please." I sighed.

Marty gave me a frustrated look as he stood and picked up his chair, carrying it to the far corner of the tiny room.

"What's going on, Diane? Celia and the girls have been trying to reach you and come and see you for months, but you won't let them. Now your lawyer is calling me and telling me you're refusing to eat?"

"I don't want to see them, and I can't tolerate the shit in here that they claim is food. It's not edible," I told him. "I gotta get out of here, Darnell. I need your help."

"Di, you're facing some serious drug charges, not to mention the fraud and money wiring stuff you got going on behind that GoFundMe. I mean, I can put some money on your books, but I ain't got money for no high-ass bail."

"I ain't talking about no money, Darnell," I told him. "I need you to do something else."

"Something else like what?" He frowned.

"Since you're still in here, you tell him, Marty," I said and sat back.

"Well, Mr. Caldwell," Marty said from where he sat. "Ms. Hughes has decided to explain to the DA handling the case about her previous addiction to narcotics and agree to enter a supervised drug rehabilitation program."

"What? Diane, what the hell is he talking about? The only drugs you've ever done was smoke weed and pop an X every now and then. Get the hell out of here with that bullshit." Darnell shook his head.

"Look, Darnell, the DA will allow me to be placed under house arrest and attend the rehab program, but like Marty here said, it's gotta be supervised. I need for you and Celia to sign off on this," I said. "And let me come live at the crib with y'all."

"Now you've really lost your damn mind. You know good and damn well that shit ain't happening. Hell, I don't even live there anymore," Darnell said.

"What?" I said, surprised by his announcement.

"Cele and I separated, Diane. After she found out about you and me, we were done. We've filed for divorce. I can't help you." He went to stand up.

"You can, and you will," I told him. "You call Celia, and you tell her y'all are getting the fuck back together so I can get out of here."

"I'm not doing that," Darnell said.

"Yes, you are." I turned to Marty and said, "If he leaves, I'm not eating."

"Mr. Caldwell, please . . ." Marty pleaded.

"I don't give a shit if she doesn't eat. Let her ass starve," Darnell told him.

"She has to eat, Mr. Caldwell—"

"Look, I'm not staying here and dealing with another one of Diane's tantrums just so she can get her way. She don't wanna eat? That's on her," Darnell said.

"If she continues starving herself, then the baby will die," Marty said.

Suddenly, the room became eerily quiet. Darnell slowly turned around, and I stood up. For the first time since he had entered the room, he really looked at me. His eyes went from my face to my fuller breasts, then landed on the slight pouch of my stomach.

"Di, what is he talking about?"

"Congrats. You're going to be a father," I said, my voice void of emotion. I had found out I was pregnant right after I was arrested. For the first few weeks, I was in shock. I couldn't believe I was having a baby, especially by my sister's husband. After the twins were born, I got my tubes tied. Plus, I'd always used condoms—except with Darnell.

"Shit." Darnell plopped back down in his seat.

"Touché," I said. "Now you see why you have to get me the fuck up out of here?"

"How do I know it's my baby?" He stared at me.

"Don't do that, Darnell. It's your baby, and you know it. I can tell you the exact day it was conceived. We were at the Westin, and not only did we fuck in the king-sized bed, but we also fucked on the balcony, in the shower, and on the counter in the bathroom. It was a very eventful day, remember?" I glanced over at Marty, who looked quite uncomfortable.

"What am I supposed to do? Celia isn't gonna go for this. Just tell them to release you into my custody," Darnell said.

"I'm afraid they might not go for that, especially considering that you and your wife just separated and you moved out. The home has to be a stable environment, under the circumstances," Marty told him.

"She's not—"

"She will," I said. "You go to Celia, and you tell her straight up that this is the chance for the two of you to have the one thing you wanted your entire life: a baby. Darnell, if you help me get out of here, I'll stay with you all until I have the baby and this court thing is over, and I will give custody to you and Cele. I promise. Marty has already talked to the DA, and as long as I stay out of trouble, they will give me time served and extended probation and parole."

"And what if I don't? I can just sue and get my baby myself." Darnell raised an eyebrow at me.

"No, you won't. Because if you don't help me get out of here within the next fifteen days, I will starve myself and your unborn child, and if I don't miscarry, I will still be just within the window to terminate this pregnancy."

The look of horror on Darnell's face was the same one Marty had worn when I told him about my plan. I knew how much Darnell and Celia wanted a baby. It was going to work.

"Diane . . ."

"Look, Darnell, I'm doing you a favor. I'm giving you the chance to get your wife back by giving her the one thing she's always wanted and couldn't have. You want her back, right?" I asked.

"Yes." Darnell nodded.

"Then go talk to her and give her this gift that I happen to be carrying for y'all." I rubbed my stomach.

Darnell remained quiet for a few moments, then turned and said to Marty, "Talk to the DA and see what we need to do. I'll call you tomorrow and set up a meeting with me and my wife."

"Yes, sir." Marty nodded.

Darnell knocked on the door, and the guard opened it. He left without even saying goodbye.

I sat back in my seat and smiled with satisfaction. "Great meeting, Marty. Suddenly, I'm famished and ready to eat."